Hoare and the Matter of Treason

ALSO BY WILDER PERKINS

HOARE AND THE PORTSMOUTH ATROCITIES
HOARE AND THE HEADLESS CAPTAINS

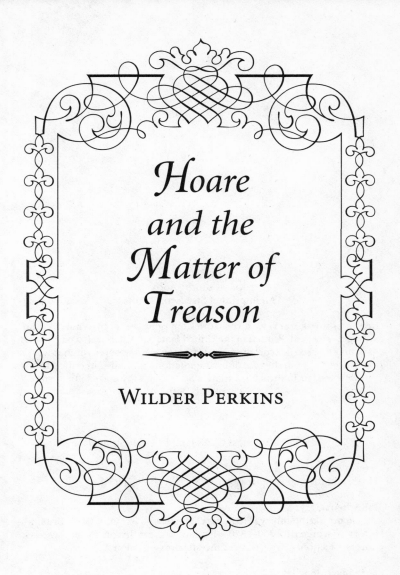

Hoare
and the
Matter of
Treason

WILDER PERKINS

THOMAS DUNNE BOOKS
ST. MARTIN'S MINOTAUR
NEW YORK

THOMAS DUNNE BOOKS.
An imprint of St. Martin's Press.

www.minotaurbooks.com

Library of Congress Cataloging-in-Publication Data

Perkins, Wilder.
  Hoare and the matter of treason / Wilder Perkins.—1st ed.
    p. cm.
  ISBN 0-312-27291-x
    1. Hoare, Bartholomew (Fictitious character)—Fiction. 2. Great Britain—History—George III, 1760–1820—Fiction. 3. Great Britain. Royal Navy—Officers—Fiction. 4. Government investigators—Fiction. I. Title.

PS3566.E6914867 H625 2001
813'.54—dc21

                                                                00-045772

First Edition: April 2001

10 9 8 7 6 5 4 3 2 1

Hoare and the Matter of Treason

Prologue

———<>———

DO YOU have it on you?" the first, smaller man asked.

"Of course not, sir," the other said. "I would hardly be carrying it about, would I now? I have it tucked away, safe at home."

"Then I have no more need for your services, sir. So I'll bid you an affectionate farewell."

The first man took his modest beaver hat from its place at his side, donned it, and tapped its top down with a decisive motion of his left hand. Below the level of the table, where it was out of sight, he drew a small, plain pistol. Aiming it in the general direction of the larger man's belly, he discharged it. At a distance of less than two feet from its target, he could hardly miss. It was just as well; the man knew himself to be an atrocious marksman.

The pistol was of small caliber, a lady's pistol; its report was little louder than a slamming door. It went unnoticed by the raucous tavern crowd. The shock of the ball as it pierced a new hole just above the larger man's navel was another thing again.

The victim's eyes and mouth popped open like those of some huge mechanical toy.

"Buh," he said once, and—as if he wanted to make sure he had been understood—again, *"buh."* He collapsed forward onto the table, knocking his glass over as he fell, and a trickle of blood appeared at his mouth. For now, the death-stink's swift onset was masked by the general tavern reek of sweat, tobacco, and stale liquor.

"Never mind," the killer told his victim in a serene voice. "On my way out, I'll send someone to clean up." Since he had already made his farewell unmistakable, he saw no need to remain. He rose and departed, weaving among the other customers. Just as he reached the tavern's front door, he informed a distracted waiter that the gentleman in the rearmost drinking nook appeared to have been taken ill. He had said he would do so, and he was in the habit of keeping his word whenever he found it convenient.

Chapter I

A marriage has been announced, and will shortly take place, between Mrs. Eleanor Graves (née Swan) and Commander Bartholomew Hoare of the Navy.

— *Naval Chronicle,* 18 November 1805

S HALL I lift you aboard, Miss Austen?" Bartholomew Hoare whispered with all his force into the cold, hazy morning air. Hoare had been deprived of his full voice eleven years ago when he was struck in the throat by a musket ball while defending His Majesty George III's plan. He saw the cloud of his breath blow away with the stiff breeze.

Now, although some years had passed since he had faced ocean weather, Hoare was still generally brown. It was his natural color. He was long, stringy, wiry, and, for the next few minutes, still a solitary, lonely widower.

"Thank you very kindly, sir," Miss Austen replied with some asperity, "but after all, with two brothers in the navy, I must already be quite familiar, must I not, with the process of boarding and leaving a ship upon visiting them, especially in harbor? And especially when, like this one, it is a very small ship?"

So saying, she withdrew her mitted hands from her muff, leaving it to dangle around her neck by its ribbon harness. She reached up, took hold of the handiest of the lanyards bracing down *Royal Duke*'s shrouds, placed one leg in the entry port and hoisted herself easily out of the wherry. With her other hand, the one with the reticule dangling on the wrist, she reached out and grasped the hand that her host, the groom, extended her. The hood of her cloak, which she had drawn over her brown hair, presumably to guard its precious curl against the wind, fell back.

When boarding from a small boat, even Jane Austen could not wholly preserve her modesty; the stocking she revealed over her surprisingly well-turned ankle was not a blue one but a scalding cochineal red, embroidered with a seasonal clock of holly leaves.

"Delighted to welcome you aboard," Hoare whispered with an insincere smile, "particularly on this joyful occasion." In the face of her unaccountable distaste for him and for the connection he was about to make, he found it difficult to summon up genuine warmth.

"And delighted to come aboard, sir," she replied, "although I do think it rather thoughtless of dear Eleanor not to have summoned me aboard before, so that I could assist her in preparing for the ceremony. Pray take me to her immediately," she added in a commanding voice, without so much as a polite exclamation about *Royal Duke*'s charming and shipshape appearance.

Fearing that his smile was degenerating into an accommodating smirk, Hoare gave her his arm and escorted her the few feet farther aft to where the hatch leading below to his quarters lay open over a newly carpeted ladder. The lady turned, smiled coolly back at Hoare, and waited for him to precede her below, so that if she were to lose her footing despite her assurances of sure-footedness, she would fall upon him instead of the deck beneath. It was clear to Hoare that she remained less than

4

enthusiastic about her schoolroom friend's selection of a second spouse.

These past days, he had found himself regretting even more the contingency that had required him to hand over almost half his spacious living quarters to the brig's homing pigeons. Now, hidden behind a bulkhead of hastily painted deal, *Royal Duke*'s graceful glazed stern ports and miniature gallery were aflutter with cooing Columbidal instead of chattering female humans; the remaining rump of a cabin was dark, airless, tainted with a faint, inappropriate odor of guano that seeped through the partition. A flutter of another kind came from behind the curtain rigged athwartships that, while it shrank Hoare's usable space still further, protected Eleanor Graves and her attendants from the prying eyes of men.

Miss Austen disappeared behind the curtain, where her appearance was greeted with shrill, happy voices. Seeing that she was in safe hands, Hoare returned topside to deal with the next arrivals.

Royal Duke lay cozily at a mooring less than a cable's length offshore, protected by Weymouth's exiguous mole. She was already lying low in the water with the weight of wedding guests who had come aboard. More, Hoare knew, were yet to come. He shuddered for his ship's center of gravity. Was his little brig fated to loll over at her mooring and convert the wedding into a mass drowning? "Sunk by matrimony, with all hands." The navy would never live it down.

From the moment of the announcement appearing in the *Naval Chronicle,* Hoare's time had not been his own. Messages of congratulation flowed in. Even Duke of Clarence, Admiral of the Fleet Prince William, sent to wish him happy. Not only, it seemed to Hoare, had he gained a number of well-wishers in the naval community; Eleanor Graves, too, was known to it. Hoare had believed he had kept his passion secret, but it was not so. Even with its body of officers expanded beyond all peacetime belief for the endless war with the French, the Royal Navy was a family, and it took care of its own.

Hoare's wedding was to be sanctified by the Reverend Arthur Gladden, recently called to serving a flock in Maiden Bradley, some miles southwest of Warminster in Wiltshire. Before taking orders, Mr. Gladden had been third lieutenant in the ill-fated, newly commissioned frigate *Vantage*. And once a naval officer, always a naval officer.

More pertinent to the occasion: rightly or wrongly, the Gladden family credited Hoare with Arthur's acquittal of the murder of Adam Hay, *Vantage*'s first and only captain. Moreover, Hoare had assisted materially in helping Miss Anne Gladden rebuff a powerful, elderly suitor. These kindnesses, neither of which Hoare had seen as more than his duty, the Gladden family had taken as major benefactions. Indeed, Lady Caroline, mother of the family, had been heard to refer to Bartholomew Hoare as the tribe's Savior, in a reverent voice that suggested that she expected him not merely to cruise the waters of the Channel, but to walk upon them.

Accordingly, the young rector had insisted on conducting today's ceremony. Mr. Gladden had taken the further liberty of bringing his little sister with him. The Honorable Miss Anne Gladden was a beauty; she was also wee—little taller than Jenny, Hoare's girl-child ward. Since Harvey Clay, Hoare's lieutenant in *Royal Duke,* was likewise a minikin, Hoare had hopes of making a match between the two and had previously arranged for Clay to be invited to Broadmead for inspection. So now, when Hoare returned on deck, he was pleased to see the couple engrossed in each other. When he went over to them, Miss Gladden looked up at him with a dazzling smile.

"My heart is quite broken today, you know, Captain," she said.

"Desolated, I'm sure, Miss Anne," Hoare whispered in reply, "but, after all, hearts are ours to break, be broken, and heal." He could not believe what he was saying. Courtly exchanges of this kind did not become him. He must be exalted.

Since his rescue of Miss Gladden had involved a mock betrothal between them, there were those among the *ton* who, upon learning that he had given the poor little thing her congé in order to make this apparently more disadvantageous connection, had looked upon him with perplexity mixed into their coolness. However, upon discovering that Miss Gladden's own relatives, and the lady herself, continued to welcome him warmly, they had quickly subsided and gone off in search of juicier scandals.

Just then, Hoare realized that Mr. Clay, engrossed as he was with the young lady, had failed to note a barge approaching from a trim frigate newly anchored just to seaward of *Royal Duke*. The frigate's broad pendant was blue. The oncoming admiral, then, would be Rear Admiral Sir George Hardcastle, KB, Port Admiral in Portsmouth. Sir George was, to all intents and purposes, Hoare's master.

Hoare flushed and barely caught himself from whistling the officer back to his duty. Instead, recollecting that he himself was not that far removed in time or rank from the task of welcoming boarding dignitaries, he repositioned himself at the gap in his ship's starboard rail. It was a gap, he knew, that hardly deserved the title of "boarding port," since *Royal Duke* measured less than sixty-five feet on the waterline.

Sir George had made it clear that his visit was not official but entirely personal. He had agreed to give the bride away, her valetudinarian father being unable to travel from Essex all the way to Weymouth, and her resident brother being at odds with her. His flag, therefore, was not to be hoisted the moment his shoulders appeared at deck level. This was fortunate, Hoare thought as he swept off his hat in salute, since Sir George's shoulders all but topped *Royal Duke*'s low freeboard before he had even raised his bottom from his seat in the barge's stern sheets.

Nonetheless, Hoare had had Mr. Clay muster side boys in advance—eight of them, as was proper when receiving a flag officer aboard—and seen that they were kitted out with white gloves. The boys were clean and tidy. Since *Royal Duke* carried no genuine boys, none was under twenty, and two were women.

"Congratulations on the day, Hoare," the admiral said upon replacing the hat he had doffed in salute to the *Royal Duke*'s imaginary quarterdeck. "She looks sprightly enough—your command, I mean, of course. I suppose the bride looks the same."

"I cannot say, sir," Hoare whispered. "I am not permitted, you know, to see her today until the ceremony takes place."

Sir George withdrew his watch and inspected it.

"Lacks only a minute of seven bells. She had better clap on sail, or she'll be late. Hate a dilatory officer."

It being the occasion it was, Hoare dared a jest.

"Ah, Sir George," he whispered, "but you are superseded in command for the time."

"What?"

A-ha. The fish had struck.

"The bride, sir. At this moment, the bride is queen. She commands us all, even yourself."

Below his fashionable Brutus crop, the admiral's face reddened. He had arrived unrigged and unpowdered, and without his wife or daughter. He disapproved, Hoare knew, of officers who traveled with their women aboard. In fact, it seemed, he disapproved of women entirely, if they attempted to exercise the least authority. Then Sir George smiled, and Hoare felt his heart beat once more.

"Why, of course," he said. "Ungentlemanly of me. I must—" He was interrupted by the prolonged twittering of massed calls from a body of boatswains posted beside the after hatch. Hoare had hastily trained several of his unusual crew in a special call of his own composition; this was to serve as the wedding fanfare. Just in time, the Reverend Arthur Gladden assumed his place with his back to *Royal Duke*'s mainmast, fully vested and as blue as the admiral's pendant, prayer book in hand. Upon his clearing his throat meaningfully, Hoare and his admiral parted. Hoare took post to one side of the clergyman; Admiral Hardcastle darted to the hatch head, ready to accept the hand of the woman he was about to give away the moment she appeared in the hatch.

The bride was preceded on deck by two other females: Miss Austen and a skinny little girl-child, her ash-blond hair skinned back, two-blocked so that her huge black eyes bulged under their heavy brows. Both bore posies.

The pair took their places on either side of the companionway, just beyond the waiting admiral. A pause ensued.

Not by chance, the two disparate bridesmaids had chosen—or had had chosen for them—simple gowns of an identical soft peach hue, cut in the oddly seductive Directoire style, with the waist positioned just below the breasts—or, in the case of little Jenny Jaggery, whose nose was running a bit in the cold—where her breasts would make their appearance in Nature's good time. Breasts or no breasts, Hoare always found the fashion quite appealing.

The pipes rose to a crescendo as the bride rose from the depths, Persephone personified. Within its cage of ribs, Hoare's heart gave a convulsive leap. The twittering of the pipes ceased, to be replaced by the music of a trio—hand-harp, violin, and kit-fiddle. The sound was sweet, lilting, and somehow Celtic.

As a widow and still a recent one, Eleanor Graves had chosen for once to conform to custom. Her small, sturdy form was clad in a froth of black lace, without the least décolletage. Her cap and veil, however, were white, formed from the most diaphanous Mechlin. Behind the veil, she had drawn her thick black hair into a firmly disciplined knot. All told, the bride could have been charged with appearing severe, were it not for the warmth of the brown eyes and the soft smiling lips that greeted Hoare from behind the veil.

Up the deck of *Royal Duke* she marched on the arm of George Hardcastle, Knight of the Bath, Rear Admiral of the Blue, Port Admiral at Portsmouth. Composed as always, she and her escort came to a halt before Mr. Gladden. The latter cleared his throat once again.

"Dearly beloved . . . ," he began.

Despite himself, Hoare could not help remembering. The words of the Roman priest in Halifax as he united Hoare with Antoinette Laplace, a full score of years ago, had been spoken in French and in Latin, and had been openly grudging. But they had been essentially the same as those that Arthur Gladden was speaking now, as were Hoare's own whispered responses and those of the woman at his side. Hoare did not mind—nor did he care—that, for Eleanor, too, this was a second marriage. He had known and respected Dr. Simon Graves. As far as he was concerned, their previous respective marriages only went to show that each of them was capable of faithful love. When he looked down at her, and she met his eyes, his heart leapt again.

At Mr. Gladden's final words, "man and wife," the music broke out once again, jubilant. Now, the trio that had marched Eleanor Graves to the altar marched Eleanor Hoare and her husband back, supplemented now by the sound of pipes. Not the martial great pipes, but the softer, more melodious Irish version. At the sound, the bride burst forth in a gurgle of laughter, took the arm of her groom, and commenced to march back toward *Royal Duke*'s taffrail. But Hoare forestalled her and broke ranks. He seized the bride's waist in one arm, took her right hand in his left, and commenced to twirl her, laughing down the deck.

As he pranced, Hoare overheard Miss Austen murmur an aside to Miss Anne Gladden. The latter was not listening; with fondly jealous eyes, she was watching her beloved Mr. Clay spinning—or perhaps being spun—along behind the bridal couple, partnered by the powerful figure of Sarah Taylor, master's mate and cryptographer. Mr. Clay's spin was brief, for he was quickly cut out by the slightly large, navy and gold form of Sir George Hardcastle, KB, Rear Admiral of the Blue. For Sir George, as was well known, was mad for dancing.

"I do believe," Hoare had heard Miss Austen say, "that I have never before seen the happy bridegroom anything but dour. Why commonly, he could 'tak' a cup o' dourness yet' to the covenanting kilted Scots in Dumfries."

Nobody but the dour one appeared to have heard her, for thereupon decorum went overboard for the day. Without regard for rank, age, or precedence, the entire wedding party formed into as many sets as were needed to accommodate them, and set to a-dancing. Only a few, the grinning clergyman and former naval officer among them, must stand aside to watch the merriment. Even little Jenny Jaggery, squealing with excitement, found herself being half-partnered, half-carried through the figures by Leese, the yacht's lantern-jawed sergeant of marines. Long before the spirit left the crew, breath left first one and then another, and they collapsed, red, sweating in the cold damp breeze, panting and laughing. Seeing that only the most durable members of the lower deck still stood up, the musicians shifted the music into a hornpipe. In a cleared space before the yacht's wheel, four of the youngest, hardest durable hands now paired off and skipped through their proudest paces—cuts, the shuffle-and-half, buck-and-wing, the lot.

"Never saw such a show in all me days at sea," puffed Admiral Hardcastle. He had long since relinquished Taylor into the black hands of his own former coxswain, Loveable Bold. Some months ago, the admiral had lent him and Stone, now the yacht's acting gunner, to Hoare as support in the latter's assault upon the renegade Edward Morrow; somehow, Hoare had kept them from their rightful master's clutches. And he intended to do so as long as he could.

"Well done, sir, well done!" the admiral added to *Royal Duke*'s breathless commander beside him.

"I hadn't a thing to do with it, sir," Hoare replied. " 'Twas all impromptu, I do assure you."

Without orders, the invisible, stiff marine on duty at the yacht's bell gave it the eight paired rings that brought in the new day for each ship in the Royal Navy. As if on that signal, Eleanor Hoare, commanding, gave her first, last, and only order of the day.

"Splice the main brace," she said in a low but carrying voice. Cheers and grog followed, and toasts to bride, groom, and yacht. That done, Sir George plucked his hat from the scupper, where he had deposited it for the ceremony just past, and put it on his head—apparently for the express purpose of removing it again in farewell to Eleanor Hoare, the yacht, and the ship's company.

"I regret it most exceedingly, Hoare," the admiral declared over the tweeting pipes of ceremony, before he stepped from *Royal Duke* into his waiting barge, "but the service requires that you report to me at Admiralty House on Wednesday morning, for orders. At eight bells of the morning watch, shall we say? You are to proceed to London immediately thereafter. Tonight, however, I give you permission to sleep away from your ship."

"Aye, aye, sir," was all the surprised, crestfallen Hoare could say. He was both ashamed to have forgotten the requirement, set down in standing orders, that no ship's commanding officer could sleep away from his ship without his admiral's permission, and dismayed to learn that he must leave his marriage bed on the very morning after its first use.

Hat in hand, he stood at *Royal Duke*'s entry port until the barge disappeared astern. Already, obedient to some signal Hoare had failed to observe during the excitement aboard *Royal Duke,* the frigate that had conveyed Sir George to Weymouth was weighing anchor. Hoare could hear the faint scratching of the fiddler on her capstan head, and the steady stamp and go of horny feet as, inch by inch, her crew won home the single anchor she had dropped on arrival. He watched, arm about his bride's waist, while, as if by clockwork, fore topsail, jibs and spanker appeared just as the admiral swarmed up her tumble-home. And watched, too, to see her 'round the breakwater, tack nimbly, and set a course for her day's journey home.

"It was a great compliment, sir, and a deserved one, that Sir George found the time to leave his post and travel here for today's ceremony." It was the Reverend Arthur Gladden's voice at Hoare's elbow. Somehow, Hoare observed, it had already acquired a clerical cadence, even so soon after its owner's admission to holy orders.

"We can thank Lord Nelson for it, Gladden," Hoare whispered. "Since Trafalgar, the Royal Navy no longer need send to sea any bottom that can swim."

"A sad, sad loss, nonetheless," Mr. Gladden remarked.

"Indeed." While respecting the late Lord Nelson's blazing courage, which he personally deemed all but suicidal, and respecting above all the hero's ability to weld the disparate captains under his command into that famous band of brothers, Hoare could not bring himself to feel the same about either his strategic genius or his personal morals.

"Well, we must be off," Gladden said. "Come, Anne! We have a long journey ahead of us, and two services for me to prepare, together with my sermon. This Christmastide—my first as a priest of God, of course—has left me sadly behind in my duties, I fear.

"By the bye, Hoare," he added, "I had thought to weave into my Sunday's homily that 'happy outcome of all our afflictions,' which is epitomized by the union which I have just been privileged to sanctify. Come, Anne!"

Hoare paid Gladden little attention, for he was thinking about the remark he had overheard Miss Austen make. She might be sardonic, but she was perceptive. He must learn to mind his dourness. As for the lady's acidulations, she appeared to save them up until the right occasion arose to use them. Perhaps she, too, kept a commonplace book, just like the one he kept in one corner of his mind, in which he preserved his own infrequent wit and wisdom. These irreverent phrases might come in handy one day, or be passed on to an admiring younger generation.

At least, he thought, she must eventually resign herself to seeing her old friend married to this man whom she apparently deemed so unsuitable a match. He knew her to be a highly intelligent woman, yet her attempts to put a spoke in Hoare's wheel had been feeble from the first, perhaps even half-hearted. He wondered what had moved her to make them to begin with.

Gladden's little sister had already parted from her lieutenant, and was awaiting her brother in the stern sheets of one of the pair-oared wherries that were hanging about *Royal Duke* to take off her guests. She turned to wave a kerchief sadly at Mr. Clay. The little lieutenant stood now, as Hoare had, hat in hand, until he saw his special guest safe ashore. Then he stood aside for his commander to leave the ship. The bride's people loaded the couple's portmanteaux into Hoare's gig, while she thanked the weary instrumentalists. As she did so, Hoare took Mr. Clay aside.

"I'll be back aboard in the morning," he whispered. "While I'm away, you must prepare her for sea. We must be in Portsmouth on Wednesday, before four bells of the morning watch."

That order given, he handed his bride into the gig and followed her out of his command.

They would spend their wedding night in the house that Dr. Simon Graves had left to his wife, and in the bed she had shared with her late husband. The next day they would part company, since Hoare must obey his summons to Portsmouth. Sir George Hardcastle, who was known to be a hard and a merciless man, tolerated tardiness not at all. Hoare did not look forward to breaking the news to his bride that they must part so soon. They had known it must happen sooner rather than later, but—their first wedded morning? That was too much of enough.

"And how do you do this morning, my love?" Hoare looked down at his bride's figure beside him, her black hair spread across the pillow. Sleepily, she looked back at him.

"To tell you the truth, Bartholomew, I'm sore," she said. "Sore down there, and somewhat surprised at the entire proceedings. The practice is much more intriguing than the theory, I find. Thank you, my dear. You are a most understanding man, I think." She drew his head down to hers, nibbled his ear, and kissed him deeply.

As Hoare had expected, Eleanor had been a virgin. Her late husband had been paralyzed below the waist when they had married, so their union had never been physically consummated. Her imagination cannot have lain idle, however, and her new experience of the night before had apparently only aroused her enthusiasm. Hoare found its intensity startling, and arousing in its turn. The beneficent cycle took its natural course.

Downstairs in the sunny parlor, the maid Agnes and the manservant Tom served the Hoares a late breakfast with their tea— kedgeree, kippers, kidneys, and toast. The child Jenny had taken a bowl of porridge in the kitchen earlier, but now sat demurely between bride and groom, handling her tableware with extreme care and absorbing food in silence and enormous quantities. Under the care of her late father, the child had been overnourished, so she had much catching up to do. She was doing her best.

Neither servant even attempted to suppress a knowing expression, and there were audible giggles in the direction of the kitchen when Eleanor Hoare, folding her napkin and slipping it into its ring, moved to her tuffet and sat down in a somewhat gingerly manner, gathering her skirts about her.

"My, how happy I shall be when my mourning can come to a close," she said. "Mourning is most unbecoming to a person of my coloring, or lack of it."

She did not wait for Hoare to whisper his denial, but continued, "I think you are procrastinating, Bartholomew. When you were seeing him over the side yesterday, Sir George talked with you longer than mere convention would require." The sparkle in her eyes belied the severity of her tone.

"Well?"

When not preoccupied with other matters during the night, Hoare had puzzled over how to break to his bride the news that, instead of their making their wedding trip to Great

Dunmow in Essex, where she planned to introduce her new husband to her people, he must leave her here like every sailor's wife. He had best be forthright, he decided at last; this woman did not take well to being cozened.

"I must leave you this morning, my dear," he said, "and return in *Royal Duke* to Portsmouth. From there, I must leave her to ground upon her own beef bones . . . and grind up secrets for the Admiralty's bread, while I go on to London and report to their Lordships."

"Oh," she said. "Ohhh!" echoed Jenny.

"Are we to we accompany you?" Eleanor asked, preparing to rise. Hoare shook his head.

"That is not possible, I fear," he said. "As you know, Sir George frowns heavily upon captains who keep their wives aboard. And not only must I travel fast; I cannot say how long I shall be required to dangle about in London. . . .

"No, I think you have two possible courses of action. The first is to remain here in comfort, safe and sound, until I can rejoin you. The second is to proceed to Portsmouth by land, hire suitable lodgings for us all, and settle down there or in the surrounding countryside, to await me."

"There is a third possibility," Eleanor said. "We could descend upon Father and my brothers in Great Dunmow, and await you there. After all, Great Dunmow is far closer to London than we would be down here on the coast. And after all, they will already be expecting us. For poor papa, the arrival of one less guest would only be a relief; I can hardly say the same of the family's most likely reaction to the news that our stay will be indefinite."

"And me?" Jenny's voice was plaintive.

"You come with us, of course," Eleanor said firmly. "You are one of us, my dear, you must remember."

"With Order?"

Order was Jenny's cat, out of Chaos, by Jove. Or Jenny was Order's girl. It made no difference, Hoare thought; the two were inseparable.

"And Order, and his parents Chaos and Jove," he whispered reassuringly. "His parents, and his sisters and his cousins and his aunts as well. The entire family of fortunate felines. . . . In command of *that* crew, you will have enough on your hands, I give you my word."

After Hoare had assembled his personal kit, the little family walked down to the dock through a light November mist. Here, with a wave of his hat, Hoare signaled *Royal Duke* to send his gig. As they stood awaiting its approach, a man behind him cleared his throat. Startled, Hoare spun around, to find himself facing the squat batrachian figure of Martin Frobisher, with his slabsided sister on his arm. The last time Hoare had seen either of them, they had been participating in the grotesque tragicomedy at the Nine Stones Circle. The lady had been bare naked above the waist that night; she had not displayed well.

Martin Frobisher's form was made all the more froggish in appearance by his choice of a surtout. Well cut, it was a deep, warm green in color. He bore his fashionable top hat in hand.

"Go and greet the bride, Lydia," he said. "I have something to tell Captain Hoare in private." Dutiful, the sister obeyed.

"May I wish you happy, sir?" he now asked.

Ever since their first encounter, up the esplanade at the Town Club, Hoare and Sir Thomas Frobisher, this young man's father, had held each other in deep mutual disesteem. Hoare knew that Sir Thomas thought him an arrogant, taciturn coxcomb who made a habit of showing contempt for his betters and who had interfered not once, but twice, with his plans for a second, profitable marriage. He had done so first with the sturdy woman now on Hoare's arm, and, almost simultaneously, with little Miss Anne Gladden. On his own part, Hoare's contempt for the knight-baronet was quite real, and carried with it—Hoare must admit to himself—more than a touch of fear. For Sir Thomas combined a singular degree of authority in much of Dorset with the assurance, self-generated and self-perpetuating, that he, and not its present Hanoverian incumbent, was the rightful occupant of England's throne. For centuries, all the male Frobishers had resembled frogs. Like Sir Thomas's daughter, the Frobisher females were slab-sided, lacked all sheer, and had pronounced humped backs.

Martin Frobisher had inherited his father's appearance but not his quirky mind. In fact, in the course of their brief acquaintance, Hoare had found him quite likeable. He lacked Sir Thomas's overweening pride, for one thing. For another, he seemed possessed of a degree of self-deprecating humor. He was not above acknowledging himself a coward.

Now, however, Mr. Martin Frobisher's mien was grave.

"I beg a word with you, sir," he said with a gesture inviting him to step aside. Puzzled, Hoare obliged.

"I know, of course, Captain Hoare, that you and my father are not the best of friends." His voice was embarrassed. As well it should be, Hoare thought.

"No, don't deny it, sir," the young man continued, looking up into Hoare's faded gray eyes with his own yellowish ones. "You know it as well as I. But, to be frank, I do not share his feelings on the matter. Indeed, I wish you well.

"For that reason, as well as with an eye to my family's honor, I feel obliged to warn you that my father entertains plans to do you harm."

"Oh?" Hoare responded, with a lifted brow.

"I do not know how, or where, but from words I happened to overhear, his intention is real. And, as you may have discovered, once my father gets an opinion, he keeps it, nourishes it, encourages it to grow. There are those who call him mad; indeed, I fear that in some respects and on some subjects, they may be right. All I can do now, sir, as his son, is give you this warning. And hope you will walk warily. Will you take my hand?"

Mr. Frobisher looked up at Hoare with eyes that were appealing as well as goggling.

"Of course, sir," Hoare said, and shook the offered hand. Behind him, his coxswain called, "Oars!," and the gig grated lightly on the hard.

"Fare you well, Captain," Frobisher said, and walked off on his bandy legs so that Hoare could make his own good-byes in privacy. Once in the gig, Hoare turned to wave to his wife and his fosterling, then turned, wondering, to face the brig he commanded.

Chapter II

A GRAY, unremarkable figure, the visitor dominated his host's closet.

"You have assured me, sir," he said, "that this conversation cannot be overheard. Nonetheless, how am I to be certain that behind one of these linen-fold panels a secret stenographer does not lurk? Even the walls have ears."

"You insult my hospitality, sir, and my integrity!"

"Bombast, sir, bombast and fustian. Have done, pray. We are practical men, you and I, and must not permit false pride to stand between us and our objective.

"In the window seat, here, I think," the guest continued. Come, sir, join me. A pleasant view, indeed, of your garden—and of your daughter. It must be more pleasant still in the spring."

"I'll thank you to leave my daughter out of the discussion. She has nothing to do with this matter."

"Agreed. Now, as to the king—he is mad, as we all know, and that presents special problems of a tactical nature."

"First, the portrait, Mr. . . ."

The visitor raised his hand in warning. "Ah-ah-ah, sir. No

names at all, if you please, not even here. I have gone so far as to assent to your whim with respect to the portrait, as long as it is kept most closely indeed—but *names?* Not yet, not until our plans bear fruit.

"We have the names we use among ourselves, you know, and I must insist we employ them, and them only. . . ."

"Call me Ahab, then." The host's voice was surly. He was not pleased, it seemed, at taking correction—and in his own house, at that.

"And, as you will remember, I am Saul. Now, as I was saying, about the king . . ."

"This brings me to my reason for requiring your presence here so soon after the recent happy occasion at which you were a principal character and I a mere hanger-on."

The speaker was Admiral Sir George Hardcastle. Without the least ceremony, the instant *Royal Duke* had touched at Portsmouth's Camber dock, Hoare had left Mr. Clay in temporary command so he could to make all speed to Admiralty House. His timely arrival had been celebrated by the ringing of eight bells on the old Spanish trophy in the building's front hall.

"Now," the admiral continued, "do you recall my speaking of Admiral Sir Hugh Abercrombie, KB?"

"Of course, sir," Hoare said, thinking as he spoke that the implied question was absurd. Any officer who did not know his true master would be a zany.

"You will also recall, I trust," the admiral went on, "that you, and that brisk little floating counting-house you command, take orders from me only at Admiral Abercrombie's pleasure. He is your commander, and not I.

"Until now, you have been known to Sir Hugh only by reputation and not in person. Sir Hugh now wishes to further his knowledge of you. He requires you to present yourself to him, at the Admiralty, forthwith. Hammersmith here . . ."

The admiral looked to one side where his new flag lieutenant sat, looking eager. Delancey, his predecessor, had been shifted into command of the brig *Niobe*, 18, some weeks ago. After an interesting brush with the virgin *Royal Duke,* he had taken *Niobe* to the waters off Cádiz to watch over the remains of the combined Franco-Spanish fleet.

". . . has prepared vouchers for suitable lodgings at the Golden Cross Inn near Whitehall. Thank you, Hammersmith, you may go."

Admiral Hardcastle looked away. Hoare could have sworn that he was embarrassed.

Even after his flag lieutenant had closed the door behind him—and stooped to put his ear to the keyhole, if Hoare knew his flag lieutenants—Sir George paused as if he expected Hoare to comment. Hoare had never heard of the Golden Cross Inn, so he could say nothing to the point. More important, he wondered at the implied order to leave his ship. What could have prompted it? Here, too, he would have nothing to say, but must sit and await enlightenment in Sir George's own good time.

The admiral did not keep his subordinate wondering for long.

"Sir Hugh informs me that he is most alarmed," he said, "by the disappearance, without trace, of certain documents dealing with affairs in the Baltic, with which his office has been entrusted by the Foreign Office. Unfortunately—and this must go no further than our four ears—they involve more than purely naval matters. If they were to fall into Boney's hands, he could, I am told, use them to our disadvantage in the Baltic states, including Russia. The Foreign Office would view their loss with extreme concern; news of their loss would certainly produce a storm in the Cabinet. As far as the Admiralty is concerned, trouble with St. Petersburg could deny the navy the pine boles we need so desperately for masting. At worst, we might find ourselves stretched to confront a new enemy in strange, cold, and distant waters.

"I have no notion of these documents' content, nor do I

wish to have one. I have more than enough of that sort of bur-
goo on my plate now. The upshot, Hoare, is that Sir Hugh is
eager for you to investigate the matter, and get the damned
things back without anyone knowing they ever went adrift in
the first place."

This would be another Herculean task, Hoare thought. He
would find himself in "strange, cold, and distant waters,"
indeed, with no charts. There was no point in voicing his concern, however: duty was duty.

"The Admiralty," Sir George went on, "inquires why you
have not yet reported to Admiral Sir Hugh Abercrombie in
Whitehall for instruction, as ordered in their signal of such-and-
such date.

"Now, my office has no record of having received such a
signal. Somewhere between Sir Hugh's hand and mine, it went
adrift. I have so informed Sir Hugh in words that absolve you, at
least of any blame in the matter. You can hardly, after all, be justly
charged with lacking diligence in executing an order which you
never received. Besides, in all fairness, I can hardly extinguish so
soon the promising career you have so recently rekindled.

"By the by, sir, you will note that in relieving *you* of blame
for the mishap, that blame will necessarily be placed somewhere
else. Since one can hardly expect that Whitehall will shoulder it,
it will almost certainly arrive on this desk to squeak and gibber
at me like Mr. Shakespeare's sheeted dead."

Admiral Hardcastle swatted the desk as if the blame had
already arrived, a-squeaking, and he wished to put it to rest
physically.

"I am truly sorry, sir," Hoare said, "to have been responsible
in any way, even indirectly, for placing you in this situation.
How may I make recompense?"

"You cannot. I made the mess. Like a good servant, I must
clean it up.

"Today is Wednesday. I shall have Patterson post-date your
receipt of this belated order by"—he withdrew the Hunter

watch from his waistcoat—"thirty hours. After all, it is already a week overdue, so one more day will not ruin any of us.

"In presenting yourself at Sir Hugh's Admiralty office," he said, "do *not* use the main door. Those people there will delight in misdirecting you; you would be lucky to escape with your virtue intact. Go around the building, to Minching Lane, and up the alley leading to the rear of the building. Use the privy entrance.

"Hammersmith will provide you with a pass which you will show the man at the privy gate. He'll see that you reach Sir Hugh's private offices.

"Repeat what I just said."

Hoare did so.

"From that point, Hoare, your future is in Sir Hugh's hands, not mine at all.

"Sir Hugh is not as accommodating an officer as I, so you can expect something of an inquisition. However, he knows quite well that you are necessarily a man of few words. I have suggested to him that you present him with a written narrative of the Moreau affair and the matter of the Duke of Cumberland and the Nine Stones Circle. He will have read of them before, of course, through the reports I have already forwarded to him, but he is heavily burdened with paperwork, and a new statement will refresh his memory so he can interrogate you more usefully. He may be inclined to mercy in your case; sometimes he is.

"Now fill me a glass of that port, if you'd be so kind, and have one yourself before you go."

"Thank you, sir," Hoare whispered, "but if I remember correctly, the Admiralty coach is scheduled to depart in fifteen minutes' time. . . ."

"What the deuce have you to do with the Admiralty coach, pray?"

"If I am to reach London with all dispatch, sir, the coach is the fastest means of doing so. Perhaps you would direct your clerk to book me a place. . . ."

"I hardly see," the admiral said in a testy voice, "how, small though she is, you expect to fit *Royal Duke* into the Admiralty coach. You are to take her to Greenwich."

The startled Hoare could hardly believe the implication of what he had just heard. A month or two before, when he had read himself in—or rather, had Mr. Clay read him in—on the yacht's quarterdeck, Sir George himself had warned him that by Admiralty order, he was never, never to take her to sea, lest she be snapped up by some wandering Frenchman and give up all the secrets she bore. It had only been by the strongest persuasion that, before the Nine Stones affair culminated, he had persuaded Sir George to stretch the point and let her loose—but only within sight and sound of tidewater. Whether their lordships in Whitehall had taken official note of this warranted disobedience he did not know and had no wish to know.

"In convoy, then, sir?" That was how *Royal Duke* had been brought 'round to Portsmouth: not only in convoy, in fact, but in the hands of a borrowed crew. Most of her own people had then known less about seamanship than they did of the binomial theorem, or of burglary.

"Or not," Sir George said. "It makes no difference. Get her there, and without further ado."

Relenting, he added, "Whatever mission they have awaiting you, it must be one of high urgency. In the hands of the wrong people, those papers must be no less than infernal machines. Now, Hoare, if you have no more asinine remarks to make, I have much to do and little time in which to do it. Have that drop you just refused, and be off with you."

They had their parting drop. "Good. Now, be off. Good luck—you'll need it."

Then, with, "And convey my respectful duty to Sir Hugh," Sir George returned to his mound of papers.

"You're in luck, Captain Hoare," declared Hammersmith, when Hoare paused at his desk outside the admiral's sanctum to watch a clerk sand the last of the documents Hoare was to carry with him.

"Why?"

"Berrier at the Golden Cross sets the finest table in London. He don't usually receive anyone below commodore, or vice minister. Or baronet."

"A cut beyond my pocket, then," Hoare whispered. He had managed to preserve as capital the windfall of prize money he had gotten in September of '81. Nonetheless, he had just undertaken matrimony, and he had seen too many naval families fall into debt and disgrace. He had no intention of following that path. He judged that his bride was a woman of some property, but he felt unaccountably ill at ease at the notion of living off a woman. It would make him feel like a ponce.

"Perhaps," he now asked Hammersmith, "you could suggest a less exalted lodging?" He understood that the flag secretary was a London man.

"Oh, you needn't worry as to that," the other said with a smile. Was the smile just a trifle superior? "You're under Admiralty orders, so the Admiralty foots the bill. Hence the voucher he had Patterson attach to your papers. If I know anything about Berrier, he'll tremble to serve anyone who even mentions old Abercrombie's name. If you think the gentleman you just left is a merciless man, just you wait till you come up against Sir Hugh."

Perhaps Hammersmith's smile was not so much superior as knowing—knowing, like the expressions of Eleanor's servants the other morning. That recollection reminded him. As soon as he was back aboard *Royal Duke* and had gotten her underway, he would have Hancock send word to Eleanor in Weymouth about the Golden Cross Inn. He was sure he remembered that the yacht's foul-smelling pigeon handler still had a Weymouth bird.

He bade a polite farewell to the man in any case.

"Sir! Sir!"

At the familiar voice, Hoare stopped and turned. As he had thought, it belonged to Lemuel Rabbett, the Admiralty clerk who had come so near to having his head lopped off at the Nine Stones Circle while in Hoare's service. Hoare was genuinely delighted to see the little man; he had grown significantly in confidence if not in stature during their association, and Hoare had found that one always loves the one he has helped at no cost to himself. Liking the thought, he tucked it into the little commonplace book he kept in a corner of his mind.

"Why, Rabbett!" he whispered. "So you are back in the . . . saddle?"

"Back in the hutch, rather, sir," Rabbett replied. "May I make so bold as to wish you happy?" He reached out a tentative hand, and Hoare gripped it firmly.

"Thank you, Rabbett. I hope the same for you, in due course."

"Sir . . . sir, I knew you would be calling on Sir George today, so I brought with me a little memento for yourself and your good lady." Shyly, Rabbett reached into his fob pocket and produced a small object, which he offered in the palm of his hand.

"From my mother and myself," he said.

Hoare must take it, or else hurt the other's feelings. He looked down to inspect it closely. About the size of his thumb to the first joint, it was a carving in mellow ivory in the shape of a crouching rabbit. Its long ears fused near their tips, forming a hole through which a loop of plum-colored braided silk was inserted.

Hoare thought he had seen a similar object in the collection of a former captain who had spent some time attempting to break into the reclusive islands of Japan. He could not remember what they were called—something that had to do with fishing, if he remembered. It was a thing of beauty.

"But this is precious, Rabbett," he whispered. "You must not give it away."

"My mother and I wish you and Mrs. Hoare to have it, sir," the clerk said in a firm voice. "While I may not be fit to go to sea with you, you will at least have one rabbit with you. Please, sir."

"Then thank you, Rabbett, with all my heart." Again, Hoare turned to leave.

"One more thing, sir. In October, when Mr. Thoday and I

were serving you, you asked me if, when I returned to this office, I would investigate the source of some leaks of secret information. You said they had to occur somewhere between *Royal Duke,* this office, and Whitehall."

"I remember," Hoare said.

"Well sir, I have made my investigation. I can assure you—and I know whereof I speak, sir—that the leaks have not emanated from here. Of that, you may have my absolute, confident assurance."

"Which I accept, Rabbett. Thank you again, and thrive until we meet once more."

He escaped at last. The tide was on the turn; if he stepped lively, *Royal Duke* could just catch the up-Channel flood. Rabbett's replica was welcome; his news was not. If the clerk was correct—and Hoare respected his competence in the field—the leaks had to be coming from the Admiralty, or from his own command. Neither was a palatable dish. It was a good thing, perhaps, that he was taking *Royal Duke* to London.

Chapter III

S QUELCHING THROUGH the night on the oblong disks that
kept him from sinking to his knees in the foul Thames
ooze, the mudlark made his way toward the promising mound
at the edge of tidewater. If he knew his corpses, this was a
corpse. And a fresh one, too, likely. For once, he might be in
luck. But he'd best make haste, for the tide had turned already.

Yes, by God and his father, he was right for once. A dead 'un
it was. Fully clothed, too; too fresh to stink, yet with the death-
shit already washed away. A hot bath and bottle of Blue Ruin
there'd be, at the end of this night, and a willing dollymop to
share 'em both. He rolled the corpse over and began to rifle its
pockets. That there was a charred hole in the placket of the
breeches drawn tightly over its belly troubled him not at all.

And, omygawd, a *pogue*! A loaded wallet!

Off upstream, from under the bridge, the mudlark heard the
same sloshing sound he himself had made in getting out to the
bloater. More than one. He wasn't going to chance it, not he.
He'd leave 'em the joy of turning out the bloater and taking his
clothes, brass buttons, hole in the breeches an' all. It 'ud hold

'em up from chasing him through the mud, back to solid ground.

Never mind. It 'ud be *two* pretty judies for him, an' he'd be on the randy for a month.

Close-hauled, her weather shrouds humming with the strain in the raw January northerly, *Royal Duke* heeled to her task. A light wash poured into her scuppers with each leeward roll, then out again as she righted. A pair of gulls swept effortlessly across her wake, heads turning as they wheeled, in their never-ending search for nutriment. The low clouds dumped an occasional spatter to support the light spray thrown from her weather bows. There would be no need to wash down the decks this morning, Hoare told himself. Instead, the watch could continue to accustom themselves to working below while under way. In his opinion, the ordinary cipher clerks and file-matchers would have no trouble, though the two forgers—"screeners," he had learned, they were termed in thieves' cant—might find it hard to keep a steady hand.

At Hoare's side, Mr. Clay grinned ecstatically into the wind, his hair, short though it was, whipping behind him.

"Her best point of sailing, I do believe, sir," he declared. "We're overhauling that transport to windward. She bears a full point farther off the weather bow."

Hoare could hardly expect the other to hear his whisper, so he merely nodded with an answering smile. It was exhilarating travel, indeed.

"Shall I have the log cast, sir?" Clay asked. Hoare nodded assent, and Clay roared out the order.

One of Sergeant Leese's Green Marines clumped forward to handle the timing glass. Since *Royal Duke* carried no midshipman, Taylor undertook the heaving of the log. Newlywed Hoare might be, but the sight of Taylor's statuesque figure as she went about the task stirred his own maturing loins. It would, he thought, have stirred those of the yacht's coroneted figurehead, had it been so mutinous as to peer aft with its painted china-blue eyes.

"Mark!" Taylor cried, and tossed the log over the side. Its thin cord whipped through her horny hands until the marine, in belated echo, called, "Mark."

"Turn."

"Stop."

She nipped the line to check the log and release its chip, and brought the instrument back aboard with a thump. After reading the nearest marking on the line, coiling it as she overhauled it, she called out the result. "Ten knots and a fathom, sir!" she announced to Mr. Clay. She sounded triumphant. Another echo, Clay repeated the finding to the captain at his elbow, in his powerful voice.

"She moves along, doesn't she?" Clay said. Fleetingly, Hoare thought of responding with a question as to which "she" his lieutenant meant, but decided that this was no occasion for double entendres. Instead, he merely whispered, "And lies most amazing close to the wind."

His mouth was close enough above Clay's ear so he could be reasonably sure of being heard. And if not, what matter? It was a casual, trivial remark, one he was sure would not be missed.

He watched Taylor coil log line and chip, deftly and in Bristol fashion. Like a surprising number of her shipmates, almost all of whom were volunteers taken aboard on account of skills quite unrelated to the sea, she had made astonishing progress as a sea-"man" in a matter of weeks. All credit to Clay and the few seasoned hands—and the unusually high level of their intelligence. Already, out of the thirty-four Royal Dukes, he would not hesitate to rate a good ten of them topmen. As gunners, now . . . if only they could master their gunnery as well, he could rest satisfied that his peculiar command would do him credit against any other bantam brig afloat.

———

A sudden notion crystalized in his mind.

"You have the deck, Mr. Clay," he said. "Thus, thus, call me if anything untoward takes place."

"Aye, aye, sir." Bare-headed at the moment, Clay touched his forelock, gamekeeper-style. Hoare, with his notion in mind, slipped below to make a certain inquiry of Stone, *Royal Duke*'s acting gunner, and Titus Thoday, official holder of the gunner's. At this speed and with this wind, *Royal Duke* would easily reach the Straits of Dover by nightfall and, if the wind were to back, might even break into the Thames estuary by dawn. But however handy the crew might be, it lacked practical sea time, and the brig's course through these crowded waters, in darkness and with no vessel showing running lights, would be fraught with danger. An awkward encounter with some wayward Englishman was the most likely hazard, but one had to bear in mind as well that Trafalgar had not swept the Channel clean of every mischievous predatory Froggy bottom.

The orders of Sir Hugh Abercrombie himself had forbidden Hoare ever, ever, to put to sea in *Royal Duke,* yet here they both were, by that same admiral's command, hard on the wind in mid-Channel, in the gathering darkness of a raw January night, a weakling at the mercy of all comers.

Having made his inquiry of Stone and issued certain corrective instructions, Hoare now removed to his truncated cabin and called for his silent servant Whitelaw. Unlike his master, Whitelaw had a perfectly healthy man's voice; he simply forbore to use it except in extreme need, a trait that Hoare found quite desirable in a captain's servant. Within two minutes and without orders, Whitelaw brought him a supper of soft bread, a chunk of hard cheese, and a few slices of ham, with a *carafon* of adequate Burgundy to wash it down. While consuming these, Hoare jotted down his rough log for the day. He read a scene or two of *As You Like It* in the selection of Shakespeare's works, which—with the chess set whose mysteries she had not yet had time to unlock for him—had been Eleanor's wedding gift. At last he disrobed, blew out the lamp, and turned in to his swinging cot.

On the larboard, windward side of the cabin, the enormous special chair that had been kept for Sir Hugh Abercrombie swayed gently in unison with the cot. To the sound of *Royal Duke*'s quiet working and the occasional mutter of her sea-pigeons in their quarters of unearned privilege aft of the bulkhead, he fell asleep.

It seemed no more than a minute before the brig's change of course awakened him. For another minute he lay confused. He had been awakened at the climax of a highly erotic dream in which the body he embraced mingled Eleanor's firm roundness with the muscular limbs of Sarah Taylor. This must cease, he ordered himself as he swung his feet to the deck. The sound of Mr. Clay's roaring voice told him that his lieutenant was simply tacking ship; he supposed Clay had chosen to tack rather than wear, so as to give the watch the challenge of groping its way through the more difficult maneuver in the dark. The brig did not fall into irons but eased to an even keel and, with a slatting of canvas and a banging of blocks and Mr. Clay's great bellows, came 'round nimbly enough, falling off onto the larboard tack.

So far, so good. If he could put *Royal Duke* about in the dark with her half-trained crew, Clay was as good a seaman as himself. If not better, Hoare admitted. He should be as good, heaven knew. Clay had been at sea since boyhood without interruption, while Hoare had been shore-bound for eleven years. He feared he had lost the exquisite timing it took to execute even the basic maneuver Clay had just made. But the handling of small fore-and-aft-rigged craft, slooplings like his beloved pinnace *Nemesis,* now towing obediently behind *Royal Duke*, Hoare knew he still had no master.

Hoare thoughtfully dressed himself in the dark. He took down the superb set of French foul weather gear that he had brought aboard from the pinnace, donned it, and went on deck into the spitting midnight gloom.

"I was on the point of calling you, sir," Mr. Clay said into his ear. "The lookout in the fore crosstrees is sure he glimpsed the loom of some vessel to windward, off the larboard bow."

"Hail him for details."

"Deck there!" came the reply. "She be about a cable's length to windward, steerin' the same course as we be! We be closing' on 'er fast!"

"Order silence aboard, Mr. Clay," Hoare directed. "Ease the spanker sheet and slack the main topsail braces. I don't want to run aboard of her until we know more about her, and I'd rather not call her attention to us."

"Aye, aye, sir," came Mr. Clay's acknowledgment; in a quiet voice, he gave the requisite commands. In response, *Royal Duke*'s passage through the water slowed noticeably.

"How does she bear now?" This time, Clay's bellow was muted.

"Oldin' 'er own, sir!"

Hoare made a decision. He might have no voice, but his eyes were as keen as those of anyone aboard. He swung himself into the larboard main shrouds and swarmed up the ratlines as nimbly as Miss Austen would have. At least, he thought as he climbed, his cruises in *Nemesis* had left him hard-handed enough.

The lookout slid himself out onto the brig's fore crosstrees to accommodate the new arrival. He gave a startled grunt on seeing his skipper's face up here. Hoare could read his mind: "Captain Oglethorpe, bless 'is ol heart, 'ud never 'a made it up 're wifout a block an' taykle."

Sharp eyes or no, it took Hoare a good minute, even with the other's patient guidance, to find the stranger in the murk, but at last he had her. From all he could tell, she was a sharp-looking craft, a three-masted lugger with a topsail on her main. She looked at least as handy as the smuggler *Fancy* Hoare had seen founder off the Isle of Wight over a month ago. But her masts were more sharply raked, and there was that mizzen besides. There was something familiar about the rig.

"Frenchman, sir, or I miss me guess," the lookout said.

"What makes you think so?" was Hoare's whispered question.

"Seen enough of 'em in St. Malo 'arbor, sir, durin' the peace. Chaz Marie."

Hoare was slow in understanding the man's word. Then it sank in. *Chasse-marée* was what he had said, mangling the French as every good Englishman should. The *chasse-marée*, the "tide-chaser," was a fast French coaster, always lug-rigged, always three-masted.

"Smell 'er, sir? Only a Frenchman smells like that, or a Portygee. Garlic. An' she wouldn't be no Portygee, not in these waters. Besides, she don't pong of fish like a Portygee. No, sir, that's French cookin', or I'm a lobster."

"Clever man." Hoare could only agree. Now that the lookout mentioned it, even he could smell the rich scent of garlic, wine, and onions. The product of English sea-cooks was one thing, he thought sadly; French sea-cooking was another kettle of fish entirely. And now he remembered who the lookout was: he was Danny Quill, an Irishman for all his Cockney speech, cook's mate.

"She'll be a privateer, sir," Quill said, "packed as full of Frogs as a keg of sardines."

"I think you're right, Quill," Hoare whispered. "Keep a sharp eye out until you're relieved. Are you a good shot?" He had a mind to see a Frenchman served the way that unknown marksman had served him, those years ago.

"Not much of an 'and at musketry, sir, fer a fact. Need practice fer that."

"Well, then, I'll have Leese send up one of his Marines to keep you company. I plan to put a spoke in that Frog's wheel." So saying, Hoare grasped the main backstay to windward, preparatory to sliding down it to the deck.

"'Ave 'im bring a spare musket with 'im, sir," Quill suggested. "'Oo knows, I might strike it lucky."

"Aye, aye," Hoare answered, and let himself slide. He slid prudently, having seen more than one rash young man peel the skin off his palms on the harsh, tarred cordage of a backstay, just by the sliding.

"Call all hands, Mr. Clay, to quarters," he ordered once on deck, his hands burning a trifle despite his care. "But quietly, man, understand?"

How Clay was to manage preparing the brig for battle *quietly* was something he decided to leave to the lieutenant.

"Aye, aye, sir," said Clay, *quietly*, and did as Hoare had ordered. Silently, the Royal Dukes collected at their stations. The stranger's loom was ever so slightly greater.

Hoare knew what his next order must be, and his heart sank.

"And let *Nemesis* slip," he said. Towing behind *Royal Duke* as she was, she could only hold the brig back. Then he added, "Belay that. I'll do it myself."

Every man, he thought, should be man enough to shoot his own dog at need, or—if, like himself, he had no dog, at least to let go of his private bark, at need. He stepped to the taffrail and cast his sweetheart's towline off the cleat to which she had been made fast. As he watched, she disappeared astern in the mid-Channel gloom.

"Have the gunners load with chain shot, and run out the guns," Hoare now ordered. "When I whistle, they are to fire. High. *High,* Mr. Clay!" Clay relayed Hoare's order. All too well, Hoare knew the propensity for even trained gunners to hull the enemy whenever possible, the hull being the most massive target and the place where humans could be hit. Aiming high to disable was a foreign trick; hulling was the English way, and it generally worked. But if this craft was what he thought she was, he had no vestige of hope either of unmanning her or fleeing.

Now, how to assure himself absolutely of the other craft's nationality? It was all very well for Quill's culinary nose to identify her as a Frenchman, and the distinctive chasse-marée brig could belong to a prize. How to smoke out her identity without revealing *Royal Duke*'s own?

Hoare resolved upon a nocturnal version of the simple old ruse by which a ship flew false colors. As long as she hauled them down and replaced them before firing, honor was observed.

"Hail 'em—in French, Mr. Clay," he said.

"In French, sir?"

"In French, Mr. Clay."

"Aye, aye, sir," he said with a resigned shrug. "Kell vessow?" he shouted.

The awful sound he made in copying Hoare's whispered French delighted Hoare. Though his bellow was enviable, his accent was appalling, but it did as Hoare had hoped and must have left the Frenchman wondering for a precious few seconds, which was just what Hoare wanted.

The stranger gave no reply. Instead, he bore off and laid a course to cross *Royal Duke*'s bows and rake her from ahead—or, more likely, to board. This could only be a tactic of the lookout Quill's privateer, packed as full of Frogs as a keg of sardines.

"Bear away, Mr. Clay, and hoist our colors."

"Aye, aye, sir." Clay relayed Hoare's first order to the helmsmen. There were two of them now, as was normal practice when going into action, neither of them more than two feet from Hoare. They would have heard his initial order, but, as they had been taught, refrained from complying until they heard Clay's clear command. There being no signal midshipman at hand, Clay bent the Union Jack to its halliard himself and ran it up to *Royal Duke*'s gaff.

Hoare watched, watched, waited, eyes fixed on the other ship, judging their relative positions, courses and speeds, counting seconds with snap, snap, snap of his fingers as he had been taught when still a junior mid. Having the inner one of the double curve the two vessels were drawing across the midnight sea, *Royal Duke* visibly fore-reached upon the chasse-marée, while each of the two closed upon the other. By the time they were abeam, both were sailing on a broad reach, the Frenchman taking some of *Royal Duke*'s wind and commencing to draw ahead. By the nature of things, she was heeling toward the brig; in daylight, Hoare would have had a clear view of her cargo of privateersman. As it was, Hoare could hear the sound of the many men aboard her, as they nerved themselves to board.

He shut one eye. Thrusting two fingers into his mouth, he gave the shrill, piercing whistle that on this occasion his gun crews knew meant "Fire!"

Mr. Clay's command, unneeded, was drowned in the near-simultaneous *crack* of *Royal Duke*'s larboard battery—all four laughable four-pounders. Hoare opened his shielded eye. The faint afterglow of the burning powder sufficed to give him a brief picture of the broadside's effect on the chasse-marée.

Of the four chain shot, one must have gone astray, but the other three had done their duty, and more. One had struck the fore lugsail yard near where it met its mast, and left the sail drooping, useless. A second had struck the forestay, leaving the already weakened foremast unstayed forward, and the lugger herself without a rag drawing forward of her undamaged mainsail. The third ball must have struck in the neighborhood of her steering position, for Hoare could see a mass of heaving confusion about her wheel and could imagine cries of pain and rage. Her colors—the *Tricolor,* thank God—still flew.

It had been an absolute freak of luck, Hoare knew. Even at so close a range—point-blank musket shot and no more—he would have been overjoyed to see even two shots from his land-lubber-manned popgun crews even hit the enemy. Well . . .

"Rule Britannia, and take no prisoners!" he felt impelled to shout. Being unable to shout, he successfully suppressed the impulse, thanking himself fleetingly for his muteness. Such a command would have doomed *Royal Duke*'s gentle little crew, their ship, and its cargo of secrets.

As it was, Hoare could have asked for no better. Wheel or no wheel, nothing could have prevented the Frenchman, with no foresail to keep her off the wind, from losing way and falling into the wind, where she hung. There she lay, helpless against a second, raking broadside, as *Royal Duke* continued on course.

"We have her!" Mr. Clay roared, pounding his little fist on *Royal Duke*'s rail.

"Steady as you go! Reload!" Mr. Clay roared into the reddened darkness. The four gun crews commenced to scuttle about the darkened deck, preparing to reload.

"Cease fire, Mr. Clay!" Hoare ordered. "Secure from quarters, and resume our original course!"

"Sir! I protest!"

"Do as I've ordered, sir!" Hoare croaked, as forcefully as his scarred throat would allow. "Do not dismiss the watch below. I'll explain when we have stood down."

Grumbling audibly, the gun crews secured their popguns, closed the ports on both sides of the brig, and returned the rounds of chain shot to their waiting-grooves.

"A word in your ear, Mr. Clay." Hoare bent to that ear so he could be heard, and conducted his seething officer to the slight lee offered by *Royal Duke*'s coach-house coaming.

"*Think*, sir. What would have been the outcome if our people were to give battle against more than thrice our number of enraged, experienced, greedy privateersman? Why, we would have been overwhelmed within minutes, and our survivors under hatches."

"I had not . . ."

"I know, Mr. Clay. You were carried away by the rage of battle. I understand, and I honor you for it. No one, *no one,* could doubt your courage. But there's more, sir—a truly compelling reason why I turned away when I did. You . . . will remember at least as well as I the Admiralty's original stricture against our going to sea at all under our own control, and their lordships' reasons for the prohibition. . . . With that in mind, how, pray, would you explain even a victory when you gave your report to our masters? 'You,' I say, for . . . I assure you that honor would not permit me to survive long enough to give it myself." Hoare meant this with all his heart. His demeanor must have showed it, for his little lieutenant hung his head.

"I did not think, sir. I . . . as you say, I was carried away by the heat of battle."

"Now, Mr. Clay," Hoare went on, "I must do my best to

persuade our people that my refusal to do battle was not mere poltroonery . . . but was in the best interest of the service. And I must ask you, once again, to act as my mouthpiece . . . whatever your true feelings may be." With that, he had Mr. Clay summon the Royal Dukes to the purely imaginary break of the quarterdeck.

A child could have sensed the feelings that radiated from them as they stood there in the dark of the night—shame, scorn, thwarted greed. Given a lead, there would be shot rolling about the deck, the private signal that was so often the precursor of mutiny. These people had wanted to conquer, kill, and loot. The urge to violence was all the greater, perhaps, for the memory of the contemptuous laughter from the observing men-o'-war in Portsmouth harbor, when they made their first feeble, laughable attempt to handle *Royal Duke*. "The Dustbins" had been the least insulting of the watchers' mocking appellations. Now, their own commander had thwarted them. During the next few minutes, Hoare must explain himself convincingly, or his command was dead and rotting.

So, without rodomontade, he set out, with Clay's big voice at his side booming out his words, to tell his people why he had turned tail in the face of the enemy instead of leading them into what they had been sure was certain, easy victory. First, though, he praised them for the calmness and order with which they had mustered in the dark and delivered the first broadside *Royal Duke* had ever delivered in anger. Then he asked them, as he had Clay, what outcome they, a mere thirty-odd, could have expected from battle against a hundred enemies—enemies who were not cowed but enraged.

"I ask you this," he said, "now that the thing is over and you've had a chance to cool down."

"We coulda taken 'em," came a voice; there were mutters of agreement.

"They'd'a made mincemeat of us, ye lubbers." Hoare recognized Bold's deep voice.

"Aye." That was Slopey, the brig's Oriental; Hoare had yet

to determine if he was Chinese or Japanese. They all looked alike to him.

Now he reminded them of the vast treasure of vital knowledge they themselves had created and bore with them, and confessed to his own madness at having put their creation at risk. In all truth, now that the encounter was past, the thought of his recklessness appalled Hoare, and he said as much.

His offer to hear questions resulted in a few of them. Most had to do with what he thought of the crew's behavior, especially that of the individual questioners. He repeated his praise. One remark he found tough to handle.

"Ogle, sir, private of marines."

"Yes, Ogle?"

"I jest wanted to tell ye, sir. Sergeant posted me in the foretop with me rifle. I missed fire, sir."

"Shame on ye, Ogle," Leese said.

"But, sir, I brung up a musket fer Danny Quill, an 'e shot the Frog's captain, he did. Saw it wif me own eyes, I did."

Hoare knew quite well that Ogle could have seen nothing of the kind. But he believed he had, and it was a creditable thing for him to believe. The Royal Dukes were learning to pull together.

"Well done," he said through Clay's voice. "Well done, the both of you."

Three bells sounded now. He felt justified in dismissing the men with his thanks, and the feeling that his motives were better understood and his courage no longer questioned. For now.

"Thank you, Mr. Clay," he said. His lieutenant might have spoken his words in truth, or he might not. They had sounded convincing enough. Suddenly he recalled that Clay had stood watch for a good eighteen hours without relief, fought the skirmish just passed, and been rebuked by his commanding officer. The man had had enough, Hoare felt. He relieved the other and sent him below. He gave the deck to Taylor but remained on deck himself lest she run into danger.

The events of the past hour had shown him that, while Mr.

Clay was undoubtedly a gallant officer, a fine seaman, and—he believed—well-disposed toward him, he wanted the cool judgment that the commander of this little craft, with its peculiar mission, must possess. Before they went into action again . . . Here, Hoare stopped himself with a wry internal laugh. *Royal Duke* must never again go into action.

"Permission to speak, sir?" It was Taylor.

"Permission granted, Taylor."

"Before we go too far on our course, sir," she said, "the tide is just turning. Could we not take two hours—no more, sir—return in our tracks, and see if we might not recover our tender? She has been a valuable asset to the ship, and it would be almost criminal to leave her behind before we have exercised due diligence in searching for her."

Put this way, the argument was an appealing one. In a manner of speaking, his pinnace was part of the brig's equipment, just as he himself was, and all his possessions—including *Nemesis*. From that point of view, he would even be wanting in attention to his command's condition were he to leave the pinnace behind without "exercising due diligence" in preserving it.

Suddenly it struck him. Perhaps, having spent time in *Nemesis* herself during the Nine Stones affair, the little craft had seduced this big woman just as she—the pinnace, not the person, as he reminded himself sharply—had seduced Hoare himself.

He thought. The picture of his crisp little craft lying in the trough of the Channel seas, abandoned, bereft, there to be caught up by any passing stranger, made him bleed anew. By God, he'd do it.

Three hours ago, Hoare, seeing Taylor grinning triumphantly astern at the recovered *Nemesis,* had left the deck to her and turned in himself. She had handled the recovery masterfully, and without calling the watch below, though the alert Mr. Clay, weary though he was, had awakened when *Royal Duke* wore, not to return below until Hoare all but thrust him along.

Hoare himself was awakened now, as he was almost every morning, by the snuffling, scratching sound of the bear on the deck over his head. He knew the bear well; in keeping with *Royal Duke*'s size, it was a small bear. It might, in fact, be considered a bear cub, Hoare thought sleepily, for it needed only two men to draw it back and forth between them across the yacht's deck. Like an organic sandpaper, the bear's coarse coir surface smoothed the deck for the day, while producing its peaceful snuffling sound. Hoare was tempted to roll over and go back to sleep, but remembered that, upon arriving in the Thames estuary, he was to appear before his master at the Admiralty. Besides, last night's brush with the French had thrown *Royal Duke*'s schedule all awry. It had gone six bells already, he saw, yet the watch on deck was still preparing her for her arrival.

On deck, in the gray morning, he found matters had progressed well, bear or no bear. The four light smears of soot from last night's single broadside had been cleared away. A brace that must have been parted by one of the few musket shots the Frenchman had been able to get off had been spliced. The bear leaders were already returning their charge to its den in the fore-peak; and Mr. Clay, up again, stood beside the helmsman, small, brisk, and proud. The hands were cheerful enough as they moved about their duties. Hoare could sense no residue of ill temper. The brig was close-hauled on the starboard tack, sailing briskly full and bye, heeling to the icy January breeze and bowing to the short chop. Sarah Taylor, master's mate, was not to be seen.

Mr. Clay made his salute and his report. "We rounded the North Foreland an hour ago, sir, and managed a good ten miles before the wind began backing westerly. We're still making progress, but of course we'll be headed by the tide before long. At this rate, we shan't be abreast of the Isle of Sheppey this tide."

"Hmph," was all Hoare could reply. Happily, it meant that the flooding tide would start helping them up the narrowing Thames at about the time they passed Woolwich. All the same, it would be evening by then. *Royal Duke* would be lucky to make Greenwich tomorrow, and would therefore have to risk sailing at night once again, with all the risk of collision that entailed. For the Thames estuary was packed with shipping, inbound and out. This was England's great artery that brought nourishment to her heart, and delivered so much of the power that held the French the other side of the Channel, where they belonged.

"With your permission, sir," Mr. Clay said, "I'll see that the people are at work below. There are some documents—correlations, I think they call them—that should be brought to a close before we bring them to Greenwich."

"By all means, Mr. Clay," was Hoare's reply. "But, while you are about it, you might be considering a different station for Green. I suspect that Quill would make a better cook."

"Perhaps she could be attached to Leese's marines, sir," Clay offered, "as heavy infantry." With that sally, he went below. The monstrous Green had formerly been a terror among the "brutes" that served and serviced the seaman population of Portsmouth; as a member of Hoare's crew, she had wielded a lethal cleaver at the Nine Stones affray last All Hallows' Eve.

It had been a good fifteen years since Hoare had been in these waters. They had a different, grayer color than the sea along the southern coast, a more choppy motion, and—above all—a different smell. Most likely, Hoare thought, it was the effluvium of London. The river served not only as an artery but as a sewer. As that thought passed through his mind, a bulbous, greasy object bobbed past in *Royal Duke*'s leeward bow wave and disappeared in her wake. A dead dog, it would be, a long-dead dog. It was not hard to find an explanation for the name of the Isle of Dogs, which lay not too far ahead.

Hoare realized that he did not look forward at all to this mission. It was taking him out of his comfortable accustomed south-coast waters, and into the malodorous, trap-ridden capital. He would flounder, he felt certain, and fail. To jolt his mind out of this unwonted gloom, he began to compose his report to the Admiralty on last night's skirmish. It made him feel no better.

While Greenwich was a trivial port compared with the great yards at Deptford immediately adjoining, it still warranted a Port Officer of its own. Perhaps, Hoare thought, the honor was due to the town's faded glory as a favorite haunt of England's monarchs and their wives and concubines. Whatever the reason, the Port Officer existed, and it was to him that *Royal Duke* made her number and received berthing orders. She was to anchor close into shore, off the Crane Stairs.

The place was all but vacant now, deserted only a few days ago by the hordes that had assembled for the obsequies of the late Lord Nelson. His body had been landed here, had lain in state in the Painted Chamber, and then been carried, the center of a vast black-clad cortege, by barge up to London. Vacant the town might be, it remained littered with all that a great crowd can leave behind it—mislaid umbrellas, odd papers, empty bottles by the score. And little would remain in the line of sustenance, whether liquid or solid.

"So I missed him again." It was Titus Thoday, titular gunner, beside him. Hoare knew it would be all but hopeless to demand more than the most superficial respect from this dignified, proud, gentlemanly, clever, meticulous man. He was a superb . . . *detective,* would that be the word? . . . but, as a sailor, he was a king's bad bargain.

Just as the news of Nelson's death had reached Weymouth, Hoare and Thoday had been fellow passengers in the chaise bearing them and their prisoner Walter Spurrier into the town.

"I shall never forget this moment," Thoday had said then, in a voice pregnant with feeling. "The morning of November the sixth, 1805. This is the place, and the time, where I was when I learned of Nelson's death."

"I fear we have both missed him again, Thoday," Hoare now replied, and turned to ship's business. He must go ashore and make his number to the Port Officer in person.

That gentleman was occupied, as Port Officers tended to be at all times.

"He will not be long, sir," said the clerk. "Captain Horn-

45

blower is with him, and he will be wishing to speed the parting guest.

"The two gentlemen do not see eye to eye in the matter of the honors due Captain Hornblower's new midshipman, sir," he went on in a confidential whisper, little louder than Hoare's own ghost of a voice. When Hoare did not prick up his ears at his breath of gossip, he subsided into sullen silence.

Hoare had met Hornblower almost exactly two years before, during the brief, uneasy peace of Amiens with the French. In fact, it had been Hornblower from whom he had acquired *Nemesis*. They had both been lieutenants then, but Hoare had at least been employed; he had then been, as he had remained until kind Fate brought him his present command, a general dogsbody to Sir George Hardcastle. Hornblower, on the other hand, had then been without a ship, and as long as the peace endured had hardly the slightest prospects of obtaining one. Moreover, due to a spitefully meticulous Navy Board, he had been penniless. It was that situation that had forced the pinnace's change of master. Their paths had not crossed since, though—the navy being a band of brothers after all, Hoare had been aware of the other's career. Now the one was a post captain, albeit a very junior one, while Hoare would never make post. Well, that was the way the world wagged; Hornblower was a gallant officer with, as Hoare had heard, an unfortunate doting wife and no money in the family. No one deserved post rank more than he. Save Hoare himself, of course.

At this instant, Captain Hornblower himself emerged from the Port Officer's office, and stood in the doorway just long enough to bid a courteous, cold farewell to the person within. When, turning, he caught sight of Hoare, his eyes lit up.

"Hoare, by God!" he grinned. "Well met!"

"Recovered from your cold, I see, sir," Hoare replied. The day the pinnace had changed hands—another wintry day, as it happened—the other officer's nose had been streaming.

"But not until recently, I see," he added, since he saw that Hornblower's nostrils were still red.

"A *new* cold, Hoare, upon my honor."

The two men drew to one side.

"I must pay my respects to the gentleman within, sir," Hoare whispered, "but would you tarry long enough to break bread with me? I should not be but a moment."

"I am genuinely sorry, sir," Hornblower replied, looking as though he meant it, "but I have a prior duty to Mrs. Hornblower, who has just been brought to bed of a son."

"My felicitations, most sincerely, sir."

"But tell me, how do you and the pinnace suit? What did you name her?"

"She goes by *Nemesis* now. We suit very well. We have had some interesting cruises together. She lies astern of *Royal Duke*; in fact, if you peer out the window there, you may see her for yourself."

Hornblower peered, approved her new, unorthodox rig, told Hoare that he and his family were to be found at the George in Deptford, where they would . . . when the loud clearing of an official throat at the door summoned Hoare back to the formal world and they parted.

Chapter IV

———◆◆◆———

"FLOATER, ENNERY," bow oar said. "'Back water, will ye, an' I'll 'aul 'im aboard. *Ukkh.* Slimy, 'e is. Three days dead, is my guess."

"'Ole in 'is belly, too," said Ennery. "'Ead shaved for a wig, 'eavylike. Might be the man the Redbreasts want."

"Wot color eyes?" bow oar asked. "Bow Street said they was blue, I fink."

"You know better nor that, mate. You ain't no Johnny Raw. "'E ain't got no more eyes. Crabs got 'em. Come on; let's about an' take 'im 'ome to muvver. I don't care fer 'is cumpny no longer than needful."

Immediately upon paying off the wherryman he had hired at Greenwich to carry him up to London Bridge, Hoare rediscovered the dizzying effect the city had on a stranger, or at least on him. There were so many people in the crowded streets, of so many colors and callings, and of no color or calling at all; such stinks of rotten vegetables, of stale beer, of heavy perfume from some passerby of better station, and—rolling out of every alley—such a fetor of mingled human wastes; such a din, of raised voices, protesting beasts, hawkers crying their wares; such a disorganized stew of buildings old and new, stately and graceless. Confused and disoriented, he hailed the first hackney he saw and ordered the driver to take him to the Admiralty in Whitehall.

His senses overloaded, Hoare was even more confused when the hackney drew up before the gate of the Admiralty in the gathering darkness. Like a fool, he paid the driver off, and the hackney had trundled off before he discovered that the gate was locked. The marine sentry told him with some satisfaction that, with winter drawing in, the Admiralty was closed to all outsiders at five. Since three bells of the first dogwatch had just struck, he could not be admitted today, let alone be allowed to leave his portmanteau at the gate.

"'Oo knows, sir?" the sentry asked. "Yer port-mantoe could 'ave an infernal machine in it, like one of them machines the Frogs are usin' to blow up the Portsmouth fleet." Hoare forbore to tell the sentry that those particular French atrocities would not recur.

Hoare was forced to violate naval etiquette for officers and lug his portmanteau with him around to the back of the darkened building as Sir George Hardcastle had instructed him, feeling his way as he went and stepping into sundry unsavory leavings. His knocks at the privy gate went unanswered. It was too late tonight, then, to make himself known to Admiral Sir Hugh Abercrombie. He returned to Whitehall.

What now? With his means of making his needs known to strangers so limited by his lack of a voice, how was he to make his way from here to the Golden Cross Inn? He felt like a booby, and he did not like the sensation at all. Keeping the portmanteau between his legs lest it disappear into the early gloaming, he drew the boatswain's call from his bosom and blew a short trill upon it. In response, what he had hoped for happened. An alert, nautical-looking oldster came up to him and knuckled his forehead.

"Evans, sir. Late captain's cox'n in *Grampus*," he said. "At your service, sir."

Hoare beckoned the man closer, and leaned forward to whisper in his ear. Evans must have been expecting to hear some unspeakable request, for he looked nonplussed when Hoare merely whispered, "Golden Cross Inn, my man," and pointed to his portmanteau.

But he shrugged and said, "Foller me, then, sir." Shouldering the portmanteau, he led the way out the Admiralty gate and into the thronged street.

"Ye'll not have been in London for a bit, sir," he volunteered over his shoulder. Then, not hearing Hoare's reply, he apparently realized this officer must have some speech impediment, for he slowed and took station to Hoare's left.

"No, I haven't," said Hoare. "Must be fifteen years."

"The place has changed mightily since then, sir. There's lots more of us. Stretchin' out, too, and new buildin's goin' up all the time."

"Why aren't you at sea, Evans?" Hoare asked.

"Captain Dawson, 'e bought me out of the service when 'e come into his estate, an' I went into service with him as his waterman, me 'avin' been his cox'n, like I said.

"I brought him and his lady into town downriver this mornin', an' he give me leaf to see what I could pick up in the way of a shillin'. Or two," he added hopefully. "So I heard yer bosun's call back there, and 'ere we are, sir."

And here they were, indeed, Hoare saw, for just ahead, a hanging sign bearing a St. Andrew's cross, gilt on a red field, proclaimed their destination.

Gules, a saltire or, Hoare thought. An ancient and honorable coat of arms, indeed. Perhaps the inn, or at least the site, had once been the townhouse of some Plantagenet grandee.

The grandee, if there ever had been one, was gone, but his grandeur remained behind. The inn had a somewhat gloomy air of obsolete elegance. A manservant idling outside the door, a tablecloth around his waist in lieu of an apron, looked at him sneeringly. Hoare knew it was nothing but pretentiousness on the man's part, and he was damned if he would show cowed in front of any Frog, emigré or not.

"Mind yer manners, Pierre," Evans said. "Off with you, an' tell Mister Berrier 'e's a guest."

Pierre dropped his sneer, replaced it with a smirk, and vanished behind the high door.

"You're known here, it seems," Hoare whispered.

"Oh, yes, sir. This is where Captain Dawson and 'is lady puts up when they come in to town. In fact, here's the captain now. If you'll excuse me, sir?" On seeing Evans, a man paused on his way up the wide, dark stairs.

"I thought I'd given you liberty, Evans," he said.

"You did, sir," said Evans. "An' I found this officer wantin' to put up at this very inn, so I brought him along."

Evans quickly pocketed the hoped-for two shillings and knuckled his forehead again to the two gentlemen before disappearing in his turn, leaving Captain Dawson and Hoare to stare at each other. Hoare saw a pale-complexioned yet fit-looking man possibly fifteen years his senior, shorter than he by half a head, in a well-cut tailed coat of navy blue whose buttons, though brass, were plain.

"Don't think we've met, sir," said Dawson finally. "Waitin' for me wife. Name's Dawson—David Dawson."

Hoare introduced himself; the inn's hallway being silent, he had no need to fall back on one of his printed introductory explanations.

"Not Joel Hoare's boy?"

Hoare nodded assent.

"Served under him in *Vindicator* until he retired in eighty-four. Heard he'd died. Sorry to hear it."

Hoare remembered now. "Why, sir, were you not the gallant officer who lead *Vindicator*'s boarding party when she took *Bourgogne* in eighty-two?"

"The same, sir, although I cannot accept your kind description. Just did me duty, ye know."

"Nonsense, sir. I am honored."

Dawson in his turn looked at Hoare in sudden recognition.

"And aren't you the chap who found *Amazon*'s mids and cleared Grable's name?"

Hoare nodded.

"A magnificent undertaking, sir," said Dawson. "You saved one of His Majesty's most valuable officers from being put ashore in disgrace.

"I'd ask you to take wine with me, but here's me wife. We must be off.

"Late as usual, eh, Alice? We'll be late at Lady Doverdale's, and it'll be your fault."

Dawson made the introduction to his stately wife, and then without consulting Mrs. Dawson, he invited Hoare to dine with them there tomorrow evening.

"Berrier here sets a fine table. A bit Frenchified for my taste, but well worth settin' down to."

"That's right, ain't it, Berrier?" he added as the man himself bustled out from the rear of the inn, wigged, soft, and oily, washing his hands, ready to please.

"Indeed, Captain Dawson," Mr. Berrier said. "I trust you will enjoy your soirée with the Doverdales." The Dawsons swept from the inn.

"Now, let me see, Captain Hoare," Mr. Berrier said in a cultivated Frenchified accent after a swift appraising look at Hoare's spare form, "I believe the Blue Room might suit. It finds itself at the back of the building, away from the noisy street, and you will 'ave it to yourself.

"Now, if you will 'ave ze kindness to bear with me while we attend to certain trifles, I shall take the liberty of showing you ze more public facilities we offer."

Hoare was intrigued to discover that Berrier hewed to the formalities of registration, which had become universal on the continent—taking names, birthdates, and the like. Since that was neither English custom nor English law, he was puzzled at what might be done with these details. He forbore to inquire of mine host, but followed him meekly into a snug parlor to the right of the entry and thence across the hall where a number of waiters, including the man with the sneer, loitered about like whores, awaiting the first diners of the evening. At two of the white-covered tables, the chairs had been tipped forward; Hoare asked Berrier the reason.

The latter used the occasion to commence a tale of how, besides catering to resident guests, the dining salon of the Golden Cross was a popular gathering place for the better sort.

"Zat table zere, *mon capitaine*, 'as been rrresairved for Lord Allerdyce for 'imself, General Boyce and 'is ozzer guests.

"I fear it will become somewhat boisterous later this evening, *mon capitaine,* so Monsieur may wish to dine early. If so, we are at your sairveese."

Hoare followed a boy up a broad stairway and then up a second, narrower and steeper one, arriving at last at the Blue Room. The boy, Sam, unlocked the door and took a candle from a row of sconces in the corridor. Then, with a muttered apology, he preceded Hoare into the room, where he used the candle to light several others.

Small the room might be—it could have been the chamber of one of the grandee's children—it was cozy and the bed inviting.

"Will ye be wantin' the fire lit, Captain, sir?" the boy asked, and upon seeing Hoare's nod, stooped and set fire to the coals in the grate. When the door closed softly behind him, Hoare pulled off his shoes, warmed himself for a moment before the fire, then washed the dust of the road from hands and face and, pulling his shoes back on, returned below. Here he satisfied himself with an excellent though solitary dinner.

It was one of the best meals he had ever consumed. The dinner was in the French style: two removes, an amplitude of crisp vegetables, even a platter of frogs' legs, reeking with garlic, at which the officers at a neighboring table scoffed almost insultingly until they met Hoare's flat, basilisk stare.

He was weary, wearier than he could believe possible. Could he be sickening of something? Nonetheless, he let the hovering waiter persuade him to a glass of port and a slice of Blue Vinny cheese.

"Sir."

"Excuse me, sir."

Someone was shaking Hoare by the shoulder, gently but firmly. Was it time to relieve Mr. Clay on deck, so soon? He opened his eyes, to look into the tolerant face of the Golden Cross's attentive waiter.

"Oh. What's the time?" Hoare whispered.

"Gone eleven, sir. Shouldn't you be abed now?" He would be far from the first gentleman the waiter had seen fall asleep over his port. There was the rustle of dignitaries in the doorway. Clearly, the dining room staff wanted him out of the way, and Hoare was happy to oblige.

He shook his head to clear it, thanked the man, and climbed the two flights of stairs to the Blue Room. There he blew out the one guttering candle that remained and fell asleep on the counterpane without even removing his shoes.

London, Hoare decided the next morning, offered even tougher navigational challenges than pine-clad, rockbound Penobscot Bay or the blockaded, cannon-girt shallows around Brest. On making his way from the Golden Cross, he took himself into and out of three blind alleys in the warren surrounding White-hall before he finally tracked down the privy entrance to the Admiralty to which Sir George Hardcastle had directed him. It was a wearisome passage, and he feared he had found his way only by fool luck.

Once found, however, the privy entrance was easily breached. Having presented his orders to an ancient, he waited while the man shuffled off to return with an eager-looking mouse of a man. The mouse took out a list and read down it until he found Hoare's name as one expected by Admiral Sir Hugh Abercrombie, KB. He then guided him down a series of stately corridors and through a web of unimpressive byways to the lair of the spider himself. The lair was lofty, spacious, well heated by a pair of glowing fireplaces, and overlooked the Horse Guards Parade; Hoare was reinforced in his expectation that the admiral was high in the councils of the mighty.

Sir Hugh was occupied with a ferret-shaped, sinuous man. The escorting mouse took one look at the ferret and fled into some bolt-hole of his own.

"You'll be Hoare," Sir Hugh rumbled from out of a pasty, puddinglike head. "Take a pew. I'll be finished with Lestrade here momentarily."

After exchanging a few more words in an undertone, Lestrade withdrew. Sir Hugh could now turn his attention to Hoare. He did not rise, for the simple act of coming to his feet would obviously have been hard for him. Now, Hoare understood why it had been necessary to devise that reinforced hanging chair in the late Captain Oglethorpe's cabin—now Hoare's own—aboard *Royal Duke*; Sir Hugh was vast.

"Stand up straight," the admiral said. Hat under arm, Hoare came to attention and stood to be inspected, staring at the invisible horizon.

"You have a report for me. Hand it over."

After receiving the papers over which Hoare had labored two nights ago, Sir Hugh steepled his hands and for several minutes examined his visitor in silence, his cold gray eyes nearly hidden in the pudding of his face. Finally, he spoke.

"So. Take a seat, sir. I have read the memoranda you drafted for Hardcastle. You're his deus ex machina, then. His Hercules. The man he uses to drag his chestnuts out of the fire. Good record at sea, respectable navy family, no voice. Pity about that.

You look as though you were otherwise fit for command. But the fleet's loss is the service's gain. Perhaps.

"Let me read these reports, however, so as not to try your voice with unnecessary questions. Be seated, if you please."

Sir Hugh drew a long churchwarden pipe from a rack behind him, packed it carefully, and lit it. When the pipe was drawing to his satisfaction, he began to read, puffing thoughtfully at the pipe as he read and giving off thick clouds of smoke. Within a minute, the room was befogged; within three minutes, his reading ended.

Setting the most recent report down, Sir Hugh now fired a fifteen-minute barrage of questions at Hoare. He covered every aspect of the *Vantage* affair, and the events surrounding the Nine Stones Circle, whether or not Hoare had set it down. He inquired about Hoare's odd little yacht, about his bride, and about the child Jenny Jaggery. He reached back into Hoare's past, to the *Amazon* and *Hebe* affair and even to his previous marriage in Halifax. He seemed to know everything.

After each question, Sir Hugh waited patiently for Hoare's increasingly painful answer, but before his cloud of pungent verbal powder smoke drifted away, Hoare was sweating freely and his feeble whisper had drifted into mere mouthing.

"Very good," Sir Hugh said at last. "Or at least, good enough. Between you and Hardcastle, the two of you may have concocted a French farrago of lies, but at least you have enough brains to be consistent with each other.

"Now. Listen carefully. You are to repeat nothing said in this or any other conversation you and I may have, and subsequently shall neither make notes of them nor prepare any writings about them. Is that clearly understood?"

Sir Hugh accepted Hoare's nod and continued. "Hardcastle will have told you a little about this office, and the activities I direct on their lordships' behalf. Those activities, of course, include your own, and those of the vessel you command.

"You have now cut off two tentacles of Bonaparte's secret service, but there are many others. Since you will have earned their extreme displeasure, you will need to walk with care henceforth. A word to the wise, sir.

"It is my task to seek out the remaining agents and destroy them, wherever they may be found, to turn them, or at least, if appropriate, to deceive them to His Majesty's advantage. It is also my task to manage the navy's own network of agents, but that is neither here nor there."

For a full hour, Sir Hugh discoursed in his low thunder of a voice upon case after case, technique upon technique. From time to time a minion padded in to place a document before his master. Without interrupting the flow of his lecture, Sir Hugh would peruse it, pen a marginal comment, sometimes sign it, and return it to the minion. The latter would then pad out. Except for an occasional remark, from Sir Hugh and never from the minion, these encounters took place in silence. Between them, Sir Hugh's deep voice droned on, and on, and on.

Just as Hoare was about to raise a hand and plead for an interval of rest, Sir Hugh said, "We now come to the immediate reason for your presence here. Hardcastle will have told you of the disappearance of certain documents of state at a time when this office had them in its charge. Their import is international and major. In the hands of the French, their misuse would be dire. They must be found. If possible, they must be recovered. If not, they must be destroyed.

"The other departments of His Majesty's government have not been notified of the loss. For them to learn of it would diminish the navy materially, to its cost and eventually to the disservice of the Crown."

So far, the admiral had told Hoare no more than he had learned from Sir George Hardcastle—less, in fact. Now, however, Sir Hugh leaned forward in his heavy chair and peered through the remaining tobacco smoke at him.

"More than that. I did not inform Sir George of this, but one of my senior confidential clerks has also gone missing. The very man, in fact, who is charged with preserving documents of confidence, among which the missing papers were to be numbered. He has not been seen since Thursday week. His nonappearance was, in fact, the event that prompted us to take the inventory of the documents in his charge, and to discover the absence of the documents in the case."

"Pray tell me about the man, sir." These were Hoare's first words since Sir Hugh had commenced his narrative.

"He is Octavius Ambler by name. Forty-four years of age, but looks older. He has been in Admiralty service for twenty-eight years, rising from apprentice writer to his present position, separated by only two degrees from myself. An only child, he has never married but lived with his widowed mother in Lambeth until her death eighteen months ago."

"His appearance, sir?"

"He is heavyset, fully fleshed, unhealthy of complexion. Much like myself, in fact. . . ." Sir Hugh looked down at his own massive, soft form with obvious distaste, and went on.

"But not so excessively bulky. Unlike me, he gets about nimbly enough for a man in his sedentary position. I am ruddy; he is pallid. Old-fashioned as to his dress. Look here."

The admiral turned, bent over his hampering belly and began to rummage through a drawer in the cabinet at his side. From where he sat, Hoare could see that the drawer was laid out with orderly labeled partitions of what might be veneer, enclosing space for files. An admirable arrangement, he thought, and one which he would see copied in *Royal Duke*'s 'tweendecks.

"Here," Sir Hugh said at last. "We have likenesses made of all our principal staff, including myself. The man who makes them apprenticed under Mr. Rowlandson or Mr. Gillray—I disremember which. This is the one he made of Ambler."

Hoare took the drawing Sir Hugh extended to him. His wiry hand and Sir Hugh's pudgy one nearly touched; with a sharp motion, the admiral snatched his paw out of danger.

Hoare examined the likeness, a silverpoint on durable hard gray paper that showed the subject's head and shoulders. As Sir Hugh had said, it also showed a full-lipped man in the worst of physical condition, heavy of jowls, petulant of expression, cleft-chinned, bewigged, and heavily pockmarked. Hoare believed the artist had tried to capture every little circular pit.

"May I see your own likeness, sir?" Hoare asked.

Sir Hugh bridled. "Damn you, sir, you see the original before you. What need have you for my simulacrum? Taken a fancy to me?" His grin was quite hideous.

"By your leave, sir," Hoare said firmly, "I would like to compare the artist's view of you with my own." He looked expectantly at his superior.

The admiral grumbled, but eventually returned to his orderly files.

"Here you are," he said. This time, he did not hold out the likeness for Hoare to take from his hand but set it on the desk between them, where Hoare could reach it easily enough without bringing their two hands too close together for his admiral's comfort.

Hoare glanced between likeness and subject. Given the artist's training and the sitter's grossness of feature, he had feared that the silverpoint would be more or less of a caricature, but it was nothing of the kind. It was neither flattering nor cruel, but coolly objective. Sir Hugh had been depicted according to Oliver Cromwell's wish, warts and all. The drawing pointed out that the admiral had two of them altogether, one just beyond his left eye and the other beside the opposite nostril. Hitherto Hoare had observed neither, but there they were. Moreover, the artist had precisely captured Admiral Abercrombie's expression of cold, experienced power. He could have been a Renaissance cardinal. It was the portrait of a master, by a master. He now believed he could count on the actual presence of those pock-marks that marred the face of the missing Octavius Ambler.

"Whoever he is, sir," Hoare whispered, "he is a man of genius. I should like to make his acquaintance." He returned the drawing.

"It took him fifteen minutes, as I recall," the admiral observed, putting his own likeness back into its slot. "He did the last one a year ago. I must have him bring me up to date; I've faded a bit since then.

"No, I lie. It took him a good half-hour of my time. I had to sit there while he fiddled, fiddled, fiddled. If you want to meet him—though damned if I can tell why—he keeps a studio in Threadneedle Street. Number fourteen, over Baker the mercer's. Pickering's his name."

Hoare had no better idea than the admiral of why he should want to meet the artist, except, perhaps, that since he had taken command of *Royal Duke*'s extraordinary crew, he was always on the lookout for new and potentially useful talents.

"To return to the man Ambler, sir," he said. "Have his lodgings been searched, and if so, by whom?"

"They *were* searched, sir, and by an expert. Lestrade. The man with whom I was closeted when you made your appearance. But the place had already been ransacked when he broke in. He found nothing of any relevance; the man's clothes were in disorder, and his personal belongings strewn about the place.

"Lestrade concluded that, whatever happened to Ambler, it is most likely that he has suffered foul play."

Hoare came to a decision, but decided that he was not quite ready to act upon it.

"I shall want to meet Mr. Lestrade, sir, if you please." Sir Hugh nodded.

"Tell me, sir, does Ambler have any particular friends, any personal habits of interest?"

The admiral was silent for a moment. He reloaded his churchwarden pipe while thinking. At last he said, "As to friends, I am unaware of any. Like so many men of our cerebral calling, he is of a solitary nature, almost cenobitical. As to habits, I can think of none.

"Any more questions? If not, I have much to do."

Hoare looked at the clock that ticked softly in a corner. Good heavens; it had gone four. For more than four hours he had been closeted with his superior officer. He rose hastily, with a whispered apology.

"Just a minute, Hoare," the admiral said. "You have not returned the sketch of Octavius Ambler. Pray do so."

"With all respect, sir," Hoare whispered, "I shall need it if I am to identify the man reliably."

He felt Sir Hugh prepared to roar, and mentally reduced sail and battened down against the blast in the offing. It did not come.

"Quite right," the admiral finally said. "Thy need is greater than mine—or that of me files. Keep it, then, and take yourself off."

"The man's address again, sir? I neglected to take it down."

With bad grace, Sir Hugh gave it.

"A last request, sir, by your leave," Hoare asked. "Has this establishment a pigeon from a Greenwich cote? I should like to send an urgent message to my ship, for one of my men to join me."

"Of course, we have, although, this tide, a pair-oar gig would be just as fast." The admiral's voice was testy. Long since, Hoare had learned that, like lamb and rosemary, admirals and testiness went together. "And ones I can send off to Portsmouth, as you must know. And several for Paris. Not, however, for St. Petersburg or Halifax or Jerusalem. There's no call for 'em. Besides, they're too far off. Hand it to Cratchit outside the door, with your instructions. He'll deliver your message.

"Tomorrow, make yourself known to Goldthwait. John Goldthwait. Eleven, Chancery Lane. He'll be expecting you."

Hoare made his bow and prepared to take his leave. Just as he had his hand on the door, the admiral addressed his back. He turned.

"Thoday would be a good man to bring into the case, Hoare." He pronounced the man's name as though it were spelled "Today," just as the man himself insisted it be pronounced. Being sensitive about matters of names himself, Hoare had understood from the first, and had obliged. As a matter of fact, Thoday was the very man he had in mind.

"Knows his way about, that man does," Sir Hugh went on. "Pity he's a Papist; otherwise, he could go far in His Majesty's service.

"Oh, and by the bye, Hoare," he said in conclusion, "I just recalled. The man Ambler is a dedicated falconer. An armchair austringer. I'm certain he never had one on his wrist, but short of that, he knows all there is to be known about falconry. Jesses, you know, and eyasses. Mutes. That sort of thing."

As he bent to his papers, Sir Hugh rang a small bell. Instantly, his mouse appeared, looked about as if to make certain the ferret Lestrade was not lying in wait to pounce upon him, and took Hoare in hand once again.

"Thank you, sir," Hoare said, and closed the door behind himself and the mouse. Sir Hugh's afterthoughts, he mused as he wrote down his message on the slip of thin paper the mouse handed him, were enlightening. He remembered both Hancock and Thoday, including their salient qualities. Hancock was a smelly man; Hoare found his presence almost unbearable. And Thoday knew his way about very well, indeed. If Hoare himself was, as he knew the Portsmouth underworld called him, the "Whispering Ferret," Titus Thoday was a sleuth-hound, a bloodhound, a born detective.

Before he left the Admiralty, he remembered, he wanted to make the acquaintance of Lestrade. He ordered Cratchit to take him to the man's lurking place. Trembling, Cratchit obeyed.

Lestrade's lair lay in one of the Admiralty cellars. He was in. He leered at Cratchit. Hoare might be a ferret in Portsmouth opinion, whispering or not, but Lestrade out-ferreted him by a cable-length or more. Hoare could have sworn he displayed small, needlelike fangs, ready to drink the blood of any wee, sleekit, cow'rin' tim'rous beastie he could catch. When Lestrade rose to greet his visitors, Cratchit squeaked, blanched, and fled.

Alone, the two creatures eyed each other.

"To what do I owe this Honor?" Lestrade asked. He stressed the "H," Hoare noticed.

"I wanted to hear about Ambler, Lestrade. Sir Hugh tells me you . . . inspected his quarters."

"Indeed I did, sir, from top to bottom, back to front. I left no stone unturned, so to speak. Hit Had been searched before me, However, and I found nothing of Hinterest. Hit seems Mr. Hambler kept His official life and His private life separate."

Lestrade also pronounced the personal pronoun as if he were referring to the Deity. He evidently Haspired to rise in this accent-conscious society.

"What do you know of Mr. Ambler's personality and habits?" Hoare asked. Before replying, Lestrade looked at him with head tilted slightly to one side, appraisingly.

"An admirable Hindividual, sir. Completely reliable. Would Have entrusted Him with me life. Yes." Lestrade nodded, Hoare remained silent, waiting for more.

"Hof course, sir, Mr. Hambler was—is—Sir Hugh's confidential Helper, and not mine. For more detail, you would be well to speak with Him, or with Mr. . . . never mind." Lestrade winced at his last words, as though he would retract them if he could. When Hoare pressed him for the name he had suppressed, he had no more to say, but pled an urgent appointment away from the building. He offered to escort Hoare to the Admiralty's principal entrance, and Hoare was glad to accept. Underground labyrinths were not to his liking.

Once outside, Hoare found it was raining. He was quite sure he could find his way back to the Golden Cross without a guide. He would try it. As he strode down Whitehall in what he hoped was the right, easterly direction, he chewed over the missing man's avocation as recalled by Sir Hugh. Falconry. He remembered the unsuitable jape he had been mad enough to utter during his first, disastrous encounter with Sir Thomas Frobisher. He had described to that powerful batrachian baronet how, while he did not hunt as the baronet had asked, he batted.

He and other like-minded folk in the north country flew trained bats, he had said, to retrieve insects, just as falconers flew their fierce birds. Sometimes, he had added to the astonished Sir Thomas, the largest species—the chiropteran equivalents of gyrfalcons or even eagles—could take on small birds.

Sir Thomas had not been long to twig, and had never forgiven him the insult. That Hoare had then interfered in the man's marriage schemes had not improved their relationship. As the man's own son had warned him, he must walk warily.

Chapter V

━━◆━━

THE PORTRAIT is finished, Mr.—er—Saul. Would you care to examine it before I hide it away until my new government is in place?"

"Indeed, Ahab, indeed."

"Here, then, sir. Come with me. Pray take two candles, while I bear the candelabra."

Saul's host led the way from the library to another room, larger but disused. He pointed toward the farther wall, and raised the candelabra above his head, the better to illumine the wide unframed canvas that leaned against a long black table, looking much like a devotional work above a Roman altar.

"My God," the visitor breathed.

A group pose in the style of a Dutch master of a century and a half past—Van Dyck, perhaps—the portrait presented eight men: the host, six others, and the visitor himself.

"What do you think of it?" its owner asked.

"I am appalled," said the visitor. "You must destroy it, now, before the authorities get wind of it."

"Destroy it, sir? Nonsense. It will be a treasure. Priceless.

65

Before very long, you will be able to admire it in surroundings more suited to its subjects."

"Destroy it, man. Destroy it, I say."

The host shook his head. "Never. You gave me your word, and you kept it. Now, you must still keep it. And remember, I have the power to compel your compliance."

"Madness," the guest responded. "Then until you can put it where you want, keep it safe, and out of sight. Give me your word, sir."

"You have it. We shall do so this very moment. Come take one end, while I take the other."

Together, the two men lugged the awkward canvas through a low service door and down a steep flight of stairs. The host bore the candelabra in one hand. By the time they reached another, locked door, both porters were puffing.

Setting down the candelabra and his end of the canvas, the host reached into a pocket and removed a bunch of keys. He selected one. When he had opened the door, he picked up his burden again and led his companion and the canvas inside. The walls of the chamber were flanked with bottles.

"Port, sir. Old port. *Very* old port. Some of it dates back to the second King Charles and the Portuguese treaty. Here, help me set it on end at the end of the cellar, and then I'll show you."

Titus Thoday appeared at Hoare's lonely candlelit table in the Golden Cross, at the point where his commander was carrying on a whispered conversation about soles with the *hotelier*. Monsieur Berrier had a pair of soles, but did not believe they should be separated. Left and right, Hoare supposed, like the new way of shoemaking in which the fabricator made pairs in mirror images. While he appreciated mine host's tender feelings, he did not see why he should be expected to cater to them, and he was saying as much. Thoday's arrival broke the impasse. Hoare ordered both soles grilled. He determined that the starboard-side sole would go to himself as the commissioned officer, while Thoday would have to be satisfied with the lesser, larboard-side one.

It was not every officer who would have stooped to dine with an enlisted man, nor was Hoare such a democrat as to dine with just any of his people. However, Titus Thoday was—Hoare chuckled to himself—a different kettle of fish. He was rated gunner's mate in *Royal Duke*, though gunnery was one of the few subjects in which Hoare had found him less than proficient. Just as Hoare had delegated the moment-to-moment seamanship in *Royal Duke* to Mr. Clay, he had rated Admiral Hardcastle's man Stone as mate's mate and instructed Thoday to treat Stone's advice as though it came from Hoare himself.

Thoday's nose was hawklike, his eyes an icy pale gray, his thin lips habitually compressed. He was respectably dressed from the yacht's unusual slop chest. He was, Hoare knew, the son of one of Sir John Fielding's best men. Sir John, the late "blind beak" of Bow Street, had been the virtual founder of London's only organization devoted to the actual control of crime. The son had taken after his father. An experienced investigator, cold, resourceful and sharp, he held himself in high esteem, and showed it. More than once his behavior toward Hoare had verged on condescension, but during the course of their collaboration in the Nine Stones affair, they had shaken down and learned to jog along well enough. Thoday had learned to keep his arrogance under hatches most of the time, while—most of the time—Hoare was able to treat him as a colleague rather than a minion.

Tonight, Thoday accepted as his due Hoare's invitation to be seated, and listened in attentive silence while Hoare whispered his story of Octavius Ambler, the missing confidential clerk, and the papers that had evidently gone missing with him. He concluded just as the two soles arrived. As he had planned, he decided that the larger sole was the starboard one, and had the waiter serve it to him with his share of the salad of cowcumbers and lettuce that he had ordered to accompany them.

When the waiter had served Thoday as well and departed

with a murmured "bon appetit," the gunner's mate made his first observations.

"From the general tone of your words, sir," he said when Hoare came to a stop at last, "I conclude that the Admiralty is less concerned about the man himself than they are about the manuscripts in his charge." He paused, inquiringly.

"A safe conclusion," Hoare replied.

"Then our first duty must be to recover them. If we should find the man himself, it is all the better, but he takes second place."

"True. But—oh dear." Hoare reached into the inner pocket of his coat for Ambler's likeness. "I forgot. Here."

"Thank you, sir." Thoday's words were discreet, but as Hoare had feared he would, he spoke them in a tone of heavy reproach. Hoare felt himself blush, and hated himself for it. He reached for his goblet of hock, and decided to forestall the advice he knew he was about to receive.

"We should search his quarters, Thoday." Thoday closed his mouth. Hoare was quite certain the other felt misused at missing his chance.

"Tonight," he went on. "Pity, I had hoped to get an uninterrupted night's sleep."

"Now I suppose we must hunt up some local to direct us," Hoare muttered. The pair had just reached the southern end of the Westminster Bridge. Since the light rain had eased, there was some hope, he thought, of finding a guide to Chantry Street where Ambler had lodged.

"No need at all, sir," Thoday said. "Chantry Street will not have moved since I was last in the area."

Hoare had forgotten that his companion, having grown up in the streets of London, would certainly have explored the alien territory south of the Thames as well, from his boyhood on. With Hoare at his side, the gunner strode confidently ahead, taking a left here and a right there, until Hoare had utterly lost his bearings. Moreover, it was dark.

At one point, Hoare was sure he heard the scraping of something more substantial than a local rat. While hardly worried—between them, they should have no difficulty disposing of any team numbering less than four venturesome footpads—he made sure his sword was loose in its scabbard.

"I'm surprised, Thoday," he whispered, more than a little out of breath, "that you have not brought a weapon with you."

"But I have, sir." Thoday raised the elegant walking stick he carried. "A sword would have been out of keeping with my present civil dress, don't you think? So . . ."

With a discreet flourish, the gunner's mate gripped the head of his sturdy stick with one hand and drew from it a slim, gleaming blade, only a little shorter than one of the épées with which Hoare was in the habit of using for his own exercises in escrime. It was much sharper than an épée; Hoare envied its owner.

"Toledo, sir," Thoday said. "Given my father in ninety-six, by the mayor of that city, for services rendered." He gave no further explanation, but sheathed the deadly thing and strode on. Hoare forbore to inquire further, or to ask him to slow down. Not for the first time, he regretted that even his occasional morning bouts with Mr. Clay did not ensure his endurance over a mile of walking, at the rate Thoday chose to travel.

"Ah. Here we are, sir." Thoday stopped at the door of a tidy dwelling. A shadowy figure was leaning against it. The gunner's voice almost concealed what Hoare was sure was a degree of pride. If so, it was well deserved.

"An' wot 'ud you be wantin', this time of night?" said the shadow in a rough voice. "Move along, you."

"You're guarding the Ambler premises?" Hoare whispered.

"An' wot 'ud you care, cully?"

Hoare threw back his boat cloak to display his uniform and the solitary epaulet that decorated his left shoulder.

"Commander Bartholomew Hoare, my man. Open the door, if you please."

"An' if I don't please, cully?"

"Then you will answer to Mr. Lestrade. Or to Sir Hugh Abercrombie, if you prefer."

Hoare did not know which name impressed the shadow the more. It made no difference, for he unlocked the door with a grind and, now revealed in the dim light of a lamp just within as a leathery man in quasi-uniform, turned obsequious.

"Never mind, Kinchin' Ned Weatherwax," Thoday said in his most patronizing voice. "I won't peach on you—not tonight."

"Jesus, Mr. Thoday," said Weatherwax. "Which I thought you'd gone to sea."

"Which I done, Weatherwax," Thoday said in the same vernacular. "Now, give us a glim up to Mr. Ambler's doss-down, there's a nifty cove."

Weatherwax, now embarrassingly eager to please, lit them up the stairs to the first-floor apartment. Hoare had been expecting the place to be noisome, but stairway and upstairs passageway were noticeably clean in appearance and odor. Stopping at a heavy door with two keyholes, the guard painstakingly inserted keys into both locks, and swung the door open. He lit the candles in several sconces before turning, doffing his cap, and standing bareheaded and upside down, expectant.

"That'll be all, Ned," Thoday said.

"Wot, no vail for me work?" Weatherwax whined.

"Yer job, Ned. No vails. Back to yer post, and close the door behind ye."

The guard's heavy steps clumped back down the stairs.

The room, one of several en suite, was clean, and its occupant had spent freely on its furnishings. Tonight, it was in great disarray. Every drawer in the sideboard had been pulled out and its contents dumped helter-skelter across the waxed and carpeted floor. A heavy chair stood upside down in the middle of the mess, its Russia leather upholstery ripped apart and the stuffing lying about like the remains of a sheep shearing. Several of the framed paintings on the walls had been pulled down, while others hung askew. To Hoare's mind, the searcher—

70

Lestrade in all likelihood—had applied the proverbial fine-tooth comb to his task of ransacking.

Titus Thoday, however, seemed less impressed. He cast a casual eye over the hurrah's-nest in the middle of the room and, lighting a candle at one of the sconces, walked into the bedroom that lay beyond. Hoare followed him.

The bedroom could have been that of a prosperous professional. But the four-poster bed's comfortable quilts, curtains, and blankets had been pulled down and discarded in the corners of the room, the bedside convenience overturned and the chamber pot lying forlorn and empty beside its owner's bed. The armoire and cupboards were likewise turned out. Someone had humped his way under the bed—not, Hoare supposed, in search of the statutory monsters. Thoday shrugged, left the bedroom as it was, and proceeded to the small kitchen via the parlor.

The kitchen looked like a china shop after the bull had left. Someone—Sir Hugh's superlative searcher Lestrade, presumably, if not his predecessor—had shattered every breakable object in the room. Slivers of glass had embedded themselves in the woodwork. In spots, the perpetrator had stamped the shards of Mr. Ambler's chinaware into the flooring; on the wide boards his footprints stood out sharply as if the man had walked through a field of gritty snow.

"Somebody found he could no longer suppress his rage," Thoday said musingly. "I believe he failed to find the papers he had come to find.

"No food," he added. Indeed, the larder was empty.

"He dined out, I suppose," Hoare observed sagely.

"Odd, don't you think, sir?" Thoday said. "Not in keeping with the man's description."

"Not at all," said Hoare, without any notion of what his man was referring to.

Thoday had kept Ambler's likeness. Now he withdrew it and looked at it again, searchingly, in the candlelight.

"Would you repeat for me the description Sir Hugh gave

you of the man's habits and personality?" he asked. Hoare obliged.

"Yes," Thoday said. "I thought I . . ." He returned to the drawing room, where he began sorting through the heap of Ambler's belongings.

"Yes," he said again. His lean face was impassive, but his voice oozed triumph. He held a figurine in his hand. A well-made bronze, after the Italian quattrocento style, it depicted a falcon, its hood opened to leave the eyes clear, glaring at the intruders over its prey, a lifelike hare. It would have stood a good eighteen inches high—life size, more or less, Hoare guessed. He had seen a similar figurine before, somewhere in the Med, in ninety-one or thereabouts—in Malta, if memory served him correctly

"Hmm," Thoday said. He inverted the figure. With a fleam withdrawn from a sheath in the skirt of his sober coat, he pried the base from the bronze and peered into the deep cavity it disclosed. With some effort, he extracted a tightly rolled cylinder, which he placed on the kitchen table and unrolled with care. It crinkled as he did so.

Thoday's discovery comprised four closely written pages of calligraphy on fine linen, headed by an engraved coat of arms unfamiliar to Hoare and ending with several impressive signatures and two seals. The language was nothing Hoare could read; looking at Thoday, he knew that the gunner's mate, too, was baffled. Even more triumphant, nonetheless.

"The missing papers, I believe, sir," he said, handing them to Hoare. His face, normally pallid, was slightly flushed, as if with pride. "I regret to admit I cannot read the language in which they are written, but from the coat of arms, I would judge it to be Swedish."

"I believe you are right," Hoare whispered. "Perhaps it's as well that neither of us knows Swedish. It will be a relief to the government to know that we, at least, are not privy to this particular secret, whatever it may be."

72

"It is irksome," Thoday declared, "to have to admit one's ignorance of such a simple thing as the Swedish language."

"Well done, Thoday, just the same," Hoare said. "Now it only remains to find Mr. Octavius Ambler." He began to blow out the candles.

"That is of lesser importance, I have been given to understand," said Thoday. "May I suggest, sir, that you instruct me to put to use my familiarity with the London underworld to see what I can do in that direction, while you return the papers to their proper place?"

"An excellent idea, Thoday. Make it so," Hoare whispered as they descended the stairs. "Again, well done. But I have an admission to make. I am a thief."

"Sir?" As Hoare had hoped he would, Thoday sounded puzzled.

"I don't think Mr. Ambler, or his heirs, if he has any, will be in any position to object to my having abstracted a little memento of our mission here."

He handed his companion the bronzen image of the hawk. He was glad to be shut of it—it was quite heavy and very cumbersome.

Chapter VI

———◆———

"Fire, sir! Fire in our cellars!"

Roused from a happy dream in which, at last, he and his tribe were receiving their due, the heavy man grunted. Then, as the message sank into his torporous brain, he roared. Without more than shoving his tender flat feet into a pair of old slippers, he took the candle from beside his bed, rushed to the door, and unlocked it. The acrid smell of smoke affronted his nostrils.

"This way, sir! This way! I have the men forming a bucket brigade from the kitchen. The house is out of danger, I am sure. But oh, sir, I fear for your port!"

Thrusting past the heaving bucket brigade, the heavy man made his way into the smoke-filled cellar. There he halted in dismay.

"What, all my port—and my portrait, too!"

By the time Hoare and Thoday had returned across the river and through the nearly deserted London streets to the Golden

Cross, it must have gone two o'clock. Hoare had arranged a separate room for his companion, on an upper floor. He would not be troubled, as he had on an earlier occasion, by the haunting strains of the pocket violin with which, he had learned, the other played himself to sleep.

The next morning, as agreed, they parted, Thoday to commence moling his way about the city's underside, while Hoare made the call on this John Goldthwait whom Sir Hugh Abercrombie was so strangely insistent he meet.

He must cudgel his memory before he recalled who Mr. Goldthwait was. At last, he remembered. A small, lean man with a weary face, he had been among the entourage of Admiral of the Fleet Prince William, Duke of Clarence, when that authentic Royal Duke had attended the trial of Arthur Gladden. If Sir Hugh saw fit to insist that Hoare attend him, Mr. Goldthwait's role on that occasion must have been something other than a mere courtier's. The one time they had met, he had spoken in a most kindly way of the role Hoare had played in the *Vantage* affair. In fact, Hoare thought, Mr. Goldthwait might well have put a good word in with Sir Hugh, and thus been instrumental in Hoare's miraculous advancement as far as the threshold of post rank.

When, after following several false trails, he finally came upon 11, Chancery Lane, his gentle raps with the knocker were without result. At last, a frowsy head stuck itself out the upstairs window of an adjoining house and informed him that he was wasting his hammering. Mr. Goldthwait was not in.

"I suppose that manservant of his has taken advantage of his master again and gone off to some boozing ken," the head volunteered.

Hoare ventured to ask the head if it would tell either Mr. Goldthwait or his manservant that Mr. Hoare of the navy had called, and it agreed to do so. Its owner then slammed the window down and left Hoare to do as he pleased. At a loss, Hoare decided he would take his discovery—or Thoday's, rather—to Sir Hugh Abercrombie. The admiral would surely be pleased.

His passage to Whitehall was a difficult one. After Hoare ended up in a warren of alleyways, a kindly passerby told him he had turned the wrong way upon leaving number 11. He should have turned left. Confused and frustrated, he retraced his steps, or at least attempted to do so. He must have taken a wrong turning again, for he found himself at length facing a dignified structure with a dome, which could only be St. Paul's. Far earlier in the day than it should, the sky had begun to darken, for it still wanted a good hour to noon. He suspected that one of the infamous London fogs was about to descend. A heavy wain almost crushed him against a wall, and its driver snarled at him in some unintelligible dialect. He was totally at sea, and he wished it true. He hated London.

He gave up, prepared to sacrifice his dignity, and hailed one of the many dirt-encrusted, starveling barefoot boy children who infested the streets hereabouts.

"Here, boy—do you know where the Admiralty is, in Whitehall?" he whispered.

"Admiralty, mister? Calls yerself a sailor-man, and can't find yer own way 'ome?" The child, wizened and wise, did nothing to hide a contemptuous sneer. "'Course I does," he said.

"Sixpence to take me there," Hoare said.

The ragamuffin tossed his head.

"Shillin'," he said.

"Sixpence now, sixpence when we get there."

"Let's see yer blunt, mister sailor-man," said the boy, and would not budge until he had bitten the coin and tucked it into his cheek for safekeeping.

"Come orn," he said, and set off.

It took Hoare's child pilot a mere fifteen minutes to lead his bewildered customer into Whitehall. Hoare knew where he was now; he could even recognize the high door of the Admiralty, from which he had been turned away two evenings before.

"I can find my own way from here," he told the boy, and handed him the other half of his fare. The other grabbed it, bit it, and disappeared.

"Mr. Hoare, Mr. Hoare! Wait for me, sir! Please!" Hoare felt himself blanch with astonishment at that clear, exclamatory, unforgettable treble, but turned all the same, however reluctantly. The owner of the voice, the visible, audible spirit of Harry Prickett, was pelting toward him. Little Prickett, he knew, late midshipman in the late frigate *Vantage,* had gone up with her while leaving Spithead one beautiful morning the previous summer, in smoke and flame.

"Aren't you glad to see me, sir?" the lad asked, looking up into Hoare's face with some anxiety.

"Why, yes. Yes, lad, I am." Hoare squatted to view Mr. Prickett at eye level, and grasped him by the shoulders. "But I thought I never would, short of Davy Jones's locker. How . . . weren't you in *Vantage,* then?" The question was silly, of course; of three hundred twenty-seven Vantages, only twenty-four had been hauled from the water when the frigate had blown up in Hoare's own presence. He had pulled in most of them himself, since he had been less than a cable's-length distant from her in his own beloved little sloop when the catastrophe occurred. Most of the survivors had been badly burned or mangled, and none had ranked higher than quarter-gunner. Like the very Christ, this so-helpful very young gentleman must have risen by divine miracle from his death in the explosion.

"Oh, no, sir! I caught the mumps, sir, from another boy who was staying at the inn, and they put me ashore before she went to sea, and sent me home! You've had the mumps, sir, haven't you?"

Hoare, who could barely remember himself and his brother being put out into the barn and nursed from that distance for a week while they bulged, sweated, and felt generally sorry for themselves, said "yes."

"Then you won't have to worry, sir! Will you?"

"No, boy. But . . . what are you doing here in London?"

"I've been taken into a ship, sir! Papa brought me up himself, all the way from Canterbury! Wasn't it sad about *Vantage*! She was a smacker, wasn't she? Poor Mrs. Watt! She's left with six daughters, all alone!" He meant Mr. Prickett's friend, *Vantage*'s clerk, who had been so helpful to Hoare, and whom he had delivered back aboard his ship just in time to share in the disaster. Watt's widow would be on the town now, of course.

"But let me introduce you to Papa! Papa! Look at what I've found! Here's Mr. Hoare! Oh, sorry, sir! *Commander* Hoare, I mean! *Captain* Hoare, I mean!"

The man who came up to them, as brisk as his son but far more stately, could only be a prosperous canon lawyer in a cathedral town. There was something episcopal about him; in fact, Hoare almost expected to see a bishop's apron shrouding the region between navel and knees. His forbidding black attire clashed with a bright, clever, humorous face.

The little mid was not shy with his papa, for he took his hand and drew him toward Hoare.

"Papa, it's Mr. Hoare! Remember? He's the officer who can't talk and he had me holloa for him!"

The two men exchanged greetings as equals.

"I am delighted, as well as astonished, to see your son alive, sir," Hoare said in all sincerity. He meant it, for the boy had radiated the cheerful confidence of a well-loved puppy. He still did. He had brains, too, and would go far in the navy.

"Not half as delighted as we were, sir," the father said. "I know, we have four more like him at home, but all of them are precious to me, and to Mrs. Prickett as well. You have children, Mr.—or should I say 'Commander' Hoare?"

"*Captain* Hoare, Papa!"

"Thank you, my boy," said the father easily. Hoare was pleased to see that, pompous though Mr. Prickett senior might appear, he was not too high in the instep to accept his child's correction willingly. Hoare explained that no, he was only recently married, but was hopeful. He forbore to mention his daughter by Antoinette, the daughter he had sought but never found, born in '84 and carried away by his late wife's people to dwell in the wilds of Quebec—if, indeed, she was still aboveground.

"Perhaps you'd like to serve with me in *Royal Duke*," Hoare whispered to Mr. Prickett. "She's small, and she doesn't go to sea often, but I can offer you a good education. We could use a handy young gentleman."

He could have bit his tongue. However appealing a safe berth of this kind might be to a master of clerical law like Prickett senior, the offer of a good education was no way to appeal to a seven-year-old boy.

For perhaps three seconds Mr. Prickett held his tongue. Then he looked up at Hoare with eyes filled with appeal.

"Oh, sir!" he said. "*Must* I? I mean, sir . . . here I am, midshipman six whole months now, but I've never been to sea! I want to go to sea *so* much, sir! Won't you let me go to sea? Captain Prothero's just offered me a berth in *Impetuous*! Papa is just now taking me to Deptford, where she lies! Can't I go with him instead? *Please*, sir?"

The lad had served Hoare well in the *Vantage* affair. He had become fond of the lad, his ebullience, his open face, his constant motion. It would have been a delight to help him mature into a seasoned sea officer. But, even in command of *Royal Duke*, he himself was as good as shorebound, as he had just let slip to Mr. Prickett, so how could he train the young gentleman to become a normal serving officer? Why, he would have to take his ship's latitude from the same spot every noon. And, as for longitude—that matter would be nugatory, since *Royal Duke* lay at Greenwich, the zero meridian. Hoare understood now how a father must feel when his favorite son leaves home to go to sea. It might be as close as he would ever get to knowing.

"Very good, Mr. Prickett. If Prothero's fool enough to want you aboard, he has a *right* to you."

The younger Mr. Prickett stifled a giggle.

Hoare had made his bow to the father and was about to part company, when the other forestalled him.

"Before we part, sir," he said, "may I beg you to take a dish of tea? To at least that extent, I am indebted to you. The Leaf lies just around the corner. It offers a fine Bohea."

Although he did not know Bohea from Yunnan, Hoare could hardly object. "With pleasure. But I am unaware of any debt you owe me, sir; if anything, the shoe is on the other foot. Your son was an invaluable aide. Had I had a dispatch to write on the subject of the *Vantage* affair, I should have mentioned him in them."

"Very kind of you, I'm sure," Mr. Prickett said. He took Hoare by the arm and, undisturbed by his son's perpetual motion about them both, escorted him to the Leaf.

When they had been seated and young Prickett's mouth stoppered with a large round sweetish bun, Hoare took the chance to ask for clarification.

"You informed me just now, sir, that me you are in my debt. As I said then, I know of no such thing. Elaborate, I pray." The attorney's stately quality appeared to prompt an equally stately mode of speech on Hoare's part.

"Had it not been for young Harry's attendance on you last summer," Mr. Prickett answered, "he would not have strayed into the inn yard and contracted the stable-boy's mumps. But for the mumps, he would have remained aboard *Vantage* when she sailed to join Lord Nelson, and would have been lost with her."

" 'The house that Jack built,' it seems to me, sir, if you will forgive me. My role in Harry's mumps was only casual. Rather than making a thank offering to me, would it not be appropriate to slaughter an ox before the altar of the Fates?"

As he spoke, Hoare realized he had just abandoned his synthetic stateliness of speech. Had he erred? No; the other nodded.

"You are perfectly correct, sir. Truth to tell, the reason I gave you was no more than a thin crust on top of a much juicier pie. I ask your forgiveness for the deception."

Mr. Prickett paused to await Hoare's reaction. Hoare took advantage of his own muteness, sat back and waited for the next disclosure.

"As it happens, Captain Hoare, I am an advocate in Admiralty law as well as a canon lawyer. Expertise in canon law alone, I found long ago, is no longer in demand sufficient to support a large and hopeful family. So now, while we reside not far from Canterbury and my related duties call for my regular presence in Lambeth, I actually spend at least as much time in Whitehall.

"It is in the latter connection that I took advantage of the fortuitous meeting young Harry unwittingly arranged. In fact, I had already been requested to—ah—curry—acquaintance with you. I prefer to be forthright, however, whenever circumstances permit. I believe that to be the case now.

"To make a long story short, Captain Hoare, you are being considered for a post which might be more permanent and more to your advantage than the one you presently occupy, and I, with others, have been charged with examining you . . . informally, that is. May I proceed?"

"Of course, sir," Hoare whispered. "But if the interview is to be a long one, will your son be willing to sit still?"

"Long since, Mrs. Prickett and I taught all our young to be silent and invisible at table. Otherwise, neither she nor I would have retained our sanity. We are at table now, Harry, you understand?"

Mr. Prickett the younger nodded. His gob-stopper was long since gone, but the gob in question remained stopped, as if the child were the mute, and not the man.

Thereupon, the father subjected Hoare to a barrage of questions about himself, his brother in Melton Mowbray, his Hoares, and his father's politics (here, Hoare could say nothing, for Captain Joel was mumchance about his doings as a member of Parliament). This was Hoare's second such inquisition today, and it was becoming irritating. He determined to bear up.

As the advocate proceeded, he unabashedly disclosed considerable previous knowledge of Hoare's own affairs; thus, he knew of the source from which Hoare had derived his own capital: the prize money from his capture of a specie-laden American privateer in September '81, while he was the sole remaining officer in the brig *Beetle*. After the navy had bought in the prize and the Halifax prize agent had done his duty for a change, Hoare had become the richer by £6,127 plus five shillings and eight pence. Shocked into good sense, the young man had promptly invested the amount in the Funds and left it at Barclays Bank to grow in peace. It had only been in '03 that he had dipped into capital in order to buy the neat little pinnace that now dawdled astern of *Royal Duke*.

All these things Mr. Prickett had known beforehand; about none of them had he a comment, save one, which bore upon Hoare's financial windfall.

"You, sir, profited by a legal technicality on that occasion, as I surely need not tell you. I venture to urge that the experience not lead you to seek out other technicalities by whose advantage you might hope to rise further. For *you,* that would be gambling. Leave that sort of thing to us lawyers."

With that cryptic caution, Mr. Prickett rose, gave his son permission to unstop his gob, brushed down his nonexistent apron, paid the reckoning, and ushered Hoare from the Leaf.

"A most enjoyable occasion," he said. "I look forward to continuing our acquaintance."

"Harry said you were taking him to join Prothero in *Impetuous,*" Hoare responded. "If I'm not mistaken, she lies in Deptford just now. That's near Greenwich. You and he would be most welcome aboard *Royal Duke* at any time."

"Very kind, sir. It will be our pleasure. Come, Harry; we must be off."

"Sir Hugh will see you directly, Captain Hoare," the clerk Cratchit said. He looked amazed; evidently, his exalted master did not commonly stoop to receive mute commanders who merely "happened to be in the neighborhood and thought they would drop in for a chat."

Some half an hour later, when the admiral's scurry of messengers had ceased, his bass call summoned Hoare within. The room had not changed. Sir Hugh was still sitting, smoking, reading swiftly and dropping each page to the carpet as he finished it. A disorderly white drift of discards lay at his feet. Once, he coughed heavily. He did not look well. He stopped reading long enough to say, "Sit, sir. Well?"

In silent answer, Hoare handed him Titus Thoday's discovery. Sir Hugh leafed through the pages, just enough, Hoare suspected, to make sure they were all present or accounted for, tapped them together, and bellowed, "Cratchit!"

The mouse appeared, like a jack-in-the-box.

"Take this to Lord Manymead, to be forwarded to Lord Hovick at the Foreign Office. My compliments, and this office has no further need of these documents."

The mouse took the papers and scuttled off.

"Jumped up counter-clerk," the admiral said.

"Cratchit, sir?"

"No, you ass, Manymead. Went to India as a junior clerk under Clive, shook the pagoda tree, came home with his stolen millions. Now, just because he's seen fit to buy his way into government, he thinks he owns the whole of Whitehall and all that pertains thereunto. Including you, sir, and me."

Hoare believed he remembered Lord Manymead as being the father of one of the four midshipmen he had gathered up a year or so ago and returned to their ship, the light frigate *Hebe*. They had been kidnapped by a ramshackle gaggle of would-be Irish rebels. If it was the same portly peer—and there would hardly be two of them—he agreed with his admiral's opinion.

"Find Ambler?" the admiral asked.

"No, sir."

"Why not?"

"I think he's dead, sir. Thoday is visiting the city's deadhouses, and . . . I believe, some of the underworld haunts he seems to know so well."

"Hmph. What did Goldthwait have to say?"

"Nothing, sir."

"*Nothing*, Captain Hoare? Goldthwait never says 'nothing.'"

"I have yet to meet with Mr. Goldthwait, sir. When I called

on him an hour or so ago, he was not in . . . nor were any of his servants."

"Nonsense, Hoare. Goldthwait never goes out—when he's in Town, that is—except to come here. And he's not here. What have you to say about that, sir?"

Did the admiral look worried? Did he fear that John Goldthwait, Esquire, had followed Octavius Ambler into the . . . *Ewigkeit*? Besides *"gnädiges Fräulein,"* *Ewigkeit* was one of the few German words Hoare knew. He was not quite sure where he had learned it or what it meant, but for him it carried connotations of a wan, empty nothingness in which lost souls wandered. A special word for which he had never found an English equivalent, it seemed appropriate to this occasion.

To Vice-Admiral Sir Hugh Abercrombie, however, there was nothing Hoare could say, so he doused sail, hove to, and sat mute while the admiral hissed at him in a soft, spiteful roar. Sir Hugh must have had an unpleasant morning, and Hoare was there to receive the backlash. For Sir Hugh, Hoare knew, it would be like kicking the cat or breaking up poor Ambler's dinnerware; futile, yet strangely satisfying.

His ire assuaged at last, Sir Hugh bade Hoare go and try again for Goldthwait.

"And if you are unsuccessful in this simple task, I have been overestimating your modest competence. In that case, you are to return to your command and await further orders."

"Aye, aye, sir," Hoare replied.

This time, Mr. Goldthwait's manservant was within, informed Hoare that his master was at home to him, and admitted him to the apartments. The place was larger than it appeared from the outside. On seeing his host, Hoare recalled him instantly, for his intimate knowledge of Hoare himself, displayed at their only previous meeting, in Portsmouth's Navy Tavern, had engraved itself in his memory. Mr Goldthwait was a small, rust-colored, lean, undistinguished-looking man; his world-weary face reminded Hoare strongly of an engraved portrait he had once seen of one François Marie Arouet, Frederick the Great's pet *philosophe*, alias Voltaire. Come to think of it, there was something Frederician about him as well.

The gentleman must have a substantial income, above and beyond the emoluments due an Admiralty official of medium rank such as Mr. Goldthwait. The easy chairs on either side of the glowing grate were covered in the finest Russia leather, as were many of the books lined tidily upon the high shelves. Where there were no books, the walls displayed an occasional piece of art, of a mildly pornographic nature. Other than these, there was no sign that humankind comprised more than one sex. Altogether, the place glowed with walnut, mahogany, polished brass, and unobtrusive prosperity.

Over the mantelpiece was a long vacant space that must have borne an object of importance to Hoare's host—a painting, presumably, a panoramic landscape of some sort.

Mr. Goldthwait's sharp eye must have detected Hoare's casual interest.

"A cluster of muses hangs there," he explained. "I have had the thing carried off for a cleaning and for the opinion of an impartial connoisseur as to the artist. It leaves an ugly gap, I must confess."

Mr. Goldthwait now made himself most agreeable. Having shown Hoare to the chair on the other side of the grate from the one he obviously used himself, he offered port and biscuits with his own hand.

"Your very good health, Captain," he said with an affable smile, raising his own glass, "and my felicitations on your promotion and your marriage."

Hoare made the appropriate appreciative noise, and waited.

Thereupon, while never dropping his show of cordiality, Mr. Goldthwait embarked on the same inquisition as Sir Hugh Abercrombie had applied to him not long before, demonstrating in doing so the same familiarity with Hoare's life as Sir Hugh and then Mr. Prickett had displayed, if not more. Before long,

Hoare felt himself being pressed beyond endurance. As a result, perhaps, he had entwined his tale first in his adventures in and around the Nine Stones Circle, and then in the story of his accidental removal to the schooner *Marie Claire*.

"The two little craft—my own pinnace and Moreau's schooner—were all ahoo, sir, I must confess," he whispered.

"Ahoo, sir?" Goldthwait's look was blank.

"Awry, sir. Out of order. A piece of nautical lingo."

A grandfather's clock chimed in one corner; Hoare realized it was sounding seven bells. From the feel of his throat, he realized he had been gabbling—as much, at least, as a mute could gabble—and he fell silent.

As if to fill in an embarrassing silence, Mr. Goldthwait shook his head.

"You sailors use as many bells, it seems, as all the parishes of London put together," he said, and renewed his inquisition.

Hoare began to feel as if he were some exotic animal that had been subject unawares, all his life, to the unwinking scrutiny of too many invisible savants. He found the sensation somewhat disquieting and not at all pleasant. These intense examinations of his doings left him feeling uneasy between the shoulder blades.

At length, Goldthwait reverted to the present.

"So Ambler is dead," he said.

"Is he, sir?" Hoare asked. "I did not know that. In fact, one of my men is going about the . . . dead-houses of every likely parish this very day, in search of him."

"He must be dead," Goldthwait answered. "For over a week now, he has not been seen in his usual places. He is—he was—a sedentary man, and his movements were circumscribed. Across the bridge to the Admiralty every morning, the same chump chop in the same chophouse at noon, back across the bridge to Lambeth in the evening. A rump steak at the inn around the corner from his dwelling place, once a month to the whorehouse . . . excuse me, sir. The reference was inadvertent."

"Not at all, sir," Hoare whispered. "I am quite accustomed

to inadvertencies of the kind. A peculiar name like my own attracts them, just as a pile of shit does flies."

With this, the interview wound down gracefully. Hoare paid his compliments and took his leave.

Mr. Goldthwait, he thought as he traced his way carefully back to the Golden Cross, had seemed remarkably knowledgeable, not only about Hoare's past life, but about Octavius Ambler's movements as well. Furthermore, the detail with which he had described Ambler's daily habits made no sense. And what had made him so certain he was dead? The matter needed thought.

Before returning to the Golden Cross, Hoare decided, he would go on to Threadneedle Street and call on Mr. Pickering. He hoped that Threadneedle Street was at the same end of London as Chancery Lane. This time, however, he would take no chances. He caught the eye of an urchin, to have him pilot him there. The child looked interchangeable with the first.

"Lorst again, mister sailor man?" The child's voice was pert, and familiar as well. Following him to Threadneedle Street, Hoare felt himself blush.

The establishment of Mr. Baker the mercer was graced by one of the newfangled bow windows, which offered more room to display his goods than the conventional flat window. Hoare paused outside the shop and negotiated with the ragamuffin to wait for him until he had finished his visit. Within, the hopeful face of the apprentice or clerk who hastened up to serve this prosperous-looking naval customer fell upon hearing Hoare's unprofitable inquiry. With a backward jerk of his head, he indicated a narrow stairway.

"Third floor," he said in a voice burdened with scorn. Up, up, and up Hoare climbed, until the stairway came to an end in front of a low garret door. On the door the tenant had nailed a little sign, neatly inscribed, which read

TIMOTHY PICKERING
PORTRAITIST AND LIMNER

He knocked, waited, and knocked again. At last, he heard a shuffling sound from behind the door, and a faint infantile grizzling. For a truth, Timothy Pickering was a husband and father as well as a portraitist and limner.

"Who's there?" It was a woman's voice, and it sounded frightened. Hoare knew his whisper hopelessly incapable of making his needs known to the party on the other side of the door, and that one of his whistled signals would only alarm her. In any case, she would not know what any of the whistles meant. He resorted to one of the pre-printed slips that he carried about with him. He drew it out of his pocket.

"Permit me to present myself," it read: "Bartholomew Hoare, Lieutenant, Royal Navy. My deepest respects. That I am not speaking to you is not a matter of intentional discourtesy but is due to my inability to speak above a whisper."

Whipping out a pencil, he promoted himself to the proper rank, reminding himself as he did so that he must have a new set of slips printed, signed the paper with a flourish, and slipped it under the door. He coughed, and watched the slip disappear.

The door was opened by an anxious-looking woman in run-over slippers, with an infant on her hip. One of the pair gave off a strong odor.

"You bring bad news, I know it," the woman said. "Tell me. I shall be brave."

Behind her, the garret managed to appear both desolate and cluttered; there were no signs of an artist's paraphernalia. The artist must carry out his commissions in his subjects' homes or other places of business. The place was cold and damp, and smelled of old mold. A pot of something dreadful was simmering on a small charcoal stove in one corner, with a scrawny cat staring up at it, looking hopeful.

"I have no news, madam," Hoare whispered. "I have simply called to see Mr. Pickering. Is he within?" Since the entire Pickering dwelling was in plain sight, he asked the question only so as to be polite.

"No, sir. Oh, no. He has been away the entire morning,

soliciting commissions. And trying to sell his hat. It's a fine hat; 'twas left him by his late brother. . . . Indeed, he departed without even waiting for me to serve his breakfast. You see, I had to attend to poor little Beatrice. . . ." Mrs. Pickering bounced her baby to show this alarming stranger whom she was referring to, and it began to grizzle again.

"But please come in, sir, and have a seat if you please." With her free hand, Mrs. Pickering brushed a strand of hair out of her eyes. It flopped right back again.

"Thank you, but no, madam," Hoare said. "I may not tarry. Pray, when do you expect him to return?"

"Why, why . . ." At this, the infant's grizzling became a full-fledged roar, and Mrs. Pickering must interrupt herself and step aside to put it to a surprisingly firm breast. Hoare took advantage of the interruption to look about the garret.

At first, his glance slipped casually over the ill-made bed, the tilted lopsided table with its unwashed dishes, and the curtained corner behind which, he presumed, lay the family's wardrobe and primitive place of easement. Then it fixed on one wall, on which daylight fell less dimly than elsewhere in the apartment. There he saw an entire portrait gallery in pencil, the superbly candid, precise, unflattering likenesses that he already recognized as uniquely Pickering's work. One of the faces, of a stern middle-aged man of a naval aspect, was hauntingly familiar, but he could not at the moment attach a name to it. Drawn on separate pieces of paper, other faces surrounded it, faces which he knew but had never seen in the flesh—Queen Charlotte, the prince—and, to his astonishment, the vivid, tapered countenance of Mrs. Selene Prettyman. As a very close companion of the Duke of Cumberland, Mrs. Prettyman had been equivocally associated with the affair of the Nine Stones Circle. She was moving in odd company today, Hoare said to himself. Why was she there? Whom did she serve?

Duke Ernest's villainous face was there as well. And, from their heavy-lidded Hanoverian eyes, so were two others of the poor king's dismal litter of princely sons, though Hoare could not be sure, having met only Cumberland and Clarence. Kent, perhaps, York, Cambridge, or Sussex.

Suddenly, he recalled whose face had been puzzling him. It was his own. He had not seen himself before as others saw him, his morning view in the mirror being reversed, like all mirror images. This new view made him look disconcertingly strange. When on earth and where, he wondered, had Mr. Pickering made this secret sketch? A look at still another face, and he realized he was staring at a likeness of Titus Thoday.

On a sudden impulse, he turned to the nursing mother.

"Will you sell me these drawings, madam?" he asked.

"Why, I hardly—I—" Mrs. Pickering's eyes wandered swiftly about her home as if she hoped that her husband would appear, like some jinni, and give her the answer. Then the poverty in which she dwelt took charge.

"How much?" she asked in a voice that was suddenly hard.

"How much does Sir Hugh pay Mr. Pickering per likeness?" he whispered.

"Seven shillings sixpence apiece, sir. But Timothy sells his royalties for as much as half a pound."

Not often, I'll be bound, Hoare silently told himself. They aren't prettified enough to sell for more. But the Pickering family is obviously poor, poor.

"There are . . . let me see . . . seventeen of them," he whispered. "That would be . . . let me see . . . six pounds, seven shillings, and sixpence. I'll give you five pounds for the lot. Have you change for a ten-pound note?"

Her answer was what he had expected.

"Change for a ten-pound note?" Her voice was bitter. "This house doesn't see ten shillings from one week to the next."

"Well, well," Hoare said as if reluctantly. "Make it ten pounds even, then." He reached into the pocket in which he did not keep his communications and withdrew his purse. At this rate, he would soon need to draw more funds, either from the Admiralty's penny-pinchers or from his own resources. He found a ten-pound note and handed it to her. She received it in a trembling hand.

"Do you have nothing smaller, sir?" she asked as she watched Hoare detach his purchases from the garret wall. "No one in the neighborhood will believe we came by a ten-pound note honestly. Indeed, I never saw one before. How *big* it is! And we *do* need some food for our larder. We have a few other drawings, sir. Perhaps . . . ?"

"Let's see them, then," Hoare said.

Still carrying the infant, Mrs. Pickering disappeared behind the curtain and came out with a small roll of sketches. "That's all we have, sir," she said.

Hoare did not stop to examine them but wrapped them around the others. He hauled out a fistful of small change and handed it to her.

"Oh, sir! Oh, oh, oh!" Mrs. Pickering cried, and burst into tears. As Hoare raced down the flights of stairs to the street where his ragamuffin guide waited, he heard her voice, fading with the distance, crying, "Oh, Beatrice, Beatrice! The heavens have opened, and rained down a full year's rent!"

Just as Hoare reached the foot of the stairs, a small hatless figure crashed into him and nearly sent him flying. Thrusting him out of his way, Timothy Pickering raced up the stairs down which Hoare had just come, shouting something about having sold poor David's hat.

Upon returning to the Golden Cross, full of self-praise for his generosity to the poor and deserving, Hoare found that Thoday had preceded him and was waiting in the private bar to make his report.

"I have made the rounds of the dead-houses, sir, as far as was needful," he told Hoare. "At the third, in Cripplegate, I found our man's body."

"Are you quite sure?" Hoare whispered.

"Quite, sir. I examined every portly corpse I saw, comparing its features with the likeness you provided me. It was, if I may say so, an experience I should not care to repeat."

Hoare could only sympathize. From time to time in his career as Sir George Hardcastle's investigative dogsbody, he had had his own occasions to inspect numbers of the dead, in conditions ranging from the still-warm to the nearly deliquescent. The sweet sickening stench of human corruption was unforgettable.

"The man I found had been dead for about a week," Thoday went on. "Since most of that time had been spent in the water, his more prominent features were missing, eaten by crabs or lobsters. But the pockmarks remained, and their pattern was identical to the one shown in the likeness of the missing man. Since, as you informed me, the artist manages to capture every salient detail of a subject's countenance, I satisfied myself that the corpse was indeed that of Mr. Ambler, and I felt no need to continue my search."

"So he was drowned, then," Hoare whispered.

"Not so, sir. He was felled by a gunshot—a pistol bullet, unless I miss my guess, fired from close enough that the explosion drove powder granules and parts of the man's clothing into the wound. I withdrew the ball and some fragments, which I have with me. Here."

From one pocket, Thoday removed a folded paper, which he unfolded and tendered to Hoare. Mentally if not physically, Hoare shrank back. None too faintly, Thoday's specimen bore the cloying odor Hoare hated.

"Never mind, Thoday. Wrap the thing up again, will you? In oilcloth, if you can find some. I'll take it to Sir Hugh in the morning, when I report to him on my meeting with Mr. John Goldthwait.

"But there is something else I must take up with you, Thoday." With this, Hoare recounted his morning's call at the establishment of Timothy Pickering, Esq.

"Here are some of the likenesses I bought from his wife." Reaching into his bulging pocket with a sense of relief that his uniform coat was now returned to a reasonable shape, Hoare produced the roll of drawings. He peeled off one after another without inspecting them, dumping them at random upon the table before him. Near the core, he slowed.

"Ah, here we are," he whispered in triumph at last, and handed the gunner's mate Pickering's drawing of him. "How do you explain *this*, Thoday?"

Thoday inspected the sketch without visible emotion.

"An excellent likeness, sir, I would say. Of course, I am looking at a reoriented image of myself, so to speak, since the familiar countenance I see in the mirror of a morning is, of course, in reverse."

"But how did Pickering come to take your likeness?"

"Why, at the behest of Sir Hugh Abercrombie, sir," Thoday replied. For the second time that day, Hoare felt the blood rush to his face. Of course. Sir Hugh's acquaintance with the Royal Dukes was close; in fact, he had probably chosen most of them himself. Hoare felt an utter fool. And in any case, why, he wondered, had he been looking forward to confounding Thoday?

"May I look at the rest of these, sir?" Thoday asked.

"Of course," Hoare whispered. "I haven't really inspected them myself. . . . But let us take them upstairs to my quarters, where we can examine them in peace, without my host peering over our shoulders." For Berrier had just bustled up, to see if he or his cellar could be at their service. Hoare took the whole batch of drawings under one arm, while instructing Berrier to have a decanter of port for himself brought to his room.

"And for you, Thoday?"

"Porter, if you please, sir. I've acquired a taste for it."

Hoare nodded his assent to the proprietor, and then withdrew, Thoday at his heels.

Upstairs, the refreshments having arrived and their porter dismissed, they undertook to sort out the likenesses, setting visages either man recognized in one pile, unfamiliar faces in another, with the doubtful ones in between. None of the drawings bore names. Hoare counted thirty-nine of them in all.

Onto the first pile went one of Mrs. Pickering and the

infant Beatrice, the only example of a rendering that included more than one head, Thoday's own portrait, and likenesses of several other Royal Dukes, including one of Sarah Taylor, master's mate, and Hoare's own.

In the middle of the heap, Hoare paused in astonishment. He heard a gulping noise from his companion; Thoday would hardly demean himself by gasping. Hoare stared into a froglike face.

"What can *he* be doing in this company?" Hoare knew perfectly well that Thoday would have no answer, but he could not forbear asking the question all the same.

"I have no notion, sir," Thoday replied as expected. "I think of the gentleman in association with Dorset and not London. It is unmistakably Sir Thomas, however. And he has nothing whatsoever to do with the Admiralty."

"Hardly," Hoare said. In fact, on the only occasion of their meeting, the knight-baronet and Sir George Hardcastle had nearly come to fisticuffs.

Hoare and Thoday leafed on.

"I know that one," Hoare whispered. "I saw him this very day."

"Indeed, sir?"

"John Goldthwait, Esquire, of Chancery Lane."

"Like the others, then," Thoday said. "I suppose them to be trials which the artist chose to save for his own records. Perhaps he hopes to find an engraver and earn a few shillings by hawking them to him."

"I wonder who has the finished works. In any case, so, Thoday, I hardly think the subjects would be pleased, do you? Look here."

Hoare held up the likeness of Ernest, Duke of Cumberland, whom they both had last seen marching in dudgeon from the tragicomic Halloween ceremony in the Nine Stones Circle. The scarred face reeked with royal pride, self-indulgence, and malice.

Among the unknowns were faces unfamiliar to either of them. By their attire, most of these were visibly aristocratic. Young and old, overwhelmingly male, their visages lacked sensibility. Among them, the assortment could have been models for each and every one of the seven deadly sins.

"We must keep these portraits safe, Thoday," Hoare whispered. "I think they are very important."

"I know just the place, sir," Thoday said. "Once we have brought them safe to *Royal Duke*, you can place the roll of them in the Herschel telescope."

"An excellent thought, Thoday." The Herschel telescope was a huge thing in gleaming brass, mounted on a teakwood tripod, that lurked at the forrard end of the yacht's tweendecks. It was an acquisition of Hoare's predecessor in command of *Royal Duke*, who had been a devoted astronomer as well as a master of the intelligence trade. As far as Hoare knew, no one ever even looked through it. He found himself slightly surprised at what, for Thoday, was a flight of fancy. As a rule, he was a sobersided man.

"But where shall we stow it until we return to Greenwich?" he asked, in part to see whether the gunner would come out with something equally bizarre.

"Under your mattress, sir, of course."

So Hoare, the least bit disappointed at his aide's failure to weigh in with a further fancy, put it where he was told.

The next morning, the admiral heard Hoare's report impassively. As usual, his enormous form was so wreathed in tobacco smoke that he resembled a bull walrus on a foggy floe. The atmosphere was so thick that Hoare could barely restrain his coughs. The admiral did not trouble to do so. From time to time, the ferret Lestrade slid sinuously through the door, deposited a document, and waited for his master's instructions before winding away again. Since Portsmouth's criminal class knew Hoare himself as the Whispering Ferret, Hoare felt some kinship for the man, but little liking.

"So you have determined that Ambler is dead, eh?" Sir Hugh growled, and wheezed.

"My man Thoday did, sir," Hoare replied, and explained how.

"Never mind the details," the other said. "At the inquest—which, at the rate unexplained deaths are occurring in this city, will take place some time after 1815—the jury will bring in the usual: 'Murder, by person or persons unknown.' The man's gone, and that's all there is to it. There are dozens ready to replace him."

So much for the late Mr. Ambler, Hoare thought. He presented Mr. Goldthwait's opinion of Ambler's established habits, and remarked on the dead man's apparent prosperity.

"And Mr. Goldthwait, Hoare?" came Sir Hugh's rumble. "What did ye make of Mr. Goldthwait, once ye found him?"

Hoare's reply was ready. "He knows too much about me. If he knows so much about me . . . does it not follow that he knows as much about others, not necessarily to their good?"

"Of course, he does," Sir Hugh said. "It's his job, or part of it. If you suspect Goldthwait on *that* account, you may as well suspect me."

"About yourself, sir, for example?" Hoare ventured to add.

"Me life is an open book, sir," Sir Hugh replied, not rising to the bait. "But, being of no interest to any save myself and my family, it is a book generally closed to outsiders." Rebuffed, Hoare returned to his appraisal of John Goldthwait.

"He seems remarkably prosperous, too, sir. Has he independent means?"

"No. He does not. He comes of ordinary folk—his father was a farrier, as I recall, and he has never married. No, Hoare, his prosperity is of his own making. In fact, that, I confess, begins to render me anxious about him."

Sir Hugh knew when to pause for effect, and he used the pause to break the stem of his cheap clay churchwarden, toss it away, and fill its successor with coarse shag tobacco. Having lit it, he blew a thick blue puff into Hoare's face—not, it seemed to the victim, out of malice, but simply out of carelessness for his guest's comfort. Before continuing his discourse, he gave a loose, satisfied cough and spat copiously into a container on the floor at his side.

"I have good reason to believe, Hoare, that he gambles. Gambles with cards, playing with men of all classes, whether high or low. And is quite a consistent winner. Has been for some years. Took poor Fox, for example, for more pounds than any Whig cares to think about.

"Yet nary a whisper has come to my ears that he is a sharper or a flake. His opponents, even though they are generally losers, seldom accuse him of cheating, and those that have done so have never made their charges stick, or attempted to follow them up."

"Is Mr. Goldthwait wont, by any chance," Hoare whispered, "to respond in the usual way to accusations of . . . ungentlemanly behavior? I mean, sir, that he may be so formidable a man to meet on the field of honor that . . . even the bravest prefer not to meet him."

"Like yourself, Captain Hoare, eh?" Puff, puff. "No, sir. If that were the case, do you not think that the headstrong young bucks about town would be forever calling him out, not so much to prove the man a sharp as to prove their own panache before their friends, and their mirrors? I expect that you, sir, are not unfamiliar with that sort of thing."

Hoare nodded. Sir Hugh was in the right. Sober men chose to avoid open conflict with him; younger men, drunken ones, and fools not uncommonly sought either to issue a challenge or to provoke one. The pretext generally had to do with his name, but lately Hoare had learned to let stupid remarks of that kind slide off in ways that did not impugn either party's honor.

"There is more, sir," the admiral said. "I am a simple sailor and no man of accounts, more than is needed to have dealt well enough with navy recordkeeping when I commanded a ship of my own."

Hoare found it impossible to conceive of this man mountain pacing the weather side of his own quarterdeck, but indeed it must at one time have been so.

"But," the mountain continued, "I cannot believe that the prosperity which you so shrewdly noted derives wholly from cards. There must be another source, and I dread what it may be.

"Look at this," he said. "The coded text came to our pigeon loft several days ago, directed to Mr. Goldthwait. Somehow, thank God, one of the idiots in my service misdirected it; otherwise, it would not have reached my eyes, or now yours. Only now has one of those idiots managed to decipher it. No thanks to them, by the way, but to your own wizard. Or 'witch,' perhaps I should say—that remarkable Taylor woman in *Royal Duke*. For, as you know, it was she that broke the code."

Hoare took the paper that Sir Hugh placed on the desk within his reach.

"Acts: nine, one and two," he read, silently.

"You know the reference, I'm sure," Sir Hugh rumbled.

"I fear it escapes me, sir."

"'And Saul,'" Sir Hugh recited, "'yet breathing out threatenings and slaughter against the disciples of the Lord, went unto the high priest, And desired of him letters to Damascus to the synagogues, that if he found any of this way, whether they were men or women, he might bring them bound unto Jerusalem.'"

"Thank you, sir." Hoare made his whisper sound as humble as he could.

"The cipher, and the content of the message it bears, have a most uncomfortable familiarity, don't ye think?" Sir Hugh asked.

"Indeed it does, sir," Hoare said. "It's an inflammatory text. It has much the same character as the messages Taylor unraveled from the documents of the late Captain Spurrier."

"Precisely so. And, as you will remember, too, the ultimate source of those messages to Spurrier has never been determined. There is, Captain Hoare, every reason to believe that it is French—or at least French-connected. One of Bonaparte's men, Hoare. Who else could it be?"

The question of the ciphers had troubled Hoare ever since he had encountered his first one, early in last year's inquiry into the blowing-up of *Vantage* and several sister ships. The texts were generally Biblical in tenor, if they were not actual quotations, and they used Biblical names for writer, recipient, and any third parties. The names were suggestive, like a nudge in the ribs, but—like nudges in the ribs—skirted specificity. The whole topic had been tantalizing; the ciphers could be read, but no one had succeeded in tracing them to their sources or identifying the owners of those nagging Biblical names. Each new accession—there had been three or four—plucked more sharply at Hoare's intellect.

Hoare had thought before of one possible source, one who, at least as far as he knew, had no connection with the French but had an odd, mad agenda of his own. He debated with himself, then decided to speak up.

"It could be Sir Thomas Frobisher, sir."

"Who?"

"Sir Thomas Frobisher, baronet and knight, of Dorset. He is by way of being virtual master of the entire county, or at least so he believes, and many Dorset folk believe with him. Including Spurrier, the Satanist, who chopped off the heads of those captains not so long ago . . . and then had the effrontery to drown in his own vomit while my prisoner."

"Never heard of 'em." Sir Hugh's rumbled admission was rueful.

Hoare was taken aback. Until now, it had seemed to him that Sir Hugh Abercrombie, like Mr. John Goldthwait, was omniscient.

"Sir Thomas was Spurrier's master, you may recall, sir, at least in county affairs. What if anything he had to do with the atrocities in the South, I cannot say."

"I had forgotten." The admiral broke his churchwarden's stem with a sharp snap, as if to exorcise his rage at having been found wanting in knowledge. "Go on about him, sir."

Hoare obeyed. As he felt he must in order to be fair, he stressed the ill feeling that stood between him and Sir Thomas. He described what he perceived as its initial cause—how he, Bartholomew Hoare, had mocked the baronet on the evening of their first encounter with his description of how, instead of riding to hounds as any gentleman would, the Hoares, father and son, engaged in battery. This, as he had explained to Sir Thomas then and explained to Sir Hugh now, involved training bats to catch large insects and return them to their handlers.

"Like falconry, sir," he explained. "It was a foolish jape, sadly mistimed and fatally misdirected. The misstep did me no good, I am ashamed to say." He paused and awaited his admiral's displeasure.

Instead, Sir Hugh, rearing back in his enormous chair, began to roar with laughter. That laughter was a daunting thing to hear. Deep and cataclysmic, it could have signaled the drowning of ancient Atlantis.

"Well, Hoare, that explains why you pricked up your ears so oddly the other day, when I mentioned falconry in connection with our man Ambler. At least, there's *that* little question answered for me. I had been wondering.

"But continue about this man Frobisher." Once again, Sir Hugh's bass voice grew grave.

"The important thing about him, sir," Hoare whispered, "in this connection at least, is his absolute conviction . . . that he, and not our present Majesty, is the proper wearer of the English crown."

"A peculiarity, to be sure," the admiral said, "but hardly a matter of gravity. After all, Bedlam is crawling with men who imagine themselves Jesus Christ. They can't all be; the Savior did not, as far as I know, claim to extend to His own person His miraculous ability to multiply the loaves and fishes. If He had, I should imagine, the matter would have preoccupied all Christian divines for centuries past, with an undoubtedly beneficial effect upon the souls of us all."

"Indeed, sir. In the case of Sir Thomas's delusion, though, the trouble is that he has a certain odd attraction . . . which has made him, as I said a moment ago, the effective dictator of Dorset. Not only that, he has extended that strange magic . . . to the House of Parliament in which he sits. I have been told, by Sir George Hardcastle and Mrs. Selene Prettyman, among others—"

"What Prettyman says, I find, is generally to be taken as absolute fact," Sir Hugh observed. Puff, puff.

"—that he has a number of adherents in Parliament who might better be described as devotees, if not worshipers. You would know more about that than I, sir."

"I blush to say that I had overlooked that," Sir Hugh said unblushingly, "probably because his claim is so typical of that sort of madness. Besides all those miraculous Jesuses, I know of a round dozen King Charleses, divided equally between father and son. As I remember now, he is an uncommon good political man, well able, as you observe, to get his own way.

"If I may leap to the conclusion to which I believe you are about to come, *you* suspect of Sir Thomas Frobisher what *I* have commenced to suspect of John Goldthwait—that he has entered into a conspiracy with the French."

"Exactly, sir. If Bonaparte should overlook an opportunity to put a spoke in Britain's wheel by fomenting an insurrection against the Crown, it would hardly be the first time. And . . . if the possibility did not occur to *him*, there is always Fouché."

"Ah, yes. That son of a bitch, that ugly little bum-worm . . ."

For some minutes, Admiral Abercrombie continued to string out maledictions about his opposite number on the far side of the Channel, as if he were signal midshipman in a flag-ship, running up orders to the Fleet. Interrupting himself only with agitated puffs at his pipe, he came to anchor only when he swallowed smoke the wrong way, gagged, and in a whisper no stronger than Hoare's, ordered the latter to pound his back. Hoare obeyed.

"I do not like Goldthwait, Hoare," the admiral gasped at last. "I never have. But you are quite right. Nothing gets past that . . . never mind. So we have two suspects, of which Frobisher is one and Goldthwait himself the other."

"Against neither of whom, sir, do we have proof sufficient to take action," Hoare whispered.

"We, sir—no, *you*, sir—must find that proof. Or satisfy us both that each of us has let his imagination run riot. I was becoming anxious enough with only Goldthwait on my hands; now you have doubled my anxiety. Go forth, young man, before I suffer an apoplexy. Do your duty; there is not a moment to be lost. You may count on my support—within reason. As you go out, pray send Lestrade in. Good day."

Chapter VII

⟵═◆═⟶

I WANT you to put together a crew of reliable men to row a watch boat across the Thames at night, say half a mile above the brig."

" 'Watch boat,' sir? I don't twig. 'Picket boat,' d'you mean?"

"Damn you, don't pick at me, or I'll pick your nose off and make that mort of yours eat it while you watch, together with its filthy contents."

The listener blew his nose nervously.

"Place yourself where you can keep an eye on any boat that approaches *Royal Duke* from upstream, day or night. You can be fishing, or lobstering, or whatever you think of. Diving for treasure, if you want. When you clap eyes on an officer passenger, you're to intercept him, apprehend him, drown him, d'ye understand?"

"Aye, yer honor."

"When you have him, strip him, weight his body, drop it over the side, and bring every speck of his possessions to me. Every speck, understand?"

"Aye, yer honor. But what if 'e's in a navy boat manned wi'

fightin' men? My boys may be wild boys, but they ain't so wild they'll go up against trained soldiers or matlows, no way, unless the odds is two to one or better."

"If that's what you see, then forget it; we'll try something else. But don't think you can fight shy with *me,* not if you want to keep your head on its shoulders. I'll know, oh yes, I'll know.

"Now, you and your moll, drink up and get out."

Titus Thoday appeared able to navigate the warren of London streets through the suffocating blanket of cold smoky fog, with ease. Hoare suspected that one could bring him anywhere into the city, blindfold, and, within minutes, he would have oriented himself and gone about his business. Now, carrying the Pickering portrait gallery under one arm, rolled up like a rather large umbrella or a small set of regimental colors, he conducted Hoare to the steps below Westminster Bridge. There he negotiated on their behalf with a double-scull wherry to take them down to Greenwich. The wherrymen grumbled, but when the price rose high enough, helped them aboard their little craft and set off downstream on the ebb.

The party approached the riptide under London Bridge without difficulty, despite the fog. Not unskilled in small craft himself, Hoare admired the oarsmen's mastery of this rushing flume. Yet even so, he tensed as they swept under the bridge to the muffled roar of invisible yellow-white waters; less than six hours from now, he knew, those waters would be reversed, and anyone wishing to travel downstream would have to begin below London Bridge, or wait.

Once through the bridge, Hoare leaned back beside Thoday and relaxed with a sigh. The sounds and the smells were the familiar ones of water, though of freshwater instead of salt. The difference was enormous, of course. He was on the water again, and not cramped into filthy alleys by the towering press of buildings. It was his turn to be at home, and Thoday's to be at sea. Fog or no fog, he could sense that Greenwich lay not far ahead, to starboard. Yes, he mused, there was nothing—absolutely nothing—half so much worth doing as simply messing about in boats. Simply messing, he thought dreamily, messing about in boats. He liked the phrase, and tucked it sleepily into his mental commonplace book. Messing . . . messing . . .

A shout from bow oar brought him back to reality with a heavy crunch. They had rammed, or been rammed by, another craft. Whoever the strangers were and whoever was at fault, they meant the wherry no good, for they neither shouted in out-raged reply nor screamed in panic, but swarmed aboard the double scull out of the fog in a confusing rush. The bow oar was quickly overwhelmed, and Hoare, as he drew his sword, heard him splash into the Thames and go gurgling off. Thames boat-men, like blue water sailors, seldom swam. Beside him, Hoare sensed that Thoday had drawn the blade of his sword cane.

Stroke oar was more alert than his mate, more courageous, or simply did not want to lose his livelihood and his craft, for he grappled with the first of the boarders. The wherry tilted alarmingly. Thoday lost his balance and began to topple over the side. Hoare heard the slim cane-sword clatter into the wherry's bilges. He grabbed his shipmate under one arm and pulled him back aboard, out of danger, as a second boarder scrambled aft with a rush past stroke oar and his struggling attacker, followed by a third. It was two against two in the dark, then.

Hoare's own particular foe clawed for his eyes, but a knee in the bollocks stopped him with an agonized gasp, and the claw-ing stopped. Hoare thrust the heel of his free hand under the man's jaw and pushed, hard. Over he went, backwards. Hoare could now turn to Thoday's aid. As far as he could tell, the man on top was a boarder, for he smelt vile. Thoday, he realized fleet-ingly, was a cleanly man, as well as lacking his adversary's weight.

Hoare had his target. Without finesse, he hacked his sword into the boarder's back. With a shriek, the man collapsed upon Thoday. Hoare freed his sword and turned to the struggling pair amidships to see if he could tell friend from enemy. If so, he could bear a hand. What with their thrashing, he could not, and stood helpless.

But still another boarder was coming aft, balancing himself carefully as he came, as though he, too, knew something about messing about in boats. But, perhaps, not quite enough. Hoare thrust down with one foot, then with the other, setting the double scull a-rocking steeply—so steeply, in fact, that a wash of Thames water came over the larboard coaming. Then he reversed the motion. Back in Canada, up the Saguenay, he had seen French lumberjacks match skills that way on a log. The one who stayed out of the river was the winner. The young Hoare had at least tried this "burling" against a Canadian friend, and had gotten well soaked every time, but he had at least tried it. This opponent had not. Hoare saw him flail his arms wildly, saw him fail to regain his balance, saw him teeter and fall. He fell flat, with a clumsy splash that soaked Hoare's face and shoulders.

He could see the other craft now, the one that had carried the boarders. Swinging in the tide, it was drawing alongside them. It was a pair-oar, propelled by sweeps and not by sculls, somewhat longer and beamier than their own craft, and it held a single passenger in its stern sheets. He was near enough to grip, and Hoare gripped him. He pulled him into the double scull, where he threw him into the bilges and sat upon him, panting heavily.

So sitting, he could give his full attention to untangling stroke oar and his opponent who were still battling in the bilges. Appearing from aft, Thoday gripped one figure's hair. Hoare dropped his sword and followed suit with the other.

"This one's ours," Thoday grunted, and struck Hoare's man behind the ear with a heavy object. There was silence, broken only by panting breath all around, the gentle wash of water in the bilge, and the smothered whimpers of the visitor upon which Hoare was perching. The perch, he now realized, was a woman. He could tell by its feel.

"Bert," stroke oar said in a muffled voice. "Where's Bert?"

Hoare was about to break the news to him that Bert had been lost overside, when the missing man hauled himself wearily up and in, over the wherry's square counter.

"'Ere I be, Matthew, no thanks to you," Bert gasped.

Thoday was breathing heavily. "Well, sir, that's the second time this thing has come in handy." In his hand, he held the falcon figurine from Mr. Ambler's rooms. Even in the dark, Hoare could tell it had drawn blood.

In the heat of battle, one of the wherry's sculls had been lost overside. Besides, the man Bert was in no condition to row, and Hoare frankly doubted that Thoday had ever learned how.

"We haven't reached Greenwich yet," he whispered to the man Matthew. "Move us along, if you please."

"Wot, all by myself, after jest fightin' off a pirate crew? Take an oar yourself, mate."

"Pipe down and row."

The man began to complain bitterly.

"You hardly have a right to complain," Hoare told Matthew between heaving breaths. "Look here . . . you've gotten yourselves a prize out of this night's work." He had quietly cleated to the scull's counter the pair-oar's painter, which its last occupant had brought aboard with him as any good waterman should.

"Come on, Bert, bear an 'and," Matthew told his mate.

"Wot, wif only one oar?" Bert's voice was slurred. "'Ere then, you, budge over and gimme room." Elbowing Thoday out of his way, Bert stuck the odd scull between the thole pins and took up Matthew's rhythm. They began to make a sidling headway through the fog, the captured pair-oar towing dismally in their wake.

With Thoday's help, Hoare busied himself with securing their captives, including the woman he had been using in lieu of a thwart. She seemed to be a young person. When she began to protest at being mishandled, in a whispered snarl he ordered her to pipe down if she knew what was good for her. The rasp he produced apparently cowed her, for she piped down and let herself be trussed.

Allowing for the state of the tide, Hoare judged, the wherry and their captive pirates might have drifted to within hailing distance of *Royal Duke*. He put his fingers in his mouth and uttered his deafening general-purpose whistle. As he did so, he saw, no more than a few fathoms to starboard, the loom of some vessel. It reached well above their heads, and the wherry was sweeping past her.

"Ahoy the boat!" came a voice from her deck. Hoare nudged Thoday.

"Identify me," he whispered.

"*Royal Duke!*" Thoday called, thus announcing that they were carrying the yacht's commander.

"Ask 'em if they know her whereabouts."

"D'ye know where she lies?"

Hoare could hear a mutter of consultation. Then, "Two or three cables downstream. *Atropos* lies next below us, then *Leopard*, then your brig."

Atropos. Twenty-two guns. Hornblower's sloop. A nothing perhaps, but vastly more powerful in comparison with his own command, just as her captain was vastly more powerful than a mere Commander Bartholomew Hoare. It would have been a pleasure to stop and pay a call on Hornblower, but it would have been neither right nor proper. Besides being a new father, Hornblower, he knew, was preparing his ship for sea and would have no time to waste on a casual midnight call from a subordinate officer, no matter how friendly he might be.

"What ship is that?" Thoday called to their guide, echoing his commander's whisper.

"*Guerrière!*" came the reply.

"Thank you, *Guerrière!*"

They rowed on past two more ghostly forms, before Hoare repeated his shrill whistle. He did so again, and then again, until, muffled perhaps by the fog, he heard a faint call in reply.

"Pull for the sound, men, pull for the sound," he whispered.

Alongside the brig at last, Hoare saw all the others, including the dead attacker and the one Thoday had stunned with the falcon, hauled aboard in safety before he hauled himself through the low entry port. Once on deck, he could sort them all out. He ordered Mr. Clay—who, sensible man, had been long abed and appeared with his uniform coat hastily donned over his nightshirt—to see that Matthew and Bert the boatmen were suitably refreshed, then turned to his captives.

Now that Hoare could see them plain, out on an open deck, he realized that between them he and Thoday, with only minimal assistance from Matthew and none at all from Bert, had defeated four opponents. Five, if one counted the woman, though one should not, for she had been of no consequence in the affray. She alone was on her feet. He himself had pushed two opponents into the Thames, on or under which he presumed they remained. One, dead of the cut into his back, lay staring blankly up into the graying sky. The man Thoday had stunned had come to his senses, more or less, but still sprawled on the deck, muttering. The young woman stood facing Hoare, shivering with fear, cold, or a combination of the two. All hands were soaking wet.

"All right," Hoare whispered to her. "Which one of you is the leader of this crew?"

" 'Im," said the woman from between her chattering teeth. She pointed at the stunned man, since he could not yet speak for himself.

"Well? Who is he? And, for that matter, who are you?"

"P-P-Poll, sir, if ye please. Floppin' Poll, they calls me."

"And he?"

"Dickson, sir. Dick Dickson. " 'E's scurf of a school o' water-flimps . . . I dabs it up wif 'im."

Thoday saw Hoare's blank expression. " 'Beds with him,' she means, sir. He commands a fleet of river-going scroungers . . . petty pirates. He is new to me."

"And how did Dick Dickson and you, and his other friends, come to take us on?" Hoare whispered.

"Dunno, sir. All I know is, Sol come to the lurk an' took Dick aside. I hollered, o' course. I 'eard 'im tell me Dick to get a crew togevver an' lay off Grinnage an' nobble any wherries wot come dahnstream. You was the first come by, sir, worse luck. The perisher, 'e din't tell us you wasn't no flats. Nah look wot ye done to me cove. I'll 'ave the lor on yez, I will."

Hoare could not help admiring Floppin' Poll's reviving spirit, so he forbore to point out to her the illogic of calling the law on him, the gang's intended victim. Besides, she was turning blue. One of the female Royal Dukes, McVitty, the librarian with permanent spectacles, was loitering about, looking anxiously at her. He should think of her as a Royal Duchess, he supposed.

"Get her below, McVitty, will you, and turn her over to Tracy?" Tracy, surgeon's mate, had been a medical student at St. Bart's, but had married unfortunately and run off, as he thought, to sea.

"Aye, aye, sir. Come on, woman." McVitty hoisted one of the other woman's arms over her shoulder and half-supported her to the yacht's fore hatch, where Hoare lost sight of them.

"Best to get this one down to Tracy, too, sir," Mr. Clay advised. "He's breathing peculiarly."

"Make it so, Mr. Clay," Hoare said. He went below to his pigeon-smelling cabin, and turned in. It had been a long, adventurous day.

Back aboard *Royal Duke* at last, weary and confused, Hoare lay long abed before he could compose himself for sleep. Sleeplessness was an unusual thing for Bartholomew Hoare; ever since his first lonely nights as a mid, he had dropped off as quickly as any other sailor. It was a skill necessary for survival, he thought as he stared up through the dark at the deck beams a foot above his nose. A sailor must learn early to take his sleep as he could find it, generally in all-too-short snatches, generally hungry, often wet. Compared with those days and with other ships, his state tonight was one of luxury.

He managed to put the late encounter behind him, and think back to the preceding day and those three damnable inquisitions, one after another.

Something, he thought, had been disturbing Sir Hugh deeply—something besides the grave matter that the massive man had described, something behind that which he had not wished to disclose. Something personal, perhaps. Certainly, Sir Hugh's state of health must be distressing him. But Hoare was too tired to think further, and fell asleep.

Upon awakening, he lay for a space, wandering idly across the meadows of his memory, stopping once in a while to browse off some pleasant morsel, and overlooking the weeds for now. He had begun to share his meadow with Eleanor, only to find that she had a similar meadow of her own, to which she was making him, too, welcome.

He paused in mid-browse, upon realizing that there was someone else in his cabin. When he opened his bleary eyes, they hit upon the face of Eleanor herself, regarding him with her usual serenity from within the depths of Sir Hugh's enormous swinging chair. He sat up too suddenly and struck his head a stunning blow on the deckhead. She was supposed to be safely tucked away with her father, well north of London. Yet here she was.

"I had . . . thought you in Great Dunmow, visiting your papa," he said as soon as he could speak coherently.

"As you can see, I am not," she answered. "I am sorry to have startled you. Does your head hurt?"

"Not much," he said, sitting up and rubbing it. "I am truly delighted to see you." Indeed, he was. Every day since they first met on the shingle of Portland Bill, he had become fonder of her.

"What moved you to change your mind and join me here?" he asked.

"Well, it was you yourself, for one thing," she said. "As time goes by, I grow fonder of you. I don't understand why.

"There was another reason," she said, somewhat later. "More than one, in fact. It seems that I have become accustomed to my independence—at least, from my father and my brothers. Jack, my childhood protector, is long gone to Pondicherry, where he is making his fortune a-shaking the pagoda tree like that Lord Manymead you tell me about. In his absence, Gerald rules the roost, our father included. He is more the bully than ever. And poor Jude—well, he always was a scrub, I fear.

"No, I prefer my own household, my own little ward, my own people. And my own husband, thank you very much, sir." She nuzzled his shoulder where it joined his neck. "Now, tell me your tale. What dragons have you slain lately, for king and country?"

Hoare gave her a drastically curtailed précis.

"You seem to have learned a great deal, Bartholomew, while on the North America station," she said. Her voice was slightly acid. "In addition, of course, to getting married. This 'burling' you described, for instance. Why, I should not be surprised to learn that you learned gambling as well as the other naughty habits—those I enjoy so much."

Hoare startled and gulped. His past, in fact, held a secret that, while it would not be held disgraceful in the eyes of the world, he preferred to keep to himself. Stationed in Halifax as second in a sloop during the closing days of the fratricidal American war, he had taken up cards. He had been almost as lucky at the table as he had been earlier in the rebellion, when he had snatched up a small fortune in prize money while still a mere midshipman.

However, his shame derived from neither the gambling itself nor his good fortune in it. The shame was that, wrongly accused of cheating by a spirited young French-Canadian seigneur who had lost heavily to him at a card game, honor had compelled him to call the man out. Georges-Louis Honoré Laplace was an inexperienced stripling, though a creditable shot like most of his fellow countrymen, but Hoare had already been out almost as many times as he had years. In the ensuing encounter, he had missed his aim, which was to inflict a mere gentle chastisement, and had severely wounded his opponent.

During his long convalescence, young Laplace was attended by his slender younger sister Antoinette. Once, when duty allowed him ashore, young Bartholomew had visited his victim's sickbed below the Citadel, met the sister, and lost his heart to her.

Hoare's eloquence—for ten years of normal speech still remained to him—had persuaded her. He had even been willing to be married in the small Roman church that served the French colony. But the fact that he could not convert and still keep his precious commission had caused an estrangement to arise between his bride's people and himself. This must have weighed, he always thought, in their decision to return to the wilds of Quebec. They took with them the daughter Antoinette had died in bearing him. All of this—the birth, Antoinette's death, the family's return to Canada, had taken place while Hoare was at sea in *Beetle*, helping to wind up the fratricidal American war. He had never seen their child—Leticie, the name the sour-faced *curé* had shown him in the baptismal register upon his return to Halifax. He had never even learned whether or not she bore her father's family name, and he was of two minds on the subject. He did not wish her to be nameless; yet on the other hand, if the girl should grow up to move in Anglophone circles, his own name would carry invidious connotations.

He was irrational on the topic, he knew, but Hoare blamed Antoinette's death on the good fortune he had experienced in play with her brother, which had resulted in his challenge. He had therefore sworn solemnly that never again would he touch a card. He had kept his pledged word.

But Eleanor was still speaking, more or less into his ear.

"Besides, Bartholomew," she said, "there is another reason for my descent upon you. There were strangers in Great Dunmow, watchful strangers, watching *me*. I did not trust them.

Now, if you compare it with Little Dunmow, Great Dunmow may be a metropolis, but it holds no more than a hundred folk, young and old, and, were something untoward to take place, I would find myself without protection. So I up and came down to Greenwich."

"Leaving our household behind, madam?" Hoare whispered. "That makes little sense."

"No, my dear. I brought the entire household along—Tom, Agnes, Jenny, Order the cat, Uncle Tom Cobbley, and all. It required the hiring of a wain."

"I should imagine so," he said. "If we are to continue junketing about England like so many gypsies, we must betake ourselves to a wainwright and have a vehicle built to our order, from the keel up."

"And you shall give it a new name for every voyage, the way you did *Devastation,* or whatever your pinnace was last named, before you decided to settle on a consistent name for her."

"*Nemesis.*" Hoare's voice was absent. "But tell me more about these strangers."

"I have little more to tell you," she answered. "In a metropolis like Great Dunmow, strangers stand out, especially when they loiter about without any visible reason for doing so. They were townsmen, it seemed, shifty, and not overly strict about leaving the possessions of others alone. As I said, I did not like them or the oh-so-subtle watch they kept on me, so I came here."

"And where did you leave your wainful of family?"

"Oh, as to that, dear Jane's cousin Augustine—imagine, Bartholomew, the foolishness of his father, John Austen, naming one of his sons Augustine—has gone off with his people to Jamaica on some business of his wife's family, and his house was to let. It is the other side of Blackheath, not more than half an hour's drive from the quay opposite *Royal Duke.* Very suitable it is, too. You shall see it and take proper command there as soon as the Service permits.

"And—oh! I quite forgot. I am sorry. Bartholomew, Tracy said I was to give you the news that his patient died. The man. He never recovered consciousness; 'a depressed fracture of the cranium,' he said. So there goes one of your sources of information. I would not care to be your prisoner, sir; they do tend to die off while in your custody."

"Damn." As Hoare drew on his breeches, he remembered, not for the first time, that his predecessor in Eleanor's affections had been an eminent physician and surgeon—much of his knowledge had rubbed off on his wife, as Hoare's own interests were evidently doing as well.

How Eleanor had guessed, Hoare did not know, but he had indeed been sure that, with skilled interrogation by Thoday and himself, he could have persuaded the leader of the river pirates to disclose the identity of the man Floppin' Poll had named as "Sol." Now only the mort herself remained as a source.

Floppin' Poll was of no help at all. Recovered from her disabling chill, she had recovered her spirits as well, and would not be coerced into more than describing the man "Sol."

Moreover, her description was null. Sol could have been a masked Chinaman or a black Fijian, for all she knew. He was utterly featureless. Besides, as Hoare and Thoday agreed when they stepped aside out of the young woman's hearing, she was hardly the most intelligent or observant creature alive.

"To tell the truth, sir, she's of no use to us as she sits," Thoday said. "I suggest that we have her followed and watched. More than likely, Sol will want to learn the outcome of the little adventure he arranged for us, and will find her to interrogate her. A competent watcher should be able to detect his approach, leave the woman, and follow him."

"An excellent idea, Thoday. Have you a recommendation among your shipmates? A 'competent watcher'?"

Hoare added hastily, "Other than yourself, of course."

Slightly chagrined, Thoday thought for a moment, then nodded.

"Collis, sir. Small, nimble, used to be a sweep, still looks like a lad. Second-story man, candidate for rating as topman, Bold tells me. Unremarkable."

"*I* don't remember him, certainly," Hoare said. "If that's a measure, he certainly is unremarkable." Though he took pride in having learned his crew by name despite his brief time in actual company with them, Hoare knew himself fallible in his memory of individuals.

"Let's have a look at him."

Summoned, Collis showed why Hoare could not recall him. He looked indeterminate, like an aged urchin, prematurely wizened. An ex-jockey, perhaps. Hoare gave him his instructions and some pocket money, showed him Floppin' Poll as she sat unwitting, sent him off to *Royal Duke*'s slop chest to be clad in appropriate rags, and saw him into the wherry to sit beside his prey.

The tide was flowing. Hoare's two ferryman, whom the Royal Dukes had filled with tots saved from their own precious rum ration, clambered somewhat unsteadily into their prize. The captured pair-oar still carried both sweeps while one of their own craft's sculls had floated down toward Gravesend and the sea. They objected to carrying Floppin' Poll as the only surviving architect of their perceived misfortunes, but subsided when Hoare summoned Mr. Clay, who bellowed them into submission. Matthew, as stroke oar and commander, pocketed their fare and a little over. Hoare watched over his own taffrail as the two rowed off upstream in the pair-oar, with their passengers in the stern sheets, towing the double scull close behind them. Like an old married couple, they bickered as they pulled.

What next? Hoare asked himself. He stood at a loss for an answer.

Chapter VIII

———◦◦◦———

*T*HE MASTER'S boot thudded again into the ribs of the man who lay prone before him. The victim no longer had the strength to howl; he merely grunted with the force of the blow, and rolled over. Kick, kick—this time, into the man's unprotected face. The master lifted him by the front of his coat, hurled him against the wall and punched him in the pit of the stomach before letting him drop again. The man gagged and choked.

"Damn you, you inept nincompoop. I told you to damage him, not kill him. And you let him kill Darby. And where's Jukes? Answer me that."

"I—I—"

"Shut up. I ought to kill you myself. You ought to know by now: I keep my enemies, and put them to use. Now give me the shiv."

"I left it be'ind, boss," the man mumbled, "like you tole me—"

"I never told you any such thing. You lie in your black teeth."

"Oh, boss—"

"Another loss like that, you shite-poke, and I'll lose you your cods and feed them to you, raw. Now get out."

By his own mistake, Hoare's request to the Admiralty for permission to sleep out of his ship was sent through the usual channels. As usual, the usual recipient rejected the request with sardonic words about idle officers and half pay. Hoare resubmitted the request, directing it to Vice-Admiral Sir Hugh Abercrombie, as he should have done in the first place. Sir Hugh granted permission forthwith, and Hoare could at last put his slender kit into his saddlebags behind him when he next traveled down across Blackheath to Dirty Mill, the house that Eleanor had found for them.

Through Greenwich town he made his way, astride the modest young cob he had procured. Since being tossed aground over and over again during childhood, he had had no use for horses and hated riding them. He admitted that they were necessary creatures, but found them disorderly, disobedient, unpredictable, and ready to tittup and fart about wherever they pleased, leaving their excrement underfoot to be trodden in by their betters. He could never understand why country gentlemen were often more enthralled by a horse than by a pretty girl. Certainly, the latter made more enjoyable mounts.

Once out of Greenwich, he took the road over Blackheath to Dirty Mill, up Cromms Hill, past various landmarks, many the villas of royal mistresses, others the follies of men like Vanbrugh, until he reached the crest and could let the cob have its way down into the narrow valley where Dirty Mill lay.

Dirty Mill it might be named forevermore, but Eleanor and her people had already made the house spotless yet comfortable. His wife, he thought, must have all but emptied her childhood home—decent, unspectacular furniture dating, Hoare guessed, from Queen Anne's reign, made its appearance, while familiar hangings from Weymouth windows were recut and commenced to hang, one after another, in Dirty Mill's narrower stone-mullioned windows. Brass and silver came out to cheer up mantelpieces; a suitable cook with knowledge of local markets was hired.

Eleanor must not be without her tuffet. The round object, resilient like her bottom, on which she so liked to nest, took its place on one side of the fireplace in the small parlor, across from an easy chair that she had bullied out from under her terror of a brother and brought with her proudly, like the cat Order bringing in an enormous mouse. Certainly, the nursery furniture that had been hers as a child found an appreciative new owner in Jenny. In no time at all, Dirty Mill had become a true home, the first home Hoare had occupied since he had left the family house in the north, never to return. His life with Antoinette in Halifax all those years ago had been that of a driven junior lieutenant and his child bride; it had been all too short.

Like the rich in the Bible, the wain went empty away, trundling back to its owner in Great Dunmow.

Aboard *Royal Duke,* affairs settled into a routine. After his ride over from Dirty Mill of a morning, Hoare and Mr. Clay generally engaged in their regular duel, rain or shine. By now, the other Royal Dukes would go about their day's business around the combatants, dodging and being dodged as their respective movements required. During more than one encounter, a crewman might edge past them with a "by your leave, sir," or even hint with an expressively cleared throat that they move their passage-at-arms away from some piece of maritime equipment that needed nursing.

Then the day's serious business began: belowdecks, the inspection and sorting of the messages received the day before, either by the irritating sea-pigeons or by the more mundane means of the daily wherry service. To augment the yacht's own boats, Mr. Clay had contracted with Matthew and Bert to take two of those trips daily, down from Whitehall Steps with the tide and back again.

On deck, Mr. Clay made certain that—at least to the extent possible while lying to a mooring—the yacht's people kept their seamanship honed. Watches were kept as if they were at sea, though each watch on deck was divided into two moieties of which one exercised on deck while the other turned to the paperwork that was the vessel's raison d'être. The *Royal Duke*'s appalling performance in Portsmouth some months gone had earned them the name of the Fleet's "dustbin." Well, then, the two officers had vowed, they would turn the jeering term on its ear and make it into a word of praise—or at least respect. The Dustbins' comportment during that little passage in the Channel had shown all hands they might even succeed.

Sergeant Leese kept his Green Marines alert and fit by frequent patrols into Greenwich and out into the surrounding countryside. Early on, a short and nasty encounter had taken place with a squad of Red Marines outside the Yacht Inn, when one of the Lobsters overheard a Green Marine explain to an interested cit that "We marines really be much like lobsters, sir. As we sings in the service, 'a Red Marine's a dead marine; a Green Marine's a live 'un.'"

"Jenny and I have something to show you, Bartholomew," Eleanor told him as they returned from Matins. Both she and her husband were free-thinkers, but the proprieties must be observed. With the child trotting between them, well bundled up against the raw cold, the two were striding homeward along one of the lanes on the back side of Blackheath. Last night had seen the season's first sprinkling of snow, and Jenny's cat was beside himself with excitement at this novel, evanescent white stuff. He danced about them in the fresh white powder, athwart their hawse, like one of those legendary Chinese boatmen Hoare had heard about but had never seen, who made it a point to scull across another vessel's bows as closely as possible. By doing so, they believed, they cut off the devils in their wake, leaving them behind to pester the other craft. Surely, Order's tidy tail would be devil-free.

"Shall I show him now, Mum?" Jenny asked eagerly.

"Why not, my dear?" Eleanor said. "Look. See if you can knock down the bird's nest in the fork of that willow tree."

"Won't the mother bird be upset?"

"No, Jenny. The baby birds are long grown and gone, and the nest will be empty now."

The trio stopped in the lane, while Jenny scrabbled under the thin snow until she found a small round pebble. Hoare watched her in perplexity, Eleanor in pride. Then she reached into her bosom and withdrew a sling—a *sling*! Eleanor looked up at her husband, her eyes brimming with mischief.

"You remember, I see, Bartholomew."

"Indeed, my dear. How could I forget?" It was with a sling that Eleanor Graves had fought off her attackers on the afternoon of their first meeting, and with the self-same sling that she had made Edouard Moreau overturn his skiff in the surf so that Bartholomew Hoare could catch up with him and drown him.

Jenny popped her pebble into the sling, took a stance, and began to twirl her sling about her head with deft flips of her wrist. Three flips and she let the pebble fly. The pebble hit the nest squarely—it was less than ten yards away—and knocked it out of its crotch. It fell into the thin snow, where the cat Order attacked it.

"A dangerous pair we have on our hands," Hoare remarked. Her cheeks pink with excitement and her black eyes snapping, Jenny stooped and chose a second stone. Erect again, she sought about for another target.

Order flushed a rabbit. It bounded away, stopped. Twirl, twirl, release, and the rabbit went head over heels. It kicked thrice, and then lay still. A trickle of red appeared from its nose. Order scampered up to the little corpse and crouched to lick the blood.

"Oh, oh, oh . . . what have I done?"

On the spot, Diana became Danae. Dropping the sling, Jenny ran to her prey and squatted over it, her hand fending off the curious cat. She looked up at Eleanor and Hoare, her eyes brimming with tears.

"What have I done?" she sobbed again, and sniveled. She swept her sleeve across her nose. "I killed it. Oh, oh, oh . . ."

Eleanor crouched down beside the child and swept her into her arms.

" 'Tis all right, lass, all right. There, there. We understand. You are a brave girl." Her words faded off into mere comforting murmurs. Hoare stood above the little Pietá, his heart sore for the blooding of his charge. In an act of mercy, he had put her father to death as he lay hopelessly pinned by a beam in a burning warehouse. Some day, perhaps, she would have to know; meanwhile, her innocence had been assailed by her own doing. Now, he pocketed her victim surreptitiously, picked her up, and, cradling her against him, walked, his wife beside him, back in the direction of Dirty Mill. Behind, around, about, between his three charges, the cat Order wove his scampering way.

"Don't you think, Bartholomew," Eleanor asked as they walked, "that it is time we adopted our Jenny formally?"

"Past time," Hoare replied over the child's head. She was getting heavy, he noted with approval. "I must spend tomorrow in London. Could you find the time tomorrow to look up a solicitor and have him draw up the necessary papers?"

"Yes. I think, though, that the Church must enter into it somehow. Have you been baptized, my dear?"

"Baptized?" the child asked sleepily. "What's that?" Curiosity had stopped her sniveling.

"I think we can assume she hasn't," Eleanor said. "Besides, a second baptism can do her no harm. I know that from my childhood. After all, Father *is* in orders. I'll see to that as well."

"Will you be back by Sunday?"

"I hope so, my dear."

"Then I'll see to it, and gladly," she said. "Jenny, would you like it if Mr. Hoare and I were to become your papa and mama?"

"But you *are* my papa and mama," Jenny said into Hoare's shoulder.

"We'll tell you all about it in the morning," Hoare whispered. "Now, it's time for tea. There'll be sandy biscuits."

So it was that, after Matins in the church that served Blackheath parish, Jenny Jaggery was at once confirmed in her Christian name and became the youngest Hoare.

Reflecting on the music he had heard, Hoare shook his head a trifle sadly.

"You won't have known it, of course, but when I had a voice, I sang quite a fair baritone. On the Halifax station, Antoinette and I made a popular duet."

"Oh?" Eleanor Hoare's own voice was rather cool.

"In fact, I do believe I miss the singing more than the speaking," he added.

"To be sure," she said. "After all, Bartholomew, you *do* speak, albeit a trifle softly, perhaps. Do you think you might take up whistling?"

"*Whistling?*"

"Yes. You *do* know how to whistle, for Simon told me that when you and we first met, you showed him off your musical prowess. 'Drink to Me Only,' was it not?"

" 'Come into the Garden, Maud.' "

"The difference is immaterial. Besides, I have heard you at it, signaling to people in your employ. The pink girl Susan at the Swallowed Anchor, for example. You could develop a very nice descant to my contralto."

"What an extraordinary idea, my love. I had not thought of making harmonies with my lips before. Let me put it to a trial."

With that, Hoare commenced to twitter. By the time the three had reached home at Dirty Mill, he was managing brief trills, and the child Jenny was looking up at him with a face that was far more full of worship than it had been at morning prayer.

Chapter IX

———◆———

"I HAVE it!"

"Eh?"

"The wife, and the child. He dotes on them, I hear."

"Come, sir. Assault on men like one's self is a matter of course. But women . . . ladies in particular . . . and their children? Surely not."

"We shall see. Excuse me, I have urgent business to undertake."

"Something must be done about your pigeon shit, Hancock. I shall not abide it another minute." Hoare was below, arguing with his foul-breathed captain of the cote, or whatever the proper title was for the post. He was tired of working in the fecal fetor that seeped continually across the partition between his truncated great cabin and the pigeons' domain, dead aft, in the most desirable spot aboard. He was in no mood to care whether or not the pigeons needed his precious wide stern window and gallery to arrive and depart on their missions.

At the knock on his door, he interrupted himself to utter the chirrup that every Royal Duke now knew meant "Come in." The sentry, one of the yacht's Green Marines as usual, appeared, sworded rifle at the carry. It was the Dutchman Frits Boom, a man who looked the perfect dullard but was no such thing.

"Dere's a man down from London, sir. Sayzz his name's Lestrade, sir, an' sayzz it's urgent."

Before Hoare could tell Boom to admit Sir Hugh's pet ferret, the man himself was before him, having slipped under the guard's elbow. He had been bleeding profusely onto his dark overgarment, and his low forehead still oozed.

"It's the admiral, sir. Admiral Abercrombie. 'E's dead."

"*What?*"

Stunned at the news, Hoare still noted that Lestrade had left elsewhere his habit of mishandling his aspirates in a futile attempt at gentility.

"Dead, sir. Stabbed, over an' over again. I tried to 'elp 'im, 'deed I did, but they was too many of 'em. W'en I saw the admiral was down, I cut an' run. You was the first I thoughta, so I come down 'ere."

"When did this happen?" Hoare asked.

"'Baht two this mornin, sir."

"And here it is four bells—ten o'clock. What kept you?"

"Tide, sir. 'Twas against me. An' besides, Hit ain't—*Hisn't*—that Heasy to find a wherry at two in the morning."

Lestrade was recovering himself, as Hoare could hear, and no longer needed to make excuses. With this returned his usual veneer of genteel accent.

"Sit down, man. Out, Hancock. Talk to me later." Sullen, the man departed.

Before Hoare could whistle up Whitelaw and have him bring the messenger some refreshment, the silent servant appeared. On one palm he balanced a carafe of brandy on a tray with a pair of small glasses. In the other hand he carried a basin. A moistened cloth hung over his arm. He spoke not a word, but set right to work and began to repair his master's guest.

"Thank you, sir," Lestrade said over his glass. "Your good Health—and my apologies for breaking in on you with such dreadful tidings."

"Tell me what happened, Lestrade," Hoare whispered.

"Well, sir, you know, of course, that Sir Hugh lodges—lodged, I should say—with Mrs. Pettibone behind Downing Street. No more than a ten-minute walk, even for Him."

Hoare had not known this, but remained silent.

"For some years past, she has kept House for Him, on her ground floor, naturally. Since Sir Hugh took me into His confidence some years ago, Hi have made it a Habit to accompany Him Home in the Hevenings, if it should be dark. Has it often His, Sir Hugh being the man of duty He His. Was.

"Hi did so last night, it being foggy as well as late. About two o'clock, Has Hi think Hi said. Just Has we were turning the corner past Downing Street, we were assaulted, Hoverwhelmed by at least three Hassassins. Poor Sir Hugh drew His sword and attempted to defend Himself, but He was knocked over, and Hi was wrestled to the pavement. My assailant simply sat on me, Holding me by the Hair and bashing my Head against the stones. Hi fear that Hi lost my senses for a moment. When Hi recovered them and sat up, the Hattackers Had disappeared, and Sir Hugh was lying on His back. His sword lay at his side. It had been broken. He was quite dead."

Lestrade seemed to choke, then went on.

"Has soon as Hi could, I shouted for the watch. Some marines came running. I told them what had occurred, and they put together a party large enough to carry Him off. To the Admiralty, Hi suppose, but Hi do not know, for Hi betook myself to the Thames and roused up a wherry to be brought Here."

Lestrade took another sip of brandy. Having patched up his patient, Whitelaw took his departure, leaving the two men alone. He returned, however, bearing Hoare's hat, sword, and boat cloak, and helped his master into them. Hoare nodded at him and led Lestrade on deck.

"Is Thoday about?" he asked Mr. Clay.

"In Whitechapel, sir, I believe."

Hoare remembered now. He had sent Thoday there himself, at the man's own suggestion—one did not order Titus Thoday about arbitrarily, he had learned. There had been word from Collis that he had seen a man in close conversation with Floppin' Poll. He had seemed a gent, out of place in that particular shebeen, and Collis was set to drop the woman and follow the man.

Bold had already brought Hoare's gig to the yacht's starboard entry port. He held it close while his captain and Lestrade boarded.

"Give way, boys," Bold told his four oarsmen. Then, turning to Hoare, he said, "If we comes along like extra, sir, we can keep the tide all the way up to Westminster Steps. Which you'll be wantin', I suppose, sir?" At Hoare's nod, he relapsed into silence, except occasionally to correct the others' stroke.

Sir Hugh's immense corpse had already been hauled away to his apartments and laid on a long black table, where candles burned at its head and foot. At the foot, too, a tiny woman stood. She was silent now, but it seemed to Hoare as if the echo of her wailing still resounded through the room.

"His wife?" he breathed to Lestrade beside him.

"His Housekeeper, sir," Lestrade whispered in reply. "He was a widower, sir."

"Next of kin?"

"Only a brother, so far as Hi know, sir, somewhere in Scotland. Or thereabouts, Hi believe. There'll be a record somewhere, of course."

In death, the admiral was sadly diminished. With the departure of his stubborn, clever spirit, Hoare thought, he looked somehow deflated, like a huge pig's bladder that had been overkicked in some cruel game. Face and limbs as well as body had been badly chopped. An edged weapon had peeled the scalp back from the forehead, so that the pale pink bulge of the skull lay exposed over the staring blue eyes and under the sparse clotted white hair. Another blow had hacked into his cheek, so that two rows of gleaming false teeth lay exposed to view. Some of these blows, it seemed, had been inflicted after death, for they had not bled significantly. The two first fingers were missing from the admiral's left hand, suggesting that he might have raised it in self-defense. His white breeches, soaked in red, suggested that here was where he had received his death wound. His sword, more decorative than practical, remained gripped in his right hand. It, too, had been bloodied. So, then, Hoare thought, Sir Hugh Abercrombie, KB, Vice-Admiral of the White, had not gone gently to his death.

"Some'un 'uz drug away, zur," one of the sentries told Hoare in confirmation. "I zaw blood trail meself, I did. Went toward river, it did. There—see?"

Like a jinni, Thoday appeared at Hoare's side. How the man always seemed to know when there was a need for him, Hoare could never understand. It was as though he controlled an invisible semaphore system, or perhaps a private flock of ghostly pigeons.

"There were three attackers, sir," he said. "The admiral killed one of them. From the amount of blood, Sir Hugh struck him in the aorta or one of his carotids. A creditable blow, I must say. The two others fled, dragging their dead confederate with them. The body will be in the Thames by now, of course."

"One of them dropped a bollock-knife, sir."

"Bollock-knife, Thoday? What's a bollock-knife?"

"An old-fashioned knife with a guard shaped like a pair of calf's bollocks, sir. Here, as you can see."

He extended this weapon to Hoare, hilt first. A good ten inches long, the blade, Hoare saw, was bloody over the rust of neglect—presumably the blood had been the admiral's. The pommel did indeed resemble the neat spheres that juvenile males of most species carried about so proudly beneath their tails.

"I never saw a knife like it before," Hoare whispered. "What can you tell me about it?"

"A very good question, sir," Thoday said. "You might have seen one like it being carried by that shepherd we met at the Nine Stones Circle. They are an ancient model, used latterly mostly by animal herders to geld the young creatures."

"So its owner would be a countryman."

"Perhaps. But I cannot help but wonder, sir, how it happened to be dropped in the first place, and abandoned in the second. The admiral's assailants were apparently in no hurry to escape after completing their assassination; they had time to cut the body up a bit more, and then drag their dead comrade off with them. Why, then, did this knife's owner not pause to retrieve his weapon? They are generally heirlooms, and this one would be a valued possession."

"You think we are intended to believe the assassin was a countryman."

"I think it a possibility, sir."

Having been the bearer of the bad tidings to their Lordships of the Admiralty that they stood in need of a new chief of intelligence, Hoare was left to sit and observe the result of his having done so. He sat humbly there, in a corner of the great room with its globes and its charts of the world's oceans, well away from the glowing fire. To his astonishment, besides the usual factotums—secretaries, flunkies like Hoare himself, and the like—the only other person in attendance who was not a flag officer was Henry Prickett, Esquire. The advocate sat, as episcopal in demeanor as always, at the long gleaming mahogany, among persons who clearly perceived him as a colleague and an equal.

An admiral unknown to Hoare leaned over to whisper in Mr. Prickett's ear. The latter shook his head.

"Too soon, sir, in my opinion. The right choice, yes, but far too soon."

"It's obvious, my lord," the First Sea Lord declared dismissively. "Hardcastle's the man."

"Oh, but my lord," the First Lord said, "while I quite understand . . . after all, though, Sir George is a mere . . . a mere"—he bent his ear to his secretary's urgent, whispered prompting—"a mere, as I was saying, rear admiral. Of the blue," he added in obvious repetition, his demeanor making it clear he was uncertain what the matter of an admiral's color had to do with the matter of settling upon Sir Hugh's successor.

Lord Manymead is interfering, Hoare mused as the First Lord droned on, in matters that he does not understand. The phrase reminded him of something he knew he had put into that mental commonplace book of his. What was it, now? Ah, he had it. It had been in connection with Miss Jane Austen, that interfering lady, who had so adroitly played matchmaking juggler with the hearts of Miss Anne Gladden and Harvey Clay. With the horrible example of this First Lord at hand, he could now improve upon the trope he had then begun. "And while the House of Peers withholds . . . its legislative hand, and noble statesmen do not itch . . . to interfere in matters which . . . they do not understand." Very good.

But he must pay attention. The First Lord was still droning away.

"Besides, there is Admiral Deere to be considered."

Richard Deere was a recent creation known to Hoare, by reputation only, as a conniving, toad-eating vindictive man with a bilious digestion and an over-accommodating wife.

At this, Mr. Henry Prickett steepled his hands.

"If a mere layman may introduce his sentiments, First Lord," he said modestly, "the interests of the service would appear in this case to override the individual personal interests of the parties involved. In these perilous days, the nation faces an insidious, deadly enemy, one whose servants—be they in his pay or merely self-deluded—have just assassinated the head of the navy's intelligence operation.

"With all due respect, my lords, I must urge the selection in his stead of the best man for the job, one who has already demonstrated courage, wisdom, and energy in a position very similar to the one which is vacant. That man is unquestionably Rear Admiral Sir George Hardcastle."

"If we were to appoint Hardcastle," the First Lord said, "Deere would be insulted and consternated. He might even resign."

"A consternation devoutly to be wished," came a powerful voice from the far end of the table. There was a murmur of agreement. Seeing that he had fated to lose this battle with the admirals, the First Lord conceded, and, mentally, at least, withdrew from the conference. In such company, he was not a very strong man.

"There, Captain Hoare," Mr. Prickett said as the room emptied of chattering dignitaries, "Upon my soul, I do believe I just struck a blow for England."

"I do believe you are right, sir," Hoare replied. "And without even getting out of your chair. Pray accept my hand, sir."

"So, Hoare, you persist in your efforts to rise up the ladder of promotion, even if it means killing off the flag officers of the navy, one by one. As if you were a French marksman in a main top, with a rifle."

By this, Hoare knew, Admiral Sir George Hardcastle intended him to understand he was jesting. Sir George knew quite well how Hoare had come to lose his voice.

"Sir," he whispered, with a properly obsequious smile. Sir George had made himself quite at home in the spot his vast predecessor had chosen; behind the vast desk, tailored for Sir Hugh's tun of a body, Hardcastle's spare, square form looked almost like a child's except for the short, coarse, white Brutus-cut hair. Hoare was still accustomed to seeing a figure there that, in bulk though not in competence, minimized the present occupant. Mr. Clay would be pleased to see the change, he supposed, then chastised himself for a lack of charity toward the afflicted.

"Tell me about your discussions with Sir Hugh. I have not time for you to write a report for me, nor to read it. So you must whisper away as best you can. I'll order shrub, if it will help you along."

At Hoare's nod, the admiral did as he had suggested. Hoare took a sip of the bland stuff, and commenced. Physically, it was hard work, but he found the intellectual part advanced by the recency of his repeated interrogations, not only by Mr. Goldthwait and Mr. Prickett but also by his late commander himself. Nonetheless, the morning was well advanced before he came to a close. Hoare barely stopped himself from mopping his forehead—instead, he refreshed himself with a sip of shrub and sat back to take his medicine.

"So," Sir George declared, "above and beyond the certainty that this office has been penetrated and its confidentiality broken, Sir Hugh believed that at least one party is engaged in a deeper, broader conspiracy against the Crown. Two, perhaps, if there are two, they may be working in concert, or they may not. The 'who's' and the 'how's' are blanks, it seems. Am I correct?"

Hoare could only nod; the dregs of the shrub filled his mouth.

"Well then, sir, since you are already underway, maintain your course. Keep me informed as necessary; avoid rocks and shoals. Now be off with you, sir; I have much to do and no time in which to do it. Hammersmith!"

As the flag secretary opened the door to let Hoare pass and enter himself, Sir George halted Hoare in place.

"Oh, and by the way, Hoare, I shall have no need for those seamen ye borrowed from me so long ago and never thought to return. Stone, I think, and Bold. You may keep 'em, with my compliments."

Since Hoare had intended to do just that, with or without permission, he merely bowed and took his leave.

Chapter X

I DON'T understand you, Saul. What have you against Hoare? I hate the bastard myself, I admit, but what do you gain by capturing him and toying with him the way you say you want to do?"

"I choose to do so, sir. It's as simple as that. He has defeated my people, opposed me. I do not brook opposition. I shall break him. . . . Break him, do ye hear? Break him, let him remain in place, and make a tool of his shards."

The tracks of hoofs and wheels marked the thin snow cover, black against the moonlit white. That was odd; Hoare had passed neither cart nor carriage on his way home from *Royal Duke,* and there were more hoofprints than even a chaise and pair could explain. As far as he could tell—for, unlike Thoday, he was no tracker—the hoofprints went in both directions. Had there been visitors at Dirty Mill, come and gone?

Out of the moon-shadow of a spinney, a horseman rushed upon Hoare pell-mell. Hoare's cob shied, swerved, bucked, tossing last week's frozen snow in a hard spray about its hoofs. Hoare was nearly unseated and saved himself only by a strong heave on the reins. He forced his animal about so that it faced the attacker. To his astonishment, the man swung a saber at him; awkwardly wielded, it gleamed silver in the moonlight. His sparse teeth gleamed likewise, in a determined grin.

Why he was being attacked in this fashion, Hoare had neither a notion nor the time to consider. This was no swordsman, he realized as he backed the cob to gain time, nor was he a highwayman. Highwaymen these days commonly stood off and aimed a pair of barkers at their prey; they did not go in for escrime. Had they both been afoot, Hoare would have had no trouble in drawing his own weapon and disarming the silly ass. As it was, though, he had never in his born days played hussar, and he felt uncertain of the outcome. Hastily and awkwardly, he grappled and drew. Before he could parry, he must duck a wild slash, and his hat flew off. Instead of taking off Hoare's head, the attacker's blade cropped the cob's left ear.

The poor beast screamed and reared, and Hoare lost a stirrup. He gripped with his thighs as tightly as he would have gripped the mizzen when a-slide deckward from the crosstrees, and began to jab-jab-jab with his own weapon. For a moment, his unorthodox jabs seemed to disconcert the attacker, but he recovered and thrust forward again with a hoarse croak, his saber raised over his head, ready to divide Bartholomew Hoare as he sat.

Hoare leaned forward and jabbed. In his onset, the other impaled himself on Hoare's point. It took him in the throat. Momentum, if nothing else, carried him on, the point sinking deeper until Hoare felt it grate on bone. The strange horse crashed into the cob, which jarred back with the shock, but the attacking horseman was lifted over his cantle. He slid off the croup, twisting Hoare's sword out of his grip and carrying it with him, and sprawled in the moonlit snow. As Hoare watched, he kicked convulsively twice before going limp.

Hoare dismounted and bent over his victim, panting heavily.

First, he withdrew his sword and wiped it on the dead man's fouled breeches before returning it to its scabbard. Then he searched the body. A purse, a kerchief . . . ahh. A slip of paper, covered with writing too small for him to read in the moonlight. It would have to wait until he reached Dirty Mill. The stranger's horse bent over the body and whickered softly, as though mourning its master.

Another smell, Hoare could tell now, accompanied the odor of death. It was not excremental, though equally unpleasant, and it was one he had smelled not so long ago. Looking at the corpse a second time, he knew now who it was: Hancock, captain of *Royal Duke*'s own pigeon loft.

With a heave, Hoare hoisted the body across the newly emptied saddle, then hoisted himself back aboard his own cob. He gave a cluck and a nudge with his heels, and the beast moved off toward home and hay, not unwilling, the other animal following in its wake. Rest was not far off.

In the distance, Dirty Mill loomed dark. That should not be. Eleanor and the child would be awaiting his arrival—why had they not lit the house properly? With his knees, Hoare urged the cob on, and it broke readily into a trot. At his unlighted door, Hoare pulled the animal to a stop before it could carry him around to the back, from whence that wonderful hay was calling it.

The front door was open. Within, all was silence.

Hoare gave his chirrup of summons for someone—Tom, he hoped—to come and take the cob off to the stable with its new companion and the corpse. He himself would not tarry, however, but dismounted and left animals and corpse to fend for themselves.

Inside, there was still no sound, until at last, with his own plaintive chirp, the gray cat Order appeared from nowhere and commenced to wind himself around Hoare's ankles. Hoare's nose detected the faintest scent of burnt powder and, once again, faint but real, the reek of recent death. He groped his way to the shelf on the other side of the hallway, where he knew flint and steel lay ready, groped on until he found them, and lit a candle. For a moment, his eyes were dazzled. When they recovered, he understood why Tom had not answered his call.

"Jesus," he breathed.

The manservant lay prone next to the open green baize door separating offices from family quarters, a dark pool spread below his face, a discharged pistol dropped from one outreached hand. Order chirruped again, impatient for attention. An overturned chair lay beyond.

Putting fingers to his mouth, Hoare produced the piercing whistle of urgent command that, to friend and stranger alike, could only mean "Attention!" or "All hands!" depending on circumstances. Surely someone would hear and come a-running. He listened. Off in the distance, somewhere toward the back of the house, he was sure he heard a faint grunting sound. Leaving Tom's remains behind, he followed his ears toward the sound, along a thin trail of crimson that led him, candle in hand, past the baize door and into the pantry. The grunts were coming from the kitchen.

Except from a faint red glow from the hearth, the kitchen was as dark as the front of the house. By the light of his candle, Hoare saw the maidservant Agnes, hair and clothing awry, slumped against a cabinet, emitting the grunting sounds. She had managed to draw her skirts partway back down her discolored thighs, but a dark stain marred the apron, usually spotless, which she wore about her waist whenever she was within doors. As he watched, the stain widened. He lifted the skirts gently and viewed what lay beneath, then covered them again. He had seen worse in his time, but not much worse.

Ignoring the cat's insistent yowls, Hoare squatted beside Agnes and took her gently by the shoulder.

"Agnes," he whispered. "It's Mr. Hoare. What has happened? Where are your mistress and Jenny?"

"Uh." The girl's eyes opened. " 'Urts."

Hoare repeated his question. Now her eyes seemed to gain focus, and fixed on his candle-lit face.

"Too—took," she muttered. "'Urts zo." She clutched her bleeding belly.

"You'll be all right, Agnes. It won't hurt much longer." He knew he spoke truth.

"Who . . . ," he whispered.

"Men," she said. "Too many for Tom." Gathering strength, she added, "Done it to me, they did. Three of 'em done it to me. No, I lie, they was more. Took turns, they did . . . 'gainst my will, tu. Town folk, they was. All but that pigeon man what smells zo bad.

"'Urts zo, zur . . . Make it stop, do. . . . That pigeon man, I think 'e left sumpin' on table."

"You say the mistress was taken?"

"Aye, took, zur. Too many for 'er, too many for Tom. Poor Tom's a-cold. Oh, it 'urts."

Candle in hand, Hoare stepped across to the kitchen table, which he found had been swept clear except for a fresh red stain that told him where Agnes's rape and gutting had taken place, and an envelope placed four-square at its midpoint. It was addressed to Commander Bartholomew Hoare, in a neat clerkly hand. He knew Hancock's semi-educated script from his work in *Royal Duke*; this writing was not his. He broke the seal and read the contents.

Mr. Hoare:

I have recently learned that you have, quite improperly and in defiance of my wishes, taken into your possession certain portrait drawings by Timothy Pickering, Esq., which he in turn had, equally improperly, retained in his own keeping in the course of his work for us. Since these drawings are the rightful property of myself and my colleagues, I now require that you return them to me forthwith, in their entirety, withholding none of them whatsoever. As you now know, I have taken steps to insure that you do so.

Immediately upon receiving this communication, therefore, you shall bring the aforesaid drawings to 18, Gracechurch

Street, presenting yourself by night. You shall, it goes without saying, be unaccompanied; I shall consider the presence of any companion, aide, or follower as exhibiting bad faith on your part, and shall act accordingly, to the certain detriment of your dependents and yourself.

The same stricture applies to your bearing any arms whatsoever; upon arrival at Gracechurch Street, I warn you, you shall be subjected to a close search.

Upon your having delivered the portraits to my satisfaction, I give you my word of honor as a gentleman that your wife and stepdaughter (or ward) will be released to you in more or less the condition in which my people gathered them.

The consequences of your deviating, whether by intent or inadvertence, from these instructions need not, I am certain, be discussed at this time.

I look forward to receiving you and your documents in Gracechurch Street, and to concluding this matter in a way that I find agreeable.

The letter was unsigned.

Hoare took a last precious moment to slip up to the bedroom he and Eleanor shared. Usually tidy, it was littered now with their personal goods; in the midst of the clutter lay a long serpentine object of tough cotton cloth—his wife's savior sling. He sought out a shawl and brought it back downstairs, where he laid it across Agnes and tucked it in.

"I must leave you, Agnes," he whispered. "Rest now. I'll send help as soon as I find it." He bent, brushed the straggling hair from the girl's forehead, and kissed her there. It was cold.

Outside Dirty Mill's door, the two horses stood, still steaming lightly in the frosty air. Hoare stopped long enough to examine his choices. He must return to *Royal Duke,* for no longer than needful to retrieve the drawings that the unknown message writer was demanding. Thence, whether by land or river, he must move at utmost speed. In all truth now, not a moment was to be lost. He checked the position of the moon and, from it, verified his estimate of the tide. It was as he feared; it would be on the ebb. He must ride. The dead Barnaby's horse looked the fresher, perhaps. . . . No, it was a stranger horse, while he and the cob at least knew each other's ways. He would take the cob. He led Barnaby's horse around to the stable and dumped in a manger the hay that the cob ought to be enjoying. Then he ran back to the cob, mounted, spurred the startled beast, and was off. Behind him, Dirty Mill and its inhabitants lay in the dark, its front door still swinging gently in the frosty, light night breeze.

Sweeping aside the startled anchor watch at *Royal Duke*'s entry port, Hoare put fingers to mouth and sounded his whistle of alarm once more. Unlike the fruitless blast he had uttered at his own doorstep, the response to this second shriek was as it should always be. From belowdecks came a humming as of a hive of enormous disturbed bees. First to come on deck was Mr. Clay, nightgowned, nightcapped, and barefoot to the icy planks, buckling his serviceable sword about his waist as he came. He was followed by Leese and two of his men, also carrying their swords, as they, like the riflemen they copied in all things, termed their long bayonets. Others followed.

As had become instinctive with him by now, Clay stepped up to his captain's side to assume his duty as stentor.

"My wife and child have been taken," Hoare began. "Kidnapped."

The hum of bees rose to an enraged pitch.

"Hancock, our pigeon man, was one of them. He's dead. Here's a letter my people's takers left behind. I'll have Mr. Clay give you its gist while I prepare to follow them. *Alone,* as you will learn."

He ducked below to his cabin forward of the orphaned pigeons. As soon as he had a chance he would slaughter them all and hang them around Hancock's neck like Mr. Coleridge's albatross. But first, he must get together the likenesses with which he must ransom his family, and bring his people home. He had lost his first family; he would never let this second one out of his sight again. They had become unutterably precious.

"After hearing what you told us about Hancock, sir"—Clay told Hoare when he reappeared, the roll of drawings slung across one shoulder like a scabbard in lieu of the sword he must leave behind tonight—"I took it upon myself to take a muster of all hands, since they were already on deck. Besides Hancock, and of course Thoday and little Collis, the cook Green is missing, sir. Run, I suspect."

From one of the many Londoners in his crew, Hoare now took directions to Gracechurch Street, absorbing them as best he could, given his present mental state. He remembered, at least, that he should cross the river by the Westminster Bridge. He shook off the man's pleas to let him guide him there. "Can't risk it, Eddison," he whispered, "but thank you."

After issuing a few last-minute instructions, in which he stressed again his absolute veto of any attempt upon the part of the Royal Dukes to follow him up to London in the hope of being helpful, Hoare wrapped the Pickering drawings into a long cylinder, strapped it to his shoulder, and mounted. As he set off in the cold moonlight, he heard Mr. Clay's astonishing roar of a voice from *Royal Duke* behind: "Now Godspeed, sir, and good luck! Bring us back your women!"

Mr. Clay's farewell was followed by three quiet, grim cheers. Well, Hoare thought, at least he had not made enemies of them all.

He must not force the cob's pace. The night air was icy, the snow could hide all sorts of traps in the London road, and he was conning the animal's nose into the moonlight. So, though his heart kept urging him to gallop, gallop, gallop to the rescue, he held the beast to a sober trot. Under close-reefed topsails, so to speak, with a leadsman in its chains. He had the time now to think about what had happened, and what lay ahead of him.

The pigeon man and the cook. For sure, the cook had run. Besides being a Portsmouth "brute" by trade as well as build, she was an evil witch as a cook, and she had not been well-liked, so it could be no surprise that she had left the ship. Perhaps she had been in league with Hancock, who was dead and could not tell his tale.

As to Hancock himself: even in as unconventional a ship's company as the Royal Dukes, there was no traditional role in a ship's company for a captain of the pigeons. Such a rating had never existed before. Besides, there was the matter of stink—the stink of his feathered, cooing charges, and worse, the stink of the man himself. Hancock had become a pariah.

The fact might well have eaten into his soul, as Hoare knew from experience could happen to any Jonah: shunned, neglected, imposed upon, often beaten up. As Hoare must now confess, to his own belated chagrin, Hancock might well have taken Hoare himself into a deep hatred, for he himself had not even tried to conceal his disgust whenever the man's stench reached his nose. Certainly, Hoare recollected with a shudder, the pigeon-master's man's grin, as he rode onto him only an hour or so ago, had been a welcoming one—of a sort. Hancock had been seeking the life of an enemy.

Besides, through his work, Hancock had been in close, frequent touch with persons off ship, and with the ciphering and deciphering task directed by Sarah Taylor. (Hoare hoped, in passing, that Taylor herself had not been tainted. Surely not.) In the eyes of whomever might be trying to penetrate the operations of *Royal Duke,* the pigeon man would have been a logical target for seduction.

By now, Hoare estimated by the sinking moon in his eyes, it would be past four bells in the middle watch—two o'clock in the morning. The London road was a street now, lined with solid buildings of a mercantile nature, clear of snow but not of clutter, and he all but alone in it. When he had rounded a jog in the street, Westminster Bridge hove into sight. He would be another half hour to Gracechurch Street, provided he did not lose himself. He had best add on still another half hour in which to untangle his way.

At the bridge's near end, he spied lantern-light, and in it two huddled men. The watch, he supposed. He came to a decision. He could not stand the idea of wandering a-horseback through the London labyrinth, lost and despondent, Gracechurch Street ever receding. He would take a pilot aboard, and throw himself on the mercy of his family's captors.

The offer of a golden half-crown was more than enough to make the younger of the two watchmen snatch at the prospect of bringing this night-bound gaby in uniform to his destination.

"Swift, safe an' sahnd, sir," he promised, "an' will exercise the 'oss while I wytes, to boot."

Hoare got the man's name from his partner—he was Job Threadneedle, as in the street where the limner Pickering lived—and hauled him onto the cob to ride pillion. The beast must be weary. But necessity knew no mercy, and besides, it was due for a rest of unknown duration.

They crossed the bridge together to the music of a travel narrative from Hoare's pilot, who had a story about every corner they passed, told in a nasal drone that sometimes Hoare failed altogether to understand. When Threadneedle spoke, he breathed, and the stench of his breath reminded Hoare of Hancock. By now, the pigeon man's body should be under the scrutiny of the team Mr. Clay had ordered sent down to Dirty Mill. When his passenger began to give his directions in rhyming cant, Hoare shut him off with a harsh whispered snarl to speak English.

"'Ere we be, sir, syfe an' sahnd, jest lyke I promised yer we'd be," Threadneedle said into Hoare's ear at last, with a final putrid puff. By Hoare's estimate, only twenty minutes had elapsed since he had brought his vile-smelling pilot aboard.

"Well done, man," Hoare whispered. He slid off the cob, and Threadneedle slid onto the warm saddle.

"Wait till they admit me," Hoare went on. "Then take the

animal to the nearest inn, stable it and have it tended to, and make yourself at home there. If you're still sober when I join you, there's another sovereign in it for you."

"Walk-*er*!" To a mere watchman, two whole golden boys would be a fortune.

"Where will you put up?" Hoare asked.

After scratching his head, Threadneedle decided.

"Bow and Forest, sir," he said, and pointed with the itching head. "No more'n a 'undred yards dahn Grycechurch, that wye. Coachin' inn, it is; tykes in all kines, so long as they got the blunt, any time o' night."

Incredibly, Hoare realized he knew where the Bow was. It was the London terminus of the coach line to Cambridge, and the Hoares would have been using it overnights on their passages to and from Great Dunmow.

"Very good, Threadneedle. By the bye, tell them you are in my employ . . . Commander Hoare, of the navy."

"Commander 'Oare, of the nyvy," the pilot repeated. "An' . . . an' good luck, sir. Don't you worry, sir, Hi'll be waitin' you. 'Opes to see you there, syfe an' sahnd."

Chapter XI

—◆—

"*I* CANNOT be troubled with your petty complaints at this time, sir," said the smaller man. "I have more important matters on my mind, and so should you, if your interest in bringing this matter to a successful conclusion is as important to yourself as you have been claiming."

The host could not stifle a gasp of outrage.

"You do not dare, sir, to adopt that tone to me—not to me, above all."

"Spare me your bombast for the nonce, sir," the guest said. "You have yet to achieve your objective, and hence to deserve the homage you believe will become your due. You need my help; you know that.

"Now, here is what we must do. The females are safe, gagged, and secured, as I directed?"

"Bound, sir, seated at opposite ends of my own bedchamber. In reasonable comfort. And guarded."

"Bedchamber, eh? So you have . . . er . . . intentions with respect to one of them? Or both, perhaps?"

"Sir!"

"Pray step up and confirm that all is well. Oh, and while you are at it, make sure that the guard is firmly instructed to remain *outside* your bedroom door. Should the least hint reach my ears that either female has been interfered with, by anyone, the person or persons responsible will be subject to my extreme displeasure."

"After what your men told us about their behavior toward the woman Agnes, I am surprised at your sudden missishness."

"She was a servant. The females abovestairs are a different matter entirely."

Hoare found the house at 18, Gracechurch Street imposing enough—little less than a mansion. The steps up to the high door were wide and marble, and the balustrades wrought iron with polished brass rails. The windows were as dark as those he had left behind at Dirty Mill. Hoare knocked sharply. After a short, endless wait, a small port appeared in the door, a darker spot in the black, and a cold neutral voice said, "You brought support, I see. You were instructed to come alone, and warned of the consequences should you disobey. Good . . ."

"*Wait!*" Hoare's whisper was an agonizing rasp. "A hired guide, and no more. I lose myself in London. Please . . ."

The craven sound of his own pleading voice revolted him, but it must have satisfied the doorman. There was a further wait. Then, "Very good. A pleasure to see you again, sir." The voice was no longer cold, but cordial. With the grinding of a rusty key, the door was opened and held for Hoare to enter. The entryway being dark, Hoare could not make out the doorman's features, but the voice was familiar.

"This way, sir," it said. "We can begin to carry out our little piece of business more comfortably in our host's library." He opened the inner door, and the lamplight from within revealed his face. A small, lean, weary-looking man, he was Mr. John Goldthwait.

Without remarking on Hoare's startle, Mr. Goldthwait led him down a hall and past a graceful sweep of stairway, to a heavy walnut door, guarded by two persons. The one to larboard was Floppin' Poll, the dollymop who had taken part in the attack on the wherry bearing Hoare and Thoday down to Greenwich. The other, a swarthy man clad in a simple livery, must belong to the owner of the house. His shock of coarse black hair was unpowdered, his cheekbones prominent, his eyes slitted. He looked oddly familiar.

When the man gave him an unmistakable wink out of one of those slits of eyes, Hoare remembered. He had seen him on the box of a certain berlin, waiting at the door of Weymouth's St. Ninian's Church. He had identified him then as an Esquimau.

Mr. Goldthwait stopped at the door.

"Oh, I almost forgot," he said, looking up at Hoare with a winning smile. "The search. Pray raise both arms in the air." He produced a small, plain pistol.

"I believe I have seen that pistol before, sir," Hoare whispered. He had secreted it in his own little pinnace. In fact, come to think of it, he had not seen it since *Nemesis* had been searched and looted last summer, off Weymouth. Like his beautiful Kentucky rifle, it had flown.

"Perhaps you have, sir," Goldthwait said dismissively. "Never mind. I told you to raise your hands."

Hoare obeyed. Mr. Goldthwait ran his left hand swiftly along both sides of Hoare's body, pausing suggestively at the bulge at his crotch. Hoare could not restrain himself from flinching. Floppin' Poll snickered.

"Hmm," said the searcher. "Well-hung. And long deprived, I see." He continued the search down Hoare's legs.

"Very good, sir. And now . . ." He opened the walnut door. Upon sighting them, the library's occupant rose, as if reluctantly, from a Russia leather chair. One of three such chairs that surrounded three sides of a well-lit mahogany table, it was identical with the two in which Hoare and Mr. Goldthwait had sat, not so long ago, in the latter's apartments, and with the ruined one in the late Mr. Ambler's chambers. The fourth side of the table faced a warm, welcoming fire of clean cannel coal.

"Here we are, then," Mr. Goldthwait said. "You know Sir Thomas Frobisher, I believe. Our roy . . . er . . . *eminent* host." His voice was loaded with ironic laughter.

"You brought the portraits, Captain? Yes, of course. I see you did. I trust you enjoyed their perusal, and that they suffered no damage while in your possession."

"They are in the same condition, sir, as when I purchased them from the artist's wife," Hoare whispered. "*Purchased* them, I say, should you wish to pursue the manner of my acquiring them.

"Now, where are Mrs. Hoare and Miss Jenny? I wish . . . to have done with this business and begone."

"Tsk, tsk." Mr. Goldthwait made the sibilant little sound seem almost reproachful. "Oh, not so fast, sir." he said. "The matter is just a wee bit more complex than you appear to believe."

Hoare felt his heart grow cold.

" 'Saul, Saul, why persecutest thou me?' " he murmured.

Mr. Goldthwait's eyes opened a trifle, only to that extent did he drop his armor of cordiality.

"I do not understand you, sir," he said.

"Oh, I believe you do, Mr. Goldthwait," Hoare whispered. For, upon the sight of the woman at the library door, the hard truth had dawned on him. The man before him was both the "Saul" mentioned in those ciphers that had puzzled him so deeply, and the "Sol" to whom Floppin' Poll had referred during her interrogation aboard *Royal Duke*.

Goldthwait shrugged. His smile returned.

"So be it, then," he said. "As I just said, the matter is more complex than you believe. As you shall learn shortly."

Out of the corner of his eye, Hoare kept Sir Thomas in view. What was the knight-baronet's part in this? How had Mr. Goldthwait come to arrange this matter in what must be Sir Thomas's townhouse, opened when he came up to Town to attend Parliament? Was the host looking more than a little displeased with the proceedings? His likeness was among the ones Hoare had brought as his womenfolks' ransom, so he must be involved in this affair—and not on the side of Britain. He could well be the "Ahab" of the ciphers. If so, it appeared from his demeanor tonight, he—though the owner of this house and therefore his host—was clearly the junior of the two kings used as code-name in the ciphers, and was discomfited with the rank.

"We shall become better acquainted, Captain, than we are now," Mr. Goldthwait said in that gratingly friendly way of his, "for we shall be working together for a long, long time. At least I hope so, for the sake of all parties involved. So perhaps Sir Thomas would be kind enough to offer us refreshment. Do take a seat."

Sir Thomas jumped, but rose awkwardly and went to a castered mahogany sideboard before a bank of neatly arrayed bookshelves, where he reached for decanter and glasses.

"I would find it distasteful to accept either Sir Thomas's directed hospitality or your own," Hoare said, without accepting the proffered chair. "I do not consider this a social occasion."

Mr. Goldthwait shrugged, and gave Sir Thomas an intimate wink. "Then it will be just you and I to enjoy your port, Sir Thomas," he said.

"I do not know you as a gentleman, sir," Hoare whispered, "nor do I wish to. And . . . while Sir Thomas and I have our differences, I am astonished to see a man of his station—a gentleman, beyond dispute—engaged in what I have begun to believe to be a matter of treason. Once again, be so kind as to bring my family to me, and we shall take ourselves off, leaving your bloody portraits behind."

Mr. Goldthwait seated himself and steepled his hands below his face. His voice remained affable.

"That is not the way I choose to proceed, sir," he said. "Your people shall be returned to you when you have won them . . . or earned them. The decision, like the power, is mine."

"I do not understand, sir."

"My meaning should be clear, Captain Hoare," Mr. Goldthwait said. "During the past year or so, you have put me to considerable trouble and inconvenience. First, you interfered in the work that Edward Morrow was doing for me, and caused his demise at a time when he was just getting into his professional stride as my aide. I did not have bombs planted in His . . . current . . . Majesty's ships out of mere pleasure, you know. I have responsibilities, and a mission."

Hoare realized that, unknowing, he had just taken a chair himself. So there went his posture of standing, defiant. Ah, well, there would be worse to come, if he was not mistaken. But what was this about "current" majesty? Oh, of course. The reference would be to the bee in Sir Thomas's bonnet. But Mr. Goldthwait was still cataloguing his shipful of grievances against Bartholomew Hoare.

"And then, there was that matter of HRH the Duke of Cumberland, the plan I had laid to bring him into alliance with me, and your breaking up of that plan. Unforgettable, sir, and difficult to forgive. I am sure that Sir Thomas will share my view of *that* matter."

Mr. Goldthwait glanced across at their host. If Hoare read the knight-baronet's expression properly, Sir Thomas was far from being at one with his colleague at this particular moment. After all, Hoare reminded himself, Mr. Goldthwait had seduced Walter Spurrier, the ringleader of the Nine Stone Circles plot, from allegiance to Sir Thomas to a similar fealty to John Goldthwait, Esquire—a mere gentleman, and a dubious one at that. That could hardly sit well with "Sir Tom."

Worse from the knight's viewpoint would be the certainty that Mr. Goldthwait's aim in inveigling Ernest, Duke of Cumberland, had been to get his participation in overthrowing the rest of the duke's own family, beginning with fat Farmer George himself and going on to Wales, Kent, Clarence, and the rest. All told, an unpalatable crew, but none quite as unsavory as Ernest, Duke of Cumberland. Since Sir Thomas had his own strong views on the subject of coronal legitimacy, conflict in the cabal was certain.

But Mr. Goldthwait was still expounding.

"In short, Captain Hoare, you are in a large though intangible debt to both Sir Thomas and myself. Matters of pride as well as pence are concerned. A debt principally to myself, of course—although, if I understand Sir Thomas correctly, he, too, has suffered indignity at your hands."

"Bats," Hoare thought he heard Sir Thomas mutter.

"Now, sir, I have the opportunity to indulge myself, for a pleasant interlude, in a bit of innocent merriment, at a modest expense of your own self-esteem. So I propose a pleasant evening at cards.

"You *do* play, sir?" Mr. Goldthwait assumed an expression of anxious hope. "Sir Thomas will stand arbiter for us, won't you, sir? Come, I'll take no denial."

This continued jovial tone of his sent a grue down Hoare's back. He hesitated, while Mr. Goldthwait watched him intently, unable to suppress a gleam of private glee. He was a cat, crouching over its prey in hopes that it would escape to be recaptured over and over again, until its heart finally gave out and it died, dishonored and besmeared.

Between them Sir Thomas Frobisher sat in a near squat, his protruding eyes switching between John Goldthwait and Bartholomew Hoare, back and forth, back and forth.

"I love to gamble, Captain Hoare," Mr. Goldthwait said, "especially when I can control the odds—as, of course, I do tonight. I always win, I must warn you. At the end of play, I am never, never out of pocket."

Now Hoare confronted Hobson's choice. In order to recover his Eleanor and his Jenny, he must take up John Goldthwait's challenge. In doing so, he would be violating his pledged word never to play again. True, he had given the word to himself alone, and no one else would know, but there it was. He would spend the rest of his life as a man who knew he had stripped himself of honor. He knew he would do it, of course.

He had done it before, and most casually, most lately when he had left Walter Spurrier in the forepeak of *Royal Duke* to drown alone in his own spew.

Hoare knew this would not be the last of it. Supposing he were to win back his wife over the cards, blackmail would almost certainly ensue, and worse. It was not Goldthwait's way, he was learning, to do away with his opponents entirely, but, cat-fashion, to use them, to turn them into his agents-in-place as well as his instruments of pleasure. Hoare would become the other's tool, a repeating infernal machine in fact, which lurked in the navy's viscera and exploded from time to time whenever John Goldthwait thought it would best serve his purposes. The prospect turned his empty stomach.

"I'll do it, sir," he whispered, even more softly than was his wont.

He heard a sigh, but in the library's darkness, relieved only by scattered tapers and the table lamp, he could not tell which man had produced it. Did it come from Mr. John Goldthwait, and if so, did it reveal relief or disappointment? Or was it from Sir Thomas Frobisher's wide lips, and if so, was it one of surprise at Hoare's boldness or of vengeful excitement at his impending downfall? Never mind. The die was cast—or rather, Hoare thought wryly, the cards were on the table.

Not yet.

"We'll ask Sir Thomas to furnish the cards, then," he said, and Mr. Goldthwait did not chide. "I'll have none of yours," he went on, "and I have none of my own, even supposing you fool enough to let me use them if I did."

For the first time, he now addressed Sir Thomas directly, deliberately loading his whisper with respect.

"Can you oblige us, Sir Thomas?"

"Yes," was the answer, tout court. Going to the sideboard, the knight-baronet pulled open a drawer and removed a small packet, wrapped and sealed.

"Simply as a precaution, Sir Thomas," Mr. Goldthwait said, "may I ask that you supply us with a fresh deck upon demand by either player? I'm certain you'll understand, Captain Hoare, and agree."

Hoare nodded.

Sir Thomas returned to the drawer and took out what was probably the balance of the packets.

"Pray tell me, Sir Thomas, the source of the cards you happen to have in such surprisingly ample supply," Hoare whispered.

"They are French in origin, sir." Sir Thomas's bass voice was courteous and quiet, but chilly. "I procure them, however, from Brooks, as you can see by the seal on each pack. They cost me a guinea apiece. Will that provide you with sufficient proof that they come honest to the table?"

Hoare, of course, had never entered London's leading gambling shop, but he knew its reputation. Every gentleman did, more often than not to his own considerable cost. With respect to honesty in play, Brooks' famous scruples were as high as a vestal virgin's. He nodded acceptance.

"What game do you propose, sir?" he asked.

Mr. Goldthwait appeared to debate within himself. Whether he did so actually or in simulation as part of his game, Hoare could not guess.

"Piquet, I think," he said at last.

"*Piquet*, sir?" Hoare whispered.

"If you are familiar with it, of course," Mr. Goldthwait said in a kindly voice. "I would not wish to take advantage of a neophyte."

"I have played the game, sir."

"Then you remember the rules, I trust." Goldthwait proceeded to set forth his expectations, most of which were reasonable. To Hoare's secret pleasure, Sir Thomas objected to one of them. Irrespective of the personal animosity the knight-baronet might bear toward Hoare, he would serve impartially. Probably.

"And the stakes you propose, sir?" Hoare asked.

"Why, sir, the lives of your wife and daughter, of course," was the jovial reply.

"*You* hold them, *I* do not. What currency do you expect *me* to stake, then?"

"The likenesses, to be sure. Neither Sir Thomas nor I wish them to remain in your hands. Under certain circumstances, as I am certain you have become aware, they could be highly disruptive."

By now, Hoare was all but certain that the several unfamiliar likenesses in the portfolio included at least some of this pair's confederates. If so, Goldthwait was quite right, for Hoare—or his successor, if Hoare did not survive but the sketches did— would be able to catch enough of them to scotch their plot, whatever it was.

Just then he remembered Selene Prettyman's words about this man, back in Portsmouth, shortly before the denouement in the Nine Stones Circle

"Do not play cards with Mr. Goldthwait, sir," she had said.

The odds did not favor him. Never mind: the stakes were too great. Play he must.

Mr. Goldthwait's smile was now both sweet and confident. "Mr. Pickering's creations are undamaged, I trust, and undiminished?"

"They are, sir."

"Word of a gentleman?"

Hoare did not dignify the question with so much as a glance of contempt.

"Well, then," Goldthwait said. "It is important to me that they not remain in your possession. I could take them from you now, of course, by force instead of in play, without recompense or return. But I choose otherwise.

"The likenesses of some of my people and Sir Thomas's as well are among them, as you will have astutely guessed. It would be most unreasonable of me to allow you to retain them in your possession; the identities must be privy to myself, and to Sir Thomas, of course."

At that, Sir Thomas uttered a croak of outrage. "Then it was *you* who destroyed the portrait I commissioned from Pickering at such great expense? You who burnt it, and my priceless port with it?"

From Sir Thomas's voice, Hoare could not tell whether it was the loss of his "portrait"—whatever it might portray—or the port that one of his guests was sipping with such evident enjoyment, that the knight-baronet missed the more deeply. Nor, at this juncture, did it seem important.

"Piffle," Goldthwait said.

"Well," the knight said in a surly voice, "thanks to you, sir, I must now pay the poor man for it, without having the pleasure of possessing it. You are in my debt for a hundred fifty guineas, sir."

A hundred fifty guineas, Hoare thought, would lift poor Pickering out of penury for good.

"When you come into your own, your . . . Sir Thomas," Goldthwait replied calmly, "neither of us will have to worry about a mere hundred fifty guineas.

"Speaking of guineas, Sir Thomas, I think that, as umpire, you are the only one of the three of us—friends—who is impartial enough to convert into nominal counters the prices of the various goods Captain Hoare and I bring to the table. More convenient than passing the goods themselves—or parts of them—across the board, don't you think? As well as being less messy? Certainly, none of the *ton* would stoop to soil his hands with anything so crass as silver, or paper, or flesh."

To this jibe, Hoare made no reposte. Under the circumstances, he felt himself hopelessly handicapped in any attempt to haggle with John Goldthwait, Esquire.

Sir Thomas went to the sideboard where he had stored the sealed decks of cards and withdrew a long rack of ivory counters, dyed in various jolly hues. He mumbled out their respective values, then, as he had been instructed, assigned values to Pickering's likenesses, counting out the markers in front of Hoare as he went and placing the sketches themselves tidily in a corner of one bookshelf. Hoare noted that the knight-baronet priced his own lineament, Goldthwait's, and those of several others considerably higher than the rest; Hoare's own, Thoday's, Selene Prettyman's would bring considerably less, while the double portrait of Mrs. Pickering and her Beatrice was a paltry affair.

"And now, Sir Tom, to set values on *my* stakes."

For this task, Sir Thomas deliberated at greater length. At last he returned to his treasure chest and took out another set of ivory markers, these cut into various suggestive shapes. After deliberating still further, he laid a small stack of high-value markers in front of Mr. Goldthwait.

"For the girl," he said.

Over his last evaluation, he procrastinated still longer. As Hoare knew well, Sir Thomas's feelings toward Eleanor were complex, and this showed. At last, he counted out markers in an amount that, as best Hoare could judge, was three or four times the value he had attributed to little Jenny. These, too, he placed in front of his associate.

"There," he said. The two piles, Hoare's and Goldthwait's, were quite unequal, and Hoare commented accordingly.

"Of course, Captain Hoare," was the reply. "After all, you hold only pieces of paper with markings drawn upon them. I, on the other hand, hold specimens of flesh and blood which, I believe, you treasure."

Since there was nothing Hoare could do, he did it. The charade must be played out, and on terms over which he had no control.

Each man placed a chip in the center of the table. Sir Thomas broke the seal on the first deck, shuffled the cards swiftly, and gave the deck to each player for him to cut. Goldthwait did so; Hoare shook his head and rapped the deck with his knuckles instead.

"A Yankee custom," he whispered in response to the puzzled looks of the other two.

Sir Thomas tossed a card in front of each player. Goldthwait's was the four of hearts, while Hoare's was the nine of hearts. Sir Thomas retrieved the cards and buried them in the pack.

"Pray deal, Sir Thomas," Mr. Goldthwait said.

In answer, Sir Thomas swiftly dealt three cards to each player, beginning with Hoare—the first two facing down, the third exposed. Goldthwait had the six of hearts, Hoare the five of the same suit.

"Your bet, sir," came Sir Thomas's voice.

Goldthwait tossed a low-value chip into the center of the table, and Hoare followed suit.

When each player had four cards face-up before him, Goldthwait had a king showing, while Hoare's highest card was a seven. Sir Thomas dealt the last card to each, facedown.

"You have the high card, Mr. Goldthwait. Bet your hand, sir," he said.

Goldthwait bet three small chips, and Hoare raised the bet. Goldthwait matched it.

"Declare your hand, Captain," Sir Thomas said.

Hoare complied, disclosing his winning hand. With that, Goldthwait gave a nod and gathered his cards, and the two passed them to the dealer. Hoare drew in his meager winnings.

So the night wore on, hand after hand after hand. Sometimes Hoare had a run of luck, sometimes Mr. Goldthwait. There was little talk, save Sir Thomas's flat, guttural declarations as the cards appeared. Arbitrarily, one or the other player might call for a fresh deck; the knight-baronet promptly complied. Once and only once, when Mr. Goldthwait echoed Hoare's demand before cards were dealt, did Hoare hear a muffled batrachian snort.

Another time, before Sir Thomas could deal the first card, Hoare intervened.

"Burn it," he whispered. Sir Thomas made to set it aside.

"No, sir," Hoare said. "Burn it, if you would be so kind." He felt in dire need of any petty victory he could achieve.

In a corner of the paneled room, a high clock ticked away the seconds, solemn and disregarded. Outside, over the sleeping city, the bells of a neighboring church tolled each hour. Each hour, unbidden, one of Sir Thomas's shabbier servants entered silently and replenished the fire before making sure his master and his guests were properly supplied with wine. By request, Hoare received coffee instead; although he was sparing in its use, he found his nerves drawing ever more tightly as the night wore on. Tonight, this was all to the good as far as he was concerned, for his vis-à-vis seemed tireless. Goldthwait smiled, bet, smiled, folded, smiled, won.

"I'll smile, and smile, and be a villain," Hoare recited to himself from some source that escaped him for the moment.

During one of their moves from labor to refreshment, Mr. Goldthwait appeared even more at ease than usual. Perhaps, Hoare thought, it was because he had just won several interesting drawings.

"I suppose you have noticed these chairs, Captain Hoare," he said.

Hoare nodded.

"They are in the nature of an award, or decoration. They are the same as those in my possession, which you may also recall. There are others."

Hoare remembered one other, which had lain, overset and ripped apart, in Mr. Ambler's lodgings.

"If you do well for me, you may become entitled to one," Mr. Goldthwait said.

"I should prefer to decline the privilege," Hoare whispered.

"Suit yourself, sir. Come to play."

"I have a winning hand, sir," Hoare said, displaying his cards. It had been a close affair; Hoare's reserve had vanished. When, after an increasingly desperate search through his pockets, he had unearthed the ivory carving Lemuel Rabbett had bestowed upon him and offered it in play, it had taken ten minutes of his hardest haggling to gain its acceptance.

"Your hand, sir, I do declare," Goldthwait said, laying down his own cards—facedown, as always when he had lost, "and your daughter. I believe the pot suffices to pay her ransom. I suppose you would like her returned to your sight, even if it be only a reprieve—"

"If you please," Hoare interrupted.

"—so, if you would be so kind, Sir Thomas, as to send one of your people for her . . ."

The knight rose and went to the door, where he issued orders to an invisible person waiting on the other side. In moments, Jenny hurtled past him and into Hoare's arms, pale hair flying, uttering muffled sounds. Her mouth was bound across with a length of dark blue silk. She was followed by the familiar, lumbering, pantalooned figure of Mary Green, *Royal Duke*'s former cook. The woman refused to meet Hoare's eyes. Hoare bent to remove his daughter's gag.

"Ah, ah, ah, Captain! Not yet, sir!" came Goldthwait's warning voice. In his thin hand, Hoare's little pistol was out again, aimed this time at the child, so Hoare desisted. Jenny made an urgent gesture.

"She needs to relieve herself, can't you tell?" Sir Thomas said in a disgusted voice. He took Jenny by the hand and led her to the commode, from which he withdrew the necessary article. He turned his back while she squatted.

"Really, Mr. Goldthwait. Have you no sensibility whatsoever?" he said.

"Not really, Sir Thomas." The man's expression, so consistently benign, appeared to crack a little. "I am little acquainted with the needs of children.

"Sit down over there, child," he said, pointing at a cricket in the far corner of the room. Jenny looked appealingly at the helpless Hoare, then obeyed his nod. Green followed, whipped a lanyard out of her pocket, and secured Jenny's legs and arms to the little walnut footstool. She was not rough, but very firm. Jenny had more sense than to struggle. Before long, she nodded and was asleep. Green disappeared—to resume her guard over Eleanor, Hoare supposed. He and Mr. Goldthwait played on, under the increasingly restive eye of their host.

A few hands later, the tension in the room rose to a quiet

peak when Mr. Goldthwait declared a complicated hand, and reached for the pot.

"Keep your hand where it is, sir," Sir Thomas said. "How do you find a winning hand in those cards?"

"Why, there they are for any man to read," was the reply.

Whether intentionally or inadvertently, Goldthwait had misread his cards.

"Unless you can improve the cards you have shown us, sir, you have not won this hand," the knight said.

Goldthwait shook his head. Hoare showed his hand and took the pot.

"Pray do not do that again, sir." Sir Thomas's voice was icy.

To his embarrassment, Hoare nearly committed the same gaffe two hands later, but caught himself before either of his companions noticed. Goldthwait must content himself with a sibilant "tsk, tsk."

Shortly after the church had rung three o'clock, they were startled in midhand by an eruption of voices outside the door. Above her silken gag, Jenny's eyes popped open in alarm.

"See what that's about, Frobisher, and silence it." Mr. Goldthwait's voice was curt, and Hoare noted that, for the first time, he omitted the honorific. Could he be tiring? Before Sir Thomas could obey, the door was flung open, and the Esquimau appeared, distraught.

"Zur, zur!" he half shouted. "Three of them Lunnon blaggards got into yer brandy, an they be a–runnin' . . ."

The racket was enough without his man's cry; Sir Thomas leapt from his seat and disappeared out the door, followed by Mr. Goldthwait.

"Damn you, sir," Hoare heard the knight croak. "Have you no decency? Bad enough that you should persist in toying . . ." His outraged voice faded into the bowels of the house.

Hoare was alone, with Jenny. Could he . . . ? Well, if he were to wait until the dispute died down, only to pick up the charade where it had left off, he would be left still helpless, his women-folk clutched between Goldthwait's mischievous paws. He might sweep Jenny away and elope out a window . . . but behind him, his Eleanor would remain trapped.

Putting his finger to his lips with a speaking look at Jenny, he removed his shoes. He tiptoed over to the cricket on which his pinioned daughter was now bouncing up and down like an India-rubber ball, untied the silken gag and pocketed it. Then he cast off the lanyards.

"Don't look, Da," Jenny whispered, scrambling again for the commode and its chamber pot. "I can't wait."

"I can't wait, either, child," Hoare whispered in answer. "I must get to your mother while the getting's good. *Hide,* girl, till I return."

On his way out, he filched a look at his opponent's hand—and paused, astonished. Both were incomplete, the interruption having taken place before Sir Thomas had dealt either Mr. Goldthwait's final card or Hoare's own. Played out, Goldthwait's cards would have made for an interesting hand.

Far more interesting—astonishing, in fact—was that each hand held the same card: the trey of clubs. Someone had been cheating. It could only have been Sir Thomas. But how? And why? And which player had the knight-baronet been attempting to help or to hinder?

Thereupon, Hoare himself cheated. Vengefully, he threw both hands into the glowing grate, and followed them with the rest of the deck.

There was no time for any more of this. He gave the air a resounding, encouraging kiss for the vanished Jenny's ears alone, and departed.

Outside the frowsty library, the hallway was empty, as was the broad, elegant stairway. The hullabaloo came from behind the baize doors behind it. He tiptoed up the stairs, ears pricked to catch the sound of anyone returning from backstairs. Up the curving treads he went, remembering the trick he had learned as a lad on the way to and from his raids on the midnight buttery and keeping well to the wall so as to minimize any possible creaks. Across a shadowy windowed landing, up the second flight to a cross corridor. To his left, he saw nothing but deeper shadows; to the right, some distance down the corridor, candle-light streamed from an open door. He would go that way first.

As he crept along, close to the side of the corridor with the candle-lit doorway, he realized that the sound of the turmoil below-stairs was now coming to him from ahead.

And he was about to be discovered. Another person was approaching him from the direction of the affray, coming through the dimness at Hoare's own cautious crawl. Hoare stopped, as did the other. He brought forward a hand, and the stranger did likewise.

The move broke Hoare's illusion. Once again, he had failed to recognize his own likeness, this time in a full-length mirror sited where the corridor made a dogleg. Who *was* he, then? he wondered fleetingly, and crept on.

At the end of the corridor, he saw more candlelight, a banis-ter, and a figure leaning over it, looking downward. So: the watch had let himself be distracted by the goings-on belowdecks.

Softly, softly, Hoare crept on, past the open door. Thinking to hear movement within, he risked a peep but could see noth-ing more than part of a dimly lit bedchamber. He must not tarry.

Sir Thomas's bullfrog roar sounded from below. On its heels came a screech of rage—Goldthwait's, Hoare hoped, as he crept, crept. And knelt, and grabbed the leaning watch by the heels, and tipped him over the banister into emptiness. He went with a little shriek of horror, crashed into the next flight below, and, as Hoare leaned over the rail in his turn to watch, tumbled onto the painted landing with a *crack* and lay still. Broke his bloody neck, Hoare hoped.

But again, he must not tarry. The men below might have overheard the watch's stifled cry; if they had, they would be upon him any second. He retraced his steps to the lighted door, knelt down and crawled into the room. As he expected, his wife was within.

The chair into which Eleanor Hoare had been bound might

be comfortable, but whoever had done the binding was a professional, and she was unable to welcome him with head and eyes. Her mouth, like Jenny's, had been bound, though in her case the silken gag was a proper widowy black. She smelled like a very small child who had been neglected.

Hoare whipped out of his pocket the keen clasp knife he had procured in Halifax and kept on his person ever since, and cut his wife out of bondage.

"Excuse me," she said in a whisper of outrage no louder than Hoare's. "I seem to have beshit myself."

She rose stiffly from the chair, dropped her befouled undergarments, petticoats and all, and hastened to the washstand by the adjacent bed. She reached under it, pulled out the usual receptacle, and squatted over it, splashing audibly as she scrubbed.

"Ahh," she said. She rose stiffly to kiss her rescuer.

"There," she said with a mischievous smile. "Let Mary Green and Floppin' Poll wring' 'em out and put 'em on if they wish. I hope they do; that way, I get to shit on 'em both." Her language was not usually so earthy. She must be quite angry.

"We must gather Jenny and be off," Hoare whispered as they left Sir Thomas's best guest bedroom and bore to starboard for the front stairs.

At the sound of voices raised still higher, in the hallway below them, they paused on the landing and peered over the banister, just as if they were the guard at the head of the back stairs. Or the occupants of a loge at the Haymarket. They could see clearly down into the well-lighted space. Like a riot between Montagues and Capulets, the civil war had burst out from behind the baize doors into the Frobisher family apartments, and the way to the front door, through which Mr. Goldthwait had passed him so many long hours ago, was blocked now by fighting figures.

"Hoare!" came an enraged squall. "Goddamn you, Frobisher, you blundering frog-faced fool, where *is* the man? How could you have let him out of the room? What will Fouché have to say to you when *he* comes?"

If only Hoare had thought to open the front door before slipping up here, to simulate his flight. The shouter below them, he could see, was Mr. John Goldthwait, who had left his eternal smile elsewhere and was shouting at the knight-baronet from eighteen inches' distance. Sir Thomas was holding his own. Each man was backed by several followers, who appeared to have called a truce to their own mutual mangling so as to watch the masters slang each other.

"Oh, for my sling," Eleanor breathed.

Goldthwait's next outcry was drowned in another of Sir Thomas's croaking roars and a *smack*. The knight had had enough, and had landed a wisty caster on the smaller man's cheek. Goldthwait went down. Round one to the gentry, Hoare said to himself, wildly. He almost imagined a voice offering five to three on the frog. Well and good, but the crowd still blocked the way downstairs and out. Goldthwait was on his feet again. Desperately, Hoare looked at Eleanor as if, in her eyes, he could find a way to freedom; calmly, she returned his look.

Behind them, a tiny clink sounded, and they spun toward the dark window in time to see Collis, *Royal Duke*'s sweep and sneak, slide up the sash in dead silence and pocket a little jemmy. Lorimer the burglar has taught him well, Hoare told himself. He slipped within, an expert eel, and moved aside to permit the entry, one at a time, of Titus Thoday, Sergeant Leese, Sarah Taylor, and Jacob Stone, gunner's mate. Stone, Hoare could not help noticing, was wearing shoes—the first time Hoare had known him to do so.

"Parm me, sir," Collis breathed, "wile I shets thisyer winder. We daresn't want them folk belowdecks a-wakin' up from no draft blowin' down their necks, now does we?"

"Never mind that now, Collis," Thoday whispered. And, to Hoare, "Well met, sir."

"Well met, indeed, Mr. Thoday," Hoare whispered. "You come just in time."

"A deus ex machina, in fact," his wife added.

"Now, let us collect Jenny and be off," Hoare said.

"With respect, sir, there's no time for that. Look yonder."

Below, the supine Goldthwait was staring up at them. Gloom or no gloom, their figures must be clearly visible.

"Get out of it, sir!" Leese cried, drawing his sword-bayonet with a hiss of steel. "You an' yer lady can't 'elp 'ere. We'll hold 'em off!" Hoare knew the marine was right; it was Leese, not he, who was the hand-to-hand fighter. Besides, he was unaccountably weary. Below, the two factions had recombined and were clustering at the foot of the stairs. Hoare saw Goldthwait raise that handy little pistol, saw the black of its muzzle pointing at his eye, heard its "pop," felt the ball tear at his left ear.

Hoare gripped Thoday by the sleeve. "Cut Jenny out, then, and bring her with you," he whispered. "She'll be hiding somewhere in the library downstairs. The room to larboard of the main door. Meet us at the Bow and Forest in Gracechurch Street."

He took a vital second to shake each rescuer's hand, climbed out the still-open window, and drew Eleanor after him. As the two Hoares swarmed down the line up which the Royal Dukes had just swarmed, they heard above them the sound of battle rejoined.

Chapter XII

I'LL NOT have it," the leathery man snarled at his companion. "The man's mine. Mine, I tell you, marked for my use and Joseph Fouché's, to help me bring the emperor to London and haul his triumphant chariot down to the Abbey. And I'll have the woman, too, before I'm through. Over and over again, before the dumb bastard's very eyes. Come along, you." He yanked at the hand of the child dragging beside him.

"I want twenty men, twenty, d'ye hear? Hard men, men of their hands. Go find them. I'll be at the warehouse.

"Find them by noontime, or I'll cut out your gut and run you into the river at the end of it. Come on, you misbegotten wench, and you, too, you draggle-tailed drab, you. Bring the child with you, and don't let her out of your grips. If she escapes, you'll wish you'd never been born."

Hoare set his empty plate and mug aside and sat back on the settle he had commandeered in the common room of the Bow and Forest. It was still early in the morning.

"O'Gock, zur," the Esquimau said. "Dan'l O'Gock, if it please yer worship. I be in Zur Tammas's service, or I were. Gamekeepers an' de like, mostly."

Hoare looked questioningly into the friendly, swarthy, leathery, heavy-boned countenance of the man. He could be an elderly juvenile Grognard from across the Channel, or perhaps a misplaced muzhik from the Siberian steppes. Hoare knew him to be neither, of course.

"Very good, Dan'l O'Gock. But you asked to speak to me. Speak on, then, man."

"I wants to say, zur, 'tis time we O'Gocks brook away from dem Frobishers and stood oop on our own."

"Go on, O'Gock."

Hoare could barely follow the man's dialect, a strange variation of heavy Dorset. But since there was no interpreter handy, he must do his best.

"Well, zur, w'en I were a lad I bin tole dat, long long ago, back in de ol' country, us 'uns was fisher-folk an' 'unters like, mostly. Zeemly us 'uns should be 'unters an' fisher-folk agin, zeein' it be in our blood. Us 'uns bean't 'oss-folk by natur' like youse folk be; no, zur."

"And what about Sir Thomas?" Hoare asked.

"'*I'm*, zur? W'y, 'e be moithered in de 'ead, 'e be, poor man. An' 'sides, w'ere 'e be a-goin', 'e won't be no 'elp to us O'Gocks, will 'e now?"

Hoare was not sure himself what was going to happen to Sir Thomas Frobisher, and he hardly knew how Dan'l O'Gock would know better. Perhaps, as the direct descendant of shamanistic savages, the man was privy to secret messages from the ether whose detection was long since lost to the civilized.

"What can I do for you, then?" he asked.

"W'y, zur, take me aboard yer brig, for now, an' let me show ye w'at kind o' zailor we'uns be. We be 'andy in zpecial boats, zur, like."

"You would be, of course," Hoare whispered. "You are of Inuit stock, are you not?"

O'Gock goggled at him, almost like Sir Thomas.

"Why, yer worship, that I be, an' my people with me. But, beggin' yer parding, 'ow do ye be knowin' de name we 'uns use to name oursel's?"

Hoare explained briefly, then asked, "How did you come to be carrying an Irish name, then?"

"Rackon 'twere best de folk could do with de name my great-great tole 'em, yer worship. We' uns don't name our families, ye'll remember. Tale goes, my great-great were named 'Okkak' or like. So de udders, dey done best dey could gettin' roun' de name, zeemly."

"Well enough. Now. As far as small craft are concerned, O'Gock, that's easily said, and easily done. Tell Stone . . . you know Stone?"

"Aye, zur. De barefoot man."

"Yes. Tell Stone I want you taken downstream to *Royal Duke*. Tell him what you'll need in the matter of a boat, or, at least, materials to build one of your own. Go now, please. I have much to do, and there is not a moment to be lost."

"Aye, zur thanky, zur."

Dan'l O'Gock knuckled his forehead below his heavy shag of coarse black hair, and was gone. If only, Hoare thought, all their needs, including his own, could be met with equal ease.

Hoare had gone through the previous night with no sleep at all, being preoccupied with chasing to London from Greenwich and then trying to cope with his womenfolks' captors. So he had slept the clock around one time and a half, and then made absentminded sleepy love with his absent minded sleepy wife. In today's dawning, he had dressed and come below, ravenous, to deal with the matters stemming from the events of the last night but one. After putting a tidier plaster over the nick in her husband's left ear, Eleanor had gone about her own affairs—to replace the undergarments she had left behind in the fracas at 18, Gracechurch Street, if Hoare had understood her mission properly in his half doze. Since Sarah Taylor accompanied her, she would not be at personal risk, but, by the same token, the two women could not go far toward rescuing his Jenny for him.

For, on his rejoining the exhausted Hoare at the inn early the day before—or was it two days?—Titus Thoday's face had been somber.

"We could not find her, sir," he said. "We ransacked the entire place. We even had Sir Thomas's assistance in pointing out several nooks and crannies that even I would have had trouble in finding without him. I must conclude, sir, that Goldthwait took Miss Jenny with him when he and his people absconded from Sir Thomas's house.

"I failed you, sir. I regret it most sincerely."

"It's all right, Thoday," Hoare had answered. "It was *I* who failed *her,* not *you* who failed *me.*

"But I do have a bone to pick with you, sir," he had gone on. He had been too weary to feel astonished at having just addressed one of his own crew as "sir"; besides, rating or no, he knew Thoday to be a natural gentleman. He must look into this, later.

"Before I left my ship, Thoday," he had said, "I gave absolute orders to all hands that under no circumstances was anyone to follow me to London . . . in some misguided hope of helping me recover my family. In the event, I am happy to admit, it was most fortunate that you disobeyed those orders, but . . .

"I owe you, Leese, Taylor, and the others my thanks for my deliverance, but I also owe you condign punishment for disobeying the direct orders of your captain."

"By your leave, sir," Thoday had answered, "I was not aboard *Royal Duke* at the time you issued those orders. In fact, I knew nothing whatsoever of the distressing happenings at Dirty Mill. You will recall that I had come up to London to back up young Collis the sweep, when he sent word that he was on the trail of the man Floppin' Poll named as 'Sol.' The one, actually a mere figment, whom we had assumed must be Solomon."

The lean investigator was quite right, Hoare had realized. So

Thoday, at least, must be acquitted of insubordination. The man had a gift for catching him aback and rolling him onto his beam ends. He gritted his teeth and apologized.

"I could get you a warrant, Thoday, as master's mate," he said, "or even midshipman, if you wish to make yourself a career as a naval officer."

"You forget my faith, sir," the other answered.

"I have taken care never to inquire about it, you may have noticed, though I assume you to be of the Roman persuasion." Openly avowed, they both knew, this would debar the communicant, by Act of Parliament, from responsible office of any kind under the king.

The other nodded gravely.

"But," Hoare went on, "consider the case of Mr. Terence O'Brien. Rumor has it that he has been named third in *Devastation,* even though rumor also has it that he is a quiet Catholic. He has simply never proclaimed his faith openly."

"It is precisely that, sir, which is a stumbling block. While I do not cry my faith before all hands, in my case my conscience would never allow me to deny it if asked, as I would be, and be damned to that recusant O'Brien.

"But there's more, sir. By upbringing, and perhaps by my inherited nature, I believe I am not a naval person but another creature entirely. As you may remember, my late father was principal aide to Sir John Fielding of Bow Street."

Hoare nodded. He remembered well.

"I believe myself," Thoday said, "to have a vocation. . . ."

He stopped in mid-sentence and even grinned slightly at Hoare's expression of sudden alarm.

"No, no, sir; not to the priesthood, not at all. In fact . . . well, never mind. A vocation, I mean, to investigate, to track down, to . . . to *detect*. A career different from any other under the sun." The sunken cheeks on either side of his hawk nose almost glowed, but not quite.

"More than possible, I agree," Hoare whispered. He remembered very well the crisp deductions that Thoday had produced, one after another, during their first adventure together. Thoday's deductions, and not his own, had been largely responsible for Walter Spurrier's being laid by the heels.

"If, sir, I were—eventually, perhaps at the end of the present war with the French—to be seconded to Sir George Hardcastle's office, or perhaps even to Mr. Prickett senior's, I believe I could become of great and enduring service to my country and the Crown."

"Well, well, Thoday. We must see."

Thereupon, Hoare sent Thoday off to take up his search for Mr. Goldthwait and his followers.

But Taylor, Stone, and Leese were not off the hook yet; all had been aboard *Royal Duke* when he had issued his "do-not-follow" command. He had seen them with his own eyes. They had heard him. So, when they all had returned to their ship, they must be brought before him and formally charged with disobedience to orders. The notion of the consequence—the mental picture of Leese's green jacket stripped of its stripes and then stripped from his body in preparation for his being lashed to a grating and flogged—the thought was purely ridiculous. And as for Sarah Taylor—Hoare's tired mind boggled. The thought of executing the navy's raw justice on that handsome, robust body might arouse the nasty, but not, he told himself, Bartholomew Hoare. No, he would, simply and quietly, call each of them before him, tell them never, never again to disobey the direct order of their captain, thank them, shake hands, and put the whole thing behind him. Duty be damned.

Dismissing Titus Thoday and the rest of his rescuers from his thoughts, Hoare went off to gather strength for his next labor.

To Hoare, it made no sense for him and so many of his people to remain at the inn now, eating up Hoare's own money—or the Admiralty's, supposing he could persuade the niggards in the navy's exchequer to honor his vouchers. In fact, it would be

best for almost all of them to withdraw to their own little floating casket of secrets lying at Greenwich, leaving behind only
Thoday and any of the Royal Dukes the latter might need to
help him track down Mr. Goldthwait and his followers.

As for his remaining in London himself, he had only the
problem of Sir Thomas Frobisher. Thoday, sensible man, had left
the knight-baronet in his disordered mansion under the close
guard of three Green Marines summoned up from *Royal Duke*.
Sir Thomas had committed high treason, there could be no
question of that. There were ample witnesses to the fact, including Hoare himself, Eleanor, and any of Sir Thomas's men who
could be gotten to peach. Dan'l O'Gock, for one, sounded like
a peach that was nearly ripe.

But how much of the knight's activity had been in pursuit
of his own delusion that he, and not that other Bedlamite who
now occupied the throne, was its rightful occupant? How much
had been in aid of John Goldthwait, Esquire, servant—as Hoare
had overheard the man himself say—of Joseph Fouché?

And how much of Sir Thomas's activity had served both
causes? Hoare must return to Gracechurch Street, confront him,
and decide what should be done with him.

He found the place guarded only by two of his own Green
Marines. Sir Thomas's servants were not to be seen. Never
mind, Hoare thought, the ones from Weymouth had been a
scurvy lot. He had had to knock one of them off Sir Thomas's
own doorstep. He could not believe the kinds of Londoner the
man could attract would be any better. He let himself in.

At the library door, he looked at the aftermath of a tornado,
a typhoon, or, more surely, of a tantrum. In what must be a
limbo of bitterness, Sir Thomas was tramping back and forth
about the wreckage of his cozy library, muttering disconsolately
to himself.

Hoare's interruption into Sir Thomas's guarded castle broke
into what was evidently the closing stage of a prolonged
tantrum. Still purple in the face, the knight was striding back
and forth through the tumble of his library, kicking at small

windows of ivory counters and fulminating heavily over his property.

"Lost, broken, and stolen," Hoare heard him say. "My Russia leather chairs, scratched beyond repair. And who's to pay for my seventeen decks of cards from Brook's, at a guinea apiece, hey?"

Upon seeing Hoare, he spun with a goggling glare and a faltering attempt to bellow and bully.

"You! How dare you show your face here?"

Suspecting the knight was ready to spring upon him, Hoare put one of the defaced Russia leather chairs between them and leaned over its high back, returning stare for stare in silence, with a hard gray basilisk eye. Gradually, Sir Thomas's snarls abated into growls, and thence into mumbles. Finally, he dropped into the opposite chair and gaped silently back at his oppressor.

"Sir Thomas," Hoare whispered, "I must inform you that you are about to be taken to Whitehall, and thence the Tower, accused of high treason against the Crown, and tried."

Here, he knew well, he was treading on air, for he had not the slightest notion of the treatment the authorities would actually accord a dubbed knight and a baronet of the realm under such circumstances. Indeed, he had no idea which of the many competing authorities he should select to receive such a person. Nor had he any authority in the case.

Sir Thomas's jaw dropped, then clamped tight as he leaned forward as if ready again to spring upon his tormentor.

"Treason, you say? *Treason?* I, a *traitor?*" His voice rose again, to the point where Hoare feared the outbreak of another tantrum. "*I,* Thomas, rightful king of England, scion of the right line of Cerdic? You're mad!"

"'Right line of Cerdic' or no, Sir Thomas," Hoare whispered in reply. "Consider. Even assuming the validity of your claim, can you imagine Edward Plantagenet betraying his kingdom to the French? Or King Alfred? Or Queen Elizabeth? Nonsense, man. . . . As Sir Thomas, you have already pled guilty of treason. If you were indeed rightful king of England, and could even prove your . . . claim before both Houses of Parliament and be crowned King Thomas the First in the Abbey, what would happen next, eh?"

"I . . ."

"Off you'd go to the Tower, that's what. And off would go your head, just like King Charles's . . . and your son's head, and your daughter's, too, as far as I know."

Even as Hoare declaimed, he knew he was speaking wild words into the wind. But, he knew, no rational ones he could summon would ever reach the squat man he was addressing.

"Think, Sir Thomas, think. Would you betray England—your England, if you will—to her enemies?"

Fustian, pure fustian. Stand aside, Garrick.

Sir Thomas slumped heavily into the ruined Russia leather, and began to talk. He needed no prompting from Hoare, who unobtrusively withdrew from his pocket the sheaf of paper slips he carried about with him for use with strangers, and began to take notes upon them. The head peach itself had ripened; it began to spill its juices into Hoare's ears, to the last drop. For the rest of the morning, Hoare only needed to listen to Sir Thomas gobble his indignant tale until it, too, came to its end. Long before then, Hoare had exhausted his slips; he had then gathered up a heap of foolscap from the desk, moved to the card table, and continued to write the knight-baronet's words down as they flowed.

It was the first time he had heard it from the man's own wide lipless mouth. Sir Thomas was the acknowledged senior of the ancient Frobisher clan, a clan that had, in the days of the Saxons, been acknowledged by the world as the inheritors of the right line of Cerdic, and the crown of Britain. Thereafter, for generation after generation, the usurping dynasts—Normans, Angevins, Plantagenets, Tudors, Stuarts, and now Hanoverians—had denied his forebears England's crown, throne, and war-cry.

For mad reasons of his own, Sir Thomas vowed he would have it no more. He had commenced to assemble around him a band of true-believing, true-blooded followers sworn to his support. To a man, they were aristocrats, "or at least armiger, sir," Sir Thomas conceded, and paused to draw breath.

He now moved into territory unknown to his listener. Hoare began to pay closer attention. As the scheme unfolded, it reminded Hoare of the notorious Babington plot, in which callow young gentlemen, followers of Mary Queen of Scots, had conspired to overthrow Elizabeth and replace her with their own choice of goddess. They had all been betrayed, tracked down, and beheaded. There was even a similarity on the matter of portraits, for one of the Babington plotters had arranged to have the joint forms of himself and the other key members of the scheme delineated, standing—or so, at least, Hoare had been told—before their royal victim's disembodied head.

Putting the concept into effect was a different matter entirely. It would involve assassinating Mr. Pitt; selected members of his cabinet, whom Sir Thomas named—Hoare noting that he did not include in this little list the name of the present First Lord; the poor demented king and all his sons, including, to Hoare's surprise, the malignant Ernest, Duke of Cumberland; and the highest-ranking admirals and generals of Britain's armed forces. Cumberland, Hoare thought, had behaved equivocally enough of late to deserve being held aside for possible use.

Most of the murderers, the knight declared, were to be drawn from among those young men of family who had committed themselves to the Frobisher cause. These individuals could be expected to have easy access to the most prominent persons on the list. As for the rest, Mr. Goldthwait offered his own ruffians as experienced assassins.

"How many murders were intended?" was Hoare's natural query.

"*Executions,* if you please, sir," Sir Thomas replied in a testy voice. "No malice was intended. But, in answer to your question, let me see. . . ." He began to count.

"Thirty-two, more or less," he said at last. "Thirty-three, if you count Sir Hugh Abercrombie. He had to be eliminated earlier than we planned."

"Why was that?"

"Goldthwait had come to believe Sir Hugh had begun to suspect him. He was no longer being made privy to state secrets. Then, too, *you* had popped up again, like a hateful jack-in-the-box."

The knight now launched himself upon a discourse upon John Goldthwait, Esquire. Although the latter seldom traveled outside London, his Admiralty duties had called him into the entourage of William, Duke of Clarence and titular Admiral of the Fleet, when that authentic royal duke had chosen to attend the court-martial of Arthur Gladden on the charge of murdering Adam Hay, captain of the new frigate *Vantage*.

It had been then, of course, that Hoare and Goldthwait had first met. On the same occasion, the latter had also met Sir Thomas Frobisher and, as was his wont, wrung his inmost thoughts from him. Mr. Goldthwait had immediately recognized the potential the knight-baronet offered his cause.

Sir Thomas and his adherents, Goldthwait was convinced, could become a powerful factor in his own rise to power as the prime English agent of Fouché. That foxy-haired trimmer Joseph Fouché, "Duke of Otranto" in Bonaparte's jury-rigged aristocracy of cut-throats and muffin-men, was now Bonaparte's master of intelligence. At least his experience was relevant to Sir Thomas's plot, for he had been among the revolutionaries who sent fat Louis and his silly wife to the guillotine.

Since Bonaparte had grabbed power, as Sir Thomas learned bit by bit, and had finally had confirmed from the man's own confident, smiling confession, Mr. Goldthwait had been in French pay. Ever since, he had been applying the growing power and the funds this gave him into achieving his self-imposed mission of becoming de facto ruler of the United Kingdom.

Upon handing his soul to Fouché, Goldthwait had become Bonaparte's principal man in London. When Bonaparte in turn raised the Tricolor over the Tower, Goldthwait knew he himself would become the secret keystone of the conqueror's regime.

King Thomas, re-establisher of the royal line of Frobisher, would become his pompous, powerless puppet, his crowned figurehead.

In combination, the plot cut straight to the objectives of both men: Sir Thomas's, to gain his family its "rightful" crown; Goldthwait's, to decapitate the present government of Britain, and replace it with one of his own selection. That, at least, was Goldthwait's own view of the situation, as Sir Thomas now understood it.

Sir Thomas, he admitted to Hoare, had been slow to realize the subordinate role he was to play in what he had deemed to be an alliance of equals and of gentlemen. His doubts had begun to reach a peak the other night, when Goldthwait's true, overweening expectation, his absolute assumption that his wish was open to challenge by neither God nor man, began to reveal itself. At last, the rift between the Goldthwait and Frobisher factions had broken out on its own, and Sir Thomas realized he was being used. From that balcony, Hoare himself had seen it happen.

"He's a madman, Hoare," the knight declared, "a Bedlamite. He believes himself superior to Bonaparte, to Jesus Christ—and, as I believe you have reason to know—to Satan."

From the recent behavior of Captain Walter Spurrier, Hoare did indeed know. Spurrier, celebrant of the black Mass in the Nine Stones Circle, had once answered to Sir Thomas but had transferred his worship to Satan's superior, and died in his cause.

"He knows himself infallible, omnipotent," Sir Thomas continued, fixing Hoare with his glittering eye. "I say again, he *knows* it, utterly and absolutely. As I learned to my own sorrow only a few nights . . . a few nights ago . . . he was *using* me, sir, using me and my just cause, to disrupt the workings of the British government."

"In short, Sir Thomas, to commit high treason," Hoare whispered.

"Treason, sir?" Sir Thomas snarled. "If this be treason, make the most of it. As for me, return to me and mine our rightful crown, or give me death!" His peroration concluded in trumpet tones of challenge.

Somehow, the words sounded familiar to Hoare. Damn him, the man was all but a plagiarist. Tat the thought, he must suppress a laugh of contempt lest his laughter provoke a new outburst of rage.

But for Sir Thomas, Hoare saw, it was too late for rage. Instead, he looked once more about his ruined room, and his bulging eyes filled with tears.

Ah, said Bartholomew Hoare to himself. Now we bite close to the pit of the peach.

"He's a devil, Hoare, a devil," Sir Thomas spat.

"*The* Devil, in fact," he added, "or at least, so he deems himself."

"And, as you should have learned by now, Sir Thomas," Hoare whispered, "he who would sup with the Devil should bring a long spoon."

"Learned too late, sir," Sir Thomas answered. "My cause is just—I know it—but the means of advancing it which I chose was . . . vile. It was my fault, my most grievous fault." He stared morosely at his feet.

Some other penitent, somewhere, had used that phrase to Hoare. At the moment he could not remember who, or where. Besides, it was of no significance. It seemed to him, on occasions like this, as though the silence enforced upon him by that French musket ball had endowed him with a father confessor's alb. Or "tool?" No, he thought, it was some other garment with ritual significance.

In any case, it was not in Hoare's power to absolve Sir Thomas Frobisher, nor was there any seal upon his confessional. The knight must go before a lay tribunal. Meanwhile, in addition to Jenny's whereabouts, another matter nagged at him. Now that the other night's play was over, it did no harm, Hoare thought, to speak as one gentleman to another, even to a self-confessed traitor.

"Would it trouble you, Sir Thomas, to know that I discovered you had been—er—trifling with the cards you dealt Mr. Goldthwait and me?"

The disconsolate knight shook his head, but almost as if he were inviting further questions.

"But to what end, sir?" Hoare whispered. "You held no stake; who was to be the gainer?"

"It made no difference to me, Hoare," Sir Thomas said. "I was merely weary of being left behind, impotent. It gave me a silly feeling that at least . . . at least . . ." His voice faded away.

"And pray where, sir, did you acquire the sleight of hand necessary to slip the false card into the decks from which you dealt the other night?"

"I prefer not to say, sir," was the answer, and Sir Thomas would not be moved.

Before picking up his wife at the Bow and Forest and finding passage downstream to Greenwich, he would betake himself to Whitehall with his prisoner, find Sir George Hardcastle, and dump the problem in his lap. He knew himself too weary to address it himself.

"Collect anything you may need, Sir Thomas," he whispered, "and come with me. Pray move with dispatch, sir; there is not a moment to be lost. I shall await you with transportation outside your door."

Upon seeing the knight-baronet nod his bowed head, he nodded his own and took his leave.

Chapter XIII

I N THE back room of a less-than-savory ordinary, the unre-
markable-looking man sat among thieves, pretending to be
at his ease. He needed them, desperately. By his captures of hard
evidence, his enemy had put the entire movement in jeopardy,
while he himself had but the one piece. A powerful piece, to be
sure, and evidently a treasured one, but solitary and therefore
limited in effect.

He struck once on the side of his mug of Blue Ruin, and
again, more sharply than before. Around him the thieves' voices
faded away.

"How would you like ten thousand pounds to be split
among you, fair and square?"

"Ten *thousand pounds!*" echoed around the room as loud as
if they had been spoken. Less clearly, of course, came the second
thoughts: how to extract a second share, and a third, and . . .

"Well, then. I invited you here, and no lesser men, because
you are all known as ready men to fight for what you want. And
are right in wanting. And deserve. Now, there's a little ship lying

in Greenwich, that sticks in my craw, and I want done with it—ship, crew, cargo, and all, right down to the anchor flaws."

One of the thieves smothered a laugh.

"No man laughs at your humble servant." A small, serviceable pistol had appeared in the speaker's hand; since the laughing thief was within eighteen inches of its muzzle, he blanched and sat mute.

"You have a count of five to get out of this room alive. One . . . two . . . As I was saying, gentlemen . . ."

Leaving his cob to be returned to Greenwich in the experienced hands of one of the insubordinate Royal Dukes, Hoare embarked with Eleanor, Taylor, and the Esquimau in a navy launch directed to take them home. There having been no occasion for an earlier craft to depart for *Royal Duke,* the outlander, in obedience to his orders, had sprung nimbly aboard just as the launch was shoving off.

It was a sorry return. Between the Hoares, as they sat in the stern sheets of the launch, there was the illusion of a space, in which one small, tubular girl-child should be seated but was not. Only the Inuit bore any cheer with him, and that was an unwitting joy at being on the water.

"A waterman I be, zur, an' no gamekeeper," he declared, "niver 'appier than messin' about in boats."

Having expressed the selfsame words to himself not so long ago or so far away, Hoare could only nod.

"Zur Thomas, 'e be landsman, frog or no frog," O'Gock added. "Puddock, more like!"

"Mph," was all Hoare could say.

Sensing her husband's puzzlement at the unfamiliar word, Eleanor leaned over and whispered "He means 'toad,' my dear. Vernacular.

"But poor Sir Thomas carries no jewel in his head," she continued, in the obvious hope of cheering up her despondent husband. "A bee in his bonnet, certainly, but no jewel." She was trying very hard, Hoare knew, and she knew she was failing. He could not remember ever before having sensed uncertainty in her. Their absent Jenny sat between them. Falling silent, his wife simply took his hand in hers.

So they sat until the launch, bucking the last of the flood, had reached its destination, the cox had announced with his cry of "Royal Duke!" that her captain was aboard, and the pitiful array of side boys had mustered at the entry port to receive their skipper and his wife.

The cob and its makeshift post-boy already waited Hard at the entrance of the Naval Hospital. Mr. Clay, clever and fore-sighted as always, had guessed that Captain Hoare and his lady would be wanting to return to Dirty Mill as quickly as possible. He had ordered the cob put between the shafts of a chaise.

He had guessed correctly. Hoare took no more time than he needed to bring his lieutenant up to date on events, and then had Eleanor and himself ferried ashore, where he handed her into the chaise and directed the boy to take them home to Dirty Mill.

The early dusk was finally drawing in when the cob, recognizing that it was nearing a place that was home for it as well as its passengers, broke into a spanking trot. Hoare had dreaded this moment. Although he knew that, immediately upon getting the news from Hoare, Mr. Clay had sent a detachment here, he still envisioned the place, naturally enough, as he had left it: cold, empty of all visible life save the cat Order, ransacked, inhabited by the corpses, or at least the ghosts, of the manservant Tom and the maid Agnes.

Instead, as the chaise drew up to the door Hoare had left ajar behind him, he found it open again indeed, but well-lit from behind. The windows on either side, too, were aglow. In the doorway stood his servant Whitelaw and the spectacled librarian McVitty.

The woman was smiling a welcome, and Hoare even

thought to detect a similar smile on his silent manservant's wooden face. With a relieved sigh, he stepped to one side and let his wife precede him.

"Welcome back, ma'am, and sir!" McVitty said, speaking for both herself and Whitelaw.

In the warmth and light of the hallway, Hoare looked first at Eleanor with more than a little anxiety. Surely she would be remembering the last time she had seen this place. She would be recalling struggle, capture, being hauled away with their daughter. How would her natural feelings express themselves?

She blinked.

"Well, Bartholomew," she said, "the place is far more peaceful than it was when I left it, I must say. Good. And do I smell cinnamon? Even better. Will you give us fifteen minutes to refresh ourselves before tea, McVitty?"

With that, she preceded Hoare up the stairs and into their bedroom.

The cat Order was curled upon their bed, occupying its very middle as though entitled to the entire bed. This had been strictly forbidden the beast by Jenny; evidently it had decided to take advantage of its mistress's absence to break all bounds of propriety.

Hoare inspected the animal from a distance.

"Well, cat, you do make yourself at home," he whispered. "But this happens to be my bed, and my wife's, not yours."

He reached for Order. The cat hissed at him, and dabbed with his paw. Resisting the impulse to swat the beast across the room, Hoare withdrew his own paw and licked off the blood.

"I don't really speak Cat very well," he confessed.

"You don't speak anything very well, Bartholomew," Eleanor said with a twinkle and a grin, and kissed him.

"It's just as well," he whispered as soon as his mouth was free. "I was half-expecting a scene."

"A scene?"

"Yes. You should know, better than I, the obligatory scene in ladies' novels, in which the heroine's favorite pet pines and moans and starves when its mistress goes adrift."

"I do know, Bartholomew," she said, "even though I seldom bother with that sort of three-volume trash, but I am surprised that *you* should know. I would have expected something more grave."

"Like *Decline and Fall of the Roman Empire,* I suppose?"

"Or *Gulliver.* Far more subtle, much nearer your taste, I would suppose.

"But come," she said. "Let us breathe for ourselves a bit, before we go belowdecks for tea. I want my own dear tuffet again."

She looked up into Hoare's face, and he looked down at hers.

"Never fear, Bartholomew, our Jenny will be back with us soon," she said. "She is a tough young person, and she will be wanting her Order in her arms."

"I shall have her back." Hoare's whisper was grim.

Later, she stirred in Hoare's arms.

"That was quite a mill, was it not, Bartholomew?"

"Eh?" he whispered sleepily.

"Sir Thomas and Goldthwait," she said, "just the other night. The frog and the weasel. Fibbed each other smartly, they did! No sense of style at all, of course, but after all, neither of them would have the wit to whip a top. But plenty of snuff . . . game chickens, both of 'em."

"What?" Hoare was now wide awake, and astonished. "Where did you learn that cant, if you please, madam?"

"Bartholomew, Bartholomew," she said. "Remember, I grew up among brothers. One was a beast, another a beau sabreur. Don't you think I witnessed more mills than you could count, between them, and among their crowd?"

"Oh dear, oh dear," whispered Hoare.

Later still, perhaps because of his assertive partridge of a wife, his next step came clear to Hoare. "Goldthwait won't lie doggo for long," he whispered to her. "It isn't in him to do anything but attack. Remember, he *knows* himself to be all-powerful. God, if you will. And whenever did God need to defend Himself?

"Besides, his masters across the Channel will be pressing him to act. The loss of Frobisher will have hurt him with Fouché. He cannot afford that—not now."

He looked down at his wife. She was asleep, curled into him like a solid brown cat, snoring ever so faintly. He would not awaken her when McVitty brought their tea.

The next morning, Hoare hoisted himself stiffly aboard the cob and took his thinking with him north across Blackheath and through Greenwich, to *Royal Duke*. There, he repeated to Mr. Clay, Taylor, and Leese the conclusion he had given Eleanor the night before.

"First, though," he asked, "could any of the ship's remaining people still be Goldthwait's?"

Clay shook his head. He looked almost insulted. Thoday's kind of people would be the most likely residual traitors, and Thoday, of course, was still upriver, hoping to put himself on Goldthwait's trace, so Hoare's question was useless in that informal division of Royal Dukes.

Sergeant Leese shook his lantern-jawed head. "My lads be too countrified for that sort of work, sir. Goldthwait 'ud deem 'em too stupid for 'im.

"More fule 'e, sir. 'Oo was it put the idee in Thoday's 'ead about that there bollock knife? Gideon Yeovil, private, that's 'oo."

Hoare had heard nothing of this. "Tell me about it," he said.

"Simple enough, sir, when you comes down to it. You know the knife I means, sir?"

Hoare nodded.

"Well, sir, Yeovil recognized it right off fer wot it was. 'E'd been by way of bein' a shepherd 'imself oncet, before 'e 'listed.

"' 'T'ain't tellin' truth,' 'e sez. ' 'Tis old bollock-knife, it be, all rusty. Ain't no live shepherd's bollock-knife. We-uns keep 'em razor sharp, Sarge, or the cut goes bad an' beast dies. Been buried in sod fer years,' 'e says.

"'E told Mr. Thoday out it musta belonged to one-a them shepherds what died in the big snow on Dartmoor in eighty-eight."

"Makes sense, I suppose, Leese," Hoare said, suspecting that the sergeant was quite ready to keep on praising his private's sharpness until it wore down.

"How about you, Taylor?" The big woman, quite unabashed by the scolding her captain had poured upon her only moments before, looked thoughtfully into space for a minute before replying.

"Once in a while, sir, I have had my doubts about Blassingame. Of course, he is not a familiar; Mr. Thoday should be speaking of him, and not I."

Blassingame was *Royal Duke*'s master prestidigitator, juggler, knife-thrower, and lock picker. As a known thief, then, he would be a natural suspect. But Taylor did not appear to have finished her remarks. Hoare waited.

"However, I learn from others that Blassingame has no love for Mr. Goldthwait, or indeed for any of the secretarial persons in Whitehall. It seems that he believes himself to have been inveigled by a group of the less savory young men of the Admiralty into burglarizing a house of ill fame. He was caught, gaoled, and nearly lost his right hand to a prison bully. I would deem him as safe as . . ." She paused.

"As Private Gideon Yeovil," Hoare said at random.

"That example will serve, sir," she said, and shut her mouth with a snap.

"Do you think, Taylor," he asked, "that Mr. Goldthwait would know of Blassingame's experience?"

"I can hardly say, sir. Let me inquire."

Sir Thomas Frobisher's trial took place as Hoare had warned the knight it would, in an obscure corner of the White Tower. Truth to tell, Hoare was surprised; he had made the prediction up out of whole cloth, feeling it romantically appropriate. He was requested and required to attend the trial, and must obey, but he did so unwillingly. After all, one way or another, the knight-baronet was sure to be put away somewhere where he could do no more harm.

Throughout his trial, Sir Thomas sat in the dock, dispirited, contributing little or nothing to his defense, and appearing, indeed, to pay little attention to counsel's struggles on his behalf. Indeed, though the knight's children came faithfully to sit in the chilly gallery of the tapestried chamber, to offer their father whatever moral support they could, he acknowledged their presence only upon being escorted into the chamber and out of it.

Sir Thomas's three judges—authority had determined that the trial should not be by jury—must be exalted men of the law, Hoare was certain, for they sat heavily on high, red-robed and wigged colossally. He neither knew nor cared, but stood up when ordered to do so, gave his evidence, and reseated himself. So, too, did others: the limner Pickering, for example, and two of Sir Thomas's servants, one from Gracechurch Street and a pimpled man whom Hoare recognized as the lackey he had once pushed down Sir Thomas's steps in Weymouth.

The two were followed by a string of the knight-baronet's confederates, the sorry well-connected imitators of the Babing-ton plot. Their trial would follow in due course. Their contributions were as mixed as their demeanor, ranging as they did from cringing contriteness on the part of one youthful weed to the belligerent posturing of a curly-headed, red-faced blond man who could only have been a champion bully at Eton. The latter, to Hoare's quiet glee, was ordered suppressed by the presiding justice, and gagged.

Concluding arguments took place close to midday on the third day of the trial, and were followed by no recess. Instead, the three justices conferred in undertones, right there on the bench, before God and everyone. Within less than half an hour, they nodded agreement among themselves, three great toy mandarins from Tartary. The flanking mandarins composed themselves and turned to their senior. Would he reach for a black cap, Hoare wondered, to cover the snowy curls of his great peruke?

He would not. Instead, he simply leaned forward, unadorned. Hoare thought he heard a sigh from where the young Frobishers sat.

"The prisoner will rise," he said. Sir Thomas obeyed, and stood as straight as he could to await sentencing.

"Thomas Frobisher," the justice said, "this court finds you guilty as charged, of high treason against the realm, in that . . ." Here he embarked on a recital of as many treasonous deeds, as it seemed to the listening Hoare, as there were Articles of War.

Concluding this array, the justice refreshed himself with a sniff from the scented sphere he bore in one hand, took a sip from a glass at his other elbow, and continued.

"Until well within the memory of living men," he said, "the penalty for high treason has been harsh; attainder and a cruel, protracted death. The latter has commonly consisted of drawing, quartering, exposure of the severed parts in the four quarters of the realm, and the like.

"However, prisoner, in your case this court finds mitigating circumstances. In the first place, no person has been made to suffer unduly as a result of your plotting. In the second place, evidence has been presented to the effect that you are not always of sound mind."

At this, the prisoner visibly bridled.

"Thirdly, prior generations of the Frobisher family have been consistently loyal, and have contributed to the welfare of the realm. To the best of this court's knowledge and belief, your children—whom I believe to be present in the courtroom—"

Necks craned.

"—took no part in the conspiracy.

"Accordingly, this court has mercifully concluded that your execution would serve no purpose, and that attainder of your family—the reversion to the Crown of all its lands, tenements, and hereditary rights—would constitute cruel and unusual punishment. The Frobisher baronetcy, and the properties associated with it, may remain intact. However, the court sentences you to be transported for the balance of your natural life to His Majesty's penal colony in Australia, sentence to be carried out at the earliest convenience of the Crown."

In the dock, Sir Thomas grunted. Alone and anonymous in the gallery, Hoare chuckled to himself. The blackfellows of the outback in the antipathies—no, antipodes—could never dream that their odd land was about to be claimed by an aristocrat who was odder still.

"Moreover," his lordship continued, "this court shall inform Bath King at Arms of your guilt, in the confident expectation that that order of knighthood will take appropriate action of its own in your case."

"No!" With this shout, the prisoner sprang to his feet. "I am—"

"The prisoner will be silent." The justice did not raise his voice, but Sir Thomas subsided nonetheless.

"I declare this court adjourned," Hoare heard the justice conclude. "I've an appointment with a brace of fine lobsters, gentlemen. Good-day."

Not many days later, realizing that he had a moment to spare before meeting with the hunters of John Goldthwait, and that the tide was about to ebb, Hoare took the short walk upstream through a thin scattering shower, to Deptford Docks. From there, he had learned, HM armed transport *Sanditon* was about to cast off, destination Sydney. Thomas Frobisher, baronet, was to be aboard.

Hoare found boarding all but complete. Convicts and their relatives, about to be parted, lined rail and dockside, howling their last farewells back and forth. Not all the howls were tragic: "Bring us back a parrot, Jem!" or "Take good care of Peggo wile I'm gone! Know wot I mean?"

A chaise drew up to the entry port, followed by a substantial wagon. From the first, the three Frobishers and Sir Thomas's guards emerged. One of the latter hailed *Sanditon,* summoned a deck officer, and the transfer of Sir Thomas's traveling chattels began. His would not be a hardship case, Hoare observed.

At last, the baronet himself embraced his ugly daughter and took the hand of his ugly son. He climbed slowly aboard the vessel that would be his home for the next hundred days or more.

"Cast off forrard!"

"Pick up the tow, there!"

"Aye, aye, sir!"

"Aloft there, the larboard watch, and loose sails! One hand there, stop in the tops and crosstrees to overhaul the gear. Leave the staysails fast.

"Lay out there, four or five of you, and loose the headsails!

"Here, you, lay down out of that; there's enough men out there to *eat* them sails!"

And so it went, that old familiar, flexible ritual of getting underway from dockside, a blend between the fighting navy's sharp commands and the casual obscenity of a merchantman. As a transport, *Sanditon* had a foot in each camp. Transports were slovenly ships, and convict transports worse yet. For all his cravings for duty at sea, Hoare hardly envied Sir Thomas Frobisher the months ahead.

The baronet had inveigled one of his servants into accompanying him, Hoare had noted, but not Dan'l O'Gock. Hoare could not imagine a solitary Inuit among those antipodean blackfellows.

Now that *Sanditon* was out of easy hail from ashore, the crowd began to wander off. Before the young Frobishers could return to their chaise, Hoare stepped up to them and doffed his hat to the lady.

"Will you take tea, sir?" he asked Martin Frobisher. The other looked at him astonished, while his sister sniffed and tossed her head.

"Sir!"

"Come on, Lyd," Martin said. "Hoare's tryin' to make amends, can't you see? Delighted, Hoare."

Blassingame, it developed from Taylor's inquiry, was more fully acquainted with the Greenwich underworld than he had revealed. The next night, he asked leave for a run ashore, to bring together a cove or two that 'mought be able to bear an 'and under the circumstances, sir.'"

Upon Blassingame's return, at four bells in the morning watch, a sprinkling of snow had begun to sift from the night sky. He was accompanied by an apparition. Or was it "apparitions"? For the moment, Hoare could not be sure.

"Bubble and Squeak, sir," Hoare understood his man to say in introducing whatever it was.

"What?" Hoare whispered.

"Bubble and Squeak, sir. This-un be Bubble, this-un be Squeak."

As if to demonstrate that two separate entities confronted Hoare, Bubble made to knuckle his forehead. There was, Hoare thought, something peculiar about his gesture. Squeak essayed a bob, and emitted an eponymous sound.

Bubble was unquestionably the most hirsute man Hoare had ever seen. In the wintry gloom, nothing could be seen from behind the wild growth on his head but the dim glow of his eyes, the protrusion of a flat nose, and the gleam of a bashful grin. More hair thrust out of his rags, and below the chopped-off sleeves that covered his arms. Now Hoare could explain the oddity of the man's salute; he was devoid of hands.

"Bubble were topman in *Diligence*, storeship, sir, when the Algerines took 'er in ninety-three," Blassingame explained. "''E were ransomed, sir, 'e's tole me, but 'e's tried to escape in a skiff, an' they chopped off 'is mauleys 'fore lettin' 'im loose."

"Barstids," Bubble declared in a low placid, voice.

"They put 'im up in 'ospital 'ere," Blassingame went on, "an' Squeak took up wif 'im."

"Squeak," said Squeak, a heap of miscellaneous rags enclosing what was surely a female being, and was clinging so closely to the handless man that Hoare could not tell where one ended and the other began.

"They jumped ship a few years back, they did," Blassingame said, "an' settled down to the hat-out lay 'ereabouts, a-beggin' off the sailors in from across river, an' a-dossin' down in the tunnels underneaf the buildin's a-runnin' back up 'ill. Between 'em, sir, they knows them tunnels up an' down, back an' forth. 'Ole warren of 'em there be, ye knows, sir."

Hoare had heard.

"That barstid Ogle, what's took up with the toff from Town, 'e knows 'oles most as good as we does, sir," Bubble declared.

"'E means Goldthwait, I'm sure, sir," Blassingame said.

"Then Goldthwait *is* hereabouts?"

"Sure of it, sir."

"Hmm," Hoare whispered. Like a snowman, a plan began to roll up and take shape in his mind.

"We are expecting snow tomorrow, I hear," he said.

"Or the next night, perhaps. Heavy at times, too," Mr. Clay said at his side.

"That would make for considerable inconvenience to all hands, I think." Snow and its accompanying ice, indeed, posed many extraordinary hazards for vessels under sail, as Hoare himself remembered much too well from the winters he had spent, on station in *Beetle,* off Cape Sable, years ago.

"No landsman, I'm sure, will be surprised if we take precautionary measures," he went on.

With this, Hoare began to prepare his battle plan. He remembered.

"You sailors use as many bells, it seems, as all the parishes of London put together," John Goldthwait had told him at that first meeting in Chancery Lane. He might consider himself not only omnipotent but omniscient as well. In fact, though, as Hoare knew from that one careless remark, beyond tidewater he was ignorant as any newborn babe. Admiralty official he might be, but he knew nothing of the sea and seamen's ways. "Keep close to my desk, and never go to sea, And I can be the ruler of the King's navee," Mr. Goldthwait might have caroled of a night. Liking the notion, Hoare promptly popped it into that little mental commonplace book of his. Its reappearance told him he had recovered from thirty-six hours on his feet.

Goldthwait's eyes might be ignorant of the sea, but they would surely be as sharp as his mind. So: to those eyes and those of any of his people, *Royal Duke* must appear unbuttoned, relaxed and roistering over her captain's escape, with his wife, from Gracechurch Street. From the Greenwich Port Captain, then, Hoare obtained permission to tow *Royal Duke* into the dock.

The memory of his first, horrible experience in command of *Royal Duke* in Portsmouth was vivid in Hoare's memory as he watched Mr. Clay and the seagoing clerks bring the brig handily in and make her fast, her larboard side next the pier, with doubled dock lines and springs leading forward from her quarter and aft from her bows.

It was not until deep dusk of the following day that they rigged the awning, and it was not until then that Hoare revealed his plan and made certain additional preparations.

After completing them, the party lay below for supper; they then left a few lucky comrades behind to roister noisily, took up their assigned positions on deck and overside in Hoare's pinnace and the green launch, and waited—in the knowledge that they might have to go through the whole rigmarole again, night after night, until the attack descended upon them. If that happened, Hoare had assured them, each Royal Duke would have his turn on roistering duty.

At the entry port squatted Blassingame, who had mysteriously gone missing for two days after introducing Bubble and Squeak and who, as punishment, had been deprived of his roistering watch and placed on anchor watch of nights. From his slurred voice, however, his shipmates had comforted him with more than apples, for Hoare could hear him moaning an endless, tuneless, tipsy song. Hoare lodged himself with a stout hatchet under the starboard shrouds of *Royal Duke*'s foremast, where he settled down, adjusted his lanky form to resemble a layabout keg as much as possible, and, his breath sweeping softly upstream on a steady easterly wind, made ready for another night of alert, snowbound idleness.

It was the second night of roistering and waiting. There was silence on deck; from below came only the cheerful sound of voices and an occasional burst of song. A faint light rose from the skylight amidships. Good. The roisterers were in full swing. The roistering, incredibly, sounded a trifle forced in Hoare's ears. It went to show, he thought sleepily, that at bottom the Royal Dukes were not true roaring seamen. The moon, just past full, was late in rising, and when it rose, it was quickly quenched by a thickening cloud layer. It began to snow, more thickly by the minute. Hoare sat against the coach-house, outboard of the awning, concealed in a loose boat cloak.

Before very long, Hoare realized that he was seeing much more than he would have expected to see under these weather conditions. In fact, despite the snowfall, the brig's full length lay open to his sight, in an eerie rosy glow. He puzzled, then realized that the light derived from the huge mass of London's lamps and candles, reflected from the clouds. Well, so be it. There was nothing he could do about it; moreover, the canopy still cast a shadow.

From between two dockside buildings came the softest of rustles, from below *Royal Duke*'s cutwater came the softest of splashes. As Hoare watched, a shadowy arm reached up, groped about, grasped *Royal Duke*'s rail at the heads, and heaved up a shadowy figure. There was the tiny snap of someone's thumb against fingers; a second figure joined the first, a third, and then a fourth. One at a time, each shadow slipped over the coaming in the bows, beyond the rigged canopy. Hoare turned his eyes aft without budging his head; he would remain a keg until every invader was well into the bag. In ones and twos, more swarmed aboard, until Hoare counted a near dozen. Three carried glowing objects—slow match, most likely. Out of the corner of his eye, he clearly saw a figure standing below *Royal Duke* in the dock's trodden snow, face upraised in his direction, just as he had last seen it: Mr. Goldthwait. Just behind him stood another form. The man Ogle?

"I shall break him!" came his enemy's enraged croak, "with a rod of iron! I shall dash him in pieces like a potter's vessel!"

Crack! The first caller's feet went out from under him, and then another's. Hoare set fingers to lips and sounded his emergency whistle. Its shriek filled the air.

"Now!" Bold cried from the fore crosstrees. He cast off the awning. From her post in the main top, Taylor followed suit. As the canvas fell flopping over the intruders, the roisterers swarmed up from the fore hatch and the lurkers overside from the boats. In an orderly circle, they began to work their way over the awning, belaying pins in hand, stomping and thumping anything that moved underneath as they went. Grunts of distress came from beneath the squirming awning. The pair on the snowy pier paused, alarmed perhaps.

A cleaver appeared from below, ripped the canvas, and a familiar head broke out.

"Welcome back aboard, Green," Leese said in a savage voice. He swatted the woman's cleaver away and batted his belaying pin into the side of her head. She dropped soundlessly.

"Hammer that man!" came Mr. Clay's roar. A Royal Duke obeyed, and a boarder, escaping from under the awning, collapsed before he could scramble back overboard. The two men alongside turned now, as if to leave their beleaguered party to its fate. At Hoare's ear, a firepot sizzled, stank, and went out.

Among the combatants, marlinespike at the ready, roved Dan'l O'Gock, Anglo-Inuit. Thrice, Hoare saw him pause over a head, examine it as if to assure himself that it belonged to a boarder, and then tap it sharply with the spike. Hoare remembered that, however much the people of his fathers craved animal blood, they were chary indeed of shedding that of humans.

Having closed his trap on the boarders, Hoare found he could barely rise from his squat. He struggled, but managed only to drop his hatchet. He was forty-four, and far too stiff and chilled for battle. The pair below—Goldthwait and his underworld guide Ogle, if that were he—were on the move, and he must follow. For Goldthwait still held Hoare's Jenny. Hoare would see which man would be broken with Goldthwait's rod of iron.

Lurching to his feet at last, he drew a belaying pin from the row in the pinrail at his knees, hurled it at the retreating pair. It skidded wildly, as he knew it would; he lacked the eye his womenfolk possessed. He stuck two more pins into his belt and clambered across *Royal Duke*'s rail, to take up the chase, while the shouts of combat aboard his command now sounded somewhat more feeble behind his back. For a stunned second, he wondered what they should do with these people, but then decided to leave the question to Mr. Clay, whose bellowed battle orders still filled the snowy air.

His quarry's double track, already filling with snow, led up the wide steps of Greenwich Palace. Knowing he was falling behind with every step, suppressing a growing sense of futility, he followed.

Set into the left-hand valve of the formal bronze palace gate, a smaller doorway stood ajar, leaving a crack of uninformative blackness within. Hoare entered here, to stand in the silent dark, his eyes helpless, ears and nose a-prick. From his left, a cold, dank zephyr brought him a tantalizingly familiar smell. He could swear he associated it with Sir Thomas and Goldthwait. Yes, by Jove! Russia leather! He turned and commenced a blind march along the marble pavement.

Within moments, he had no idea which way to go. He stood in the midst of blank, dank darkness. The darkness was not absolute; from some high clerestory, a faint glow of reflected city lights reached him, but he could make out nothing of his surroundings.

Yank.

Like a startled hare, Hoare leapt in place and dropped back to his feet, prepared to flee.

"Me, sir. Bubble. They gone that-a-way. Come along, if ye pleases."

A hand, certainly not Bubble's, took his. It was soft and gentle, yet surprisingly strong. He was in the clutches of the Struldbrug, Squeak.

"I'll show that barstid Ogle 'oo knows theseyear tunnels," Bubble growled, "'im or me. 'E'll be goin' parst the beer an' then a-takin' the spy-'ole, the eejit."

The handless man's mention of "beer" left Hoare feeling more confused than ever, but, with no alternative to hand, he let himself be towed along in Squeak's wake. The "beer" question resolved itself in the next chamber, a vast one in which rested an amorphous looming construction, ebon in the cavernous space. Close to, it revealed itself a jury-rigged thing of green lath, held together by lengths of crape—the abandoned bier where the victor of Trafalgar had lain in state before being rowed upstream by Hoare's acquaintance Hornblower. Having heard of the other's struggles, Hoare knew he could never have managed the job, even if he had had the voice for it.

"Shh, now," Bubble breathed into Hoare's ear. "They might justa took 'idin' inside. There be a bolt-'ole below 'er, an' that barstid Ogle mought knowa." Hoare drew a belaying pin from his waistband and followed the leader under a projection of the bier, into utter, Stygian gloom. Within, he heard scrabbling sounds, and hoped it was only Bubble, exploring the inner fastnesses.

"They still be a'ead of us, ye know, sir," were Bubble's next words. "If yer game fer it, we can cotch up on 'em, most of the ways, any'ow, if we jes' *eeeases* oursel's through 'ere. . . ."

Hoare returned the belaying pin to its place and let Squeak take him in tow again, along passage after turning passage, until, having long since lost all sense of direction, his sense of time followed it in going adrift. Twice, they emerged into comparative light, once in what appeared to be a long-abandoned bedchamber of state, and again onto a long loggia. It was still snowing, and Hoare found the dim gray light all but dazzling.

It was just as the three were about to duck into still another passageway—this one a good five feet high and cased in rusticated stone—that Squeak stumbled and fell, clutching an ankle in silent pain. Bubble, who had just opened the way for their entrance, turned, bent over the ankle, and held a muttered conversation with its owner. When he stood erect again, his concern was visible even through his wild growth of hair.

"That's it for us, sir. Squeak can't walk, not t'rough these narrer ways."

Hoare's heart dropped. Was he to be left here, then—where, he had no idea—not only blocked from recovering his Jenny, but even blocked from seeking his own selfish escape?

"Look, sir. If ye 'ave a steady 'ead an' a good memory, I think I can tell yer the rest of the way to w'ere yer friend an' that barstid Ogle are laid up, most likely. This gate, mebbe ye'll even get there a'ead of 'em.

"Are ye game for it?"

When Hoare, having no choice, chose with a terse nod, Bubble commenced to subject him to a memory drill that far outdid the torment he had experienced as a mid, of learning where every line in a three-masted vessel was made fast, and under which circumstances. In the earlier drills, the boatswain had embedded each line into Hoare's person for emphasis; Bubble simply thumped him with the club of his heavy right arm every time he missed a turning.

At last he declared himself satisfied. With a final shove, he propelled Hoare into the passage.

"Scrag that barstid Ogle for me!" he called in his hoarse voice as Hoare, taking a deep breath as if preparing to dive deep, plunged into the last labyrinth.

There was light at the end of the tunnel, a dull reddish light, partly obscured, once and then again, by what Hoare was certain from its motion could only be a stooped human figure. If he was right, it could only be an enemy—Goldthwait, or that barstid

Ogle. Hoare remembered the last time he had been faced with the challenge of creeping up on an enemy to do him in; it had involved the hapless upstairs watch in Gracechurch Street. This situation differed, though, for his target was not so thoughtful as to be leaning over a rail, ready to be tipped overboard. Hoare debated, pulled off his soggy shoes, drew the clasp knife he had last drawn to release his Eleanor from bondage, unclasped it—softly, *softly*—tucked it between his teeth like a pirate in a melodrama, crawled up behind the target, leapt, drew, and sliced firmly across the other man's throat. He collapsed against Hoare with a hiss of escaping life blood, and a burst of foulness accompanied his death. It was not Goldthwait, so it must be Ogle.

Beyond, the tunnel widened into a small dim grotto lit only by a glow of charcoal, easily large enough to accommodate several men. A pile of rags occupied one corner, a pile that might have hidden Squeak. Some ten feet off, an arched door opened at the grotto's farther end. Between Hoare and the doorway, John Goldthwait was just turning—in response, perhaps, to some small sound of Hoare's. He was in the act of drawing a small, serviceable pistol. Hoare squatted, sprang, and in springing, remembered that his precious clasp knife lay behind him, abandoned in Ogle's blood. Hoare prepared to die.

As Hoare was still in mid-air, Goldthwait yelped with pain, kicked up one leg as if beginning some macabre pas seul, and fired the pistol into the grotto's ceiling. Hoare fell upon him amid a sprinkle of stone from above, and grappled.

Goldthwait might be doughty, but he was smaller than Hoare, and he was quickly the underdog. Somehow, besides, Hoare found himself gripping a long shard of porcelain; it was just long enough, he discovered, to grip and thrust under and up into Goldthwait's vitals.

Beneath him, Goldthwait went limp. His mouth opened, and a thin trail of blood trickled across his cheek.

"*Maman?*" he whispered, and again, "*maman? Me voici, dans le jardin. . . . Tu m'as laissé tout soul!*"

"*Maman? Maman? Que j'ai peur. . . . Ma . . .*" His jaw dropped with a sigh, and his head fell to one side.

Utterly weary, Hoare rose, but could no more than crouch beside John Goldthwait. Absently, he reached out for the serviceable pistol. Why not? After all, it *was* his property.

Into his vacant stare swam a small, blood-smeared face, the face of Jennifer Hoare, formerly Jenny Jaggery, "orphing" of Portsmouth town.

"Oh, my dear child . . ." His whisper was broken.

"Da!" Jenny cried triumphantly into Hoare's chest. He looked down at her jubilant face.

"It worked!"

"What worked, child?" he asked.

"Why, the crumbs, of course, silly! The crumbs I kep a-droppin' as them coves drug me along through Lunnon an' down the tunnels!" In her brief return to the underworld, Jenny had let her gentility lapse, Hoare could not help noticing. Ah well, she had kept her life, and her spirit. The gentility would be back; perhaps the cat Order had it in his possession.

"Yes, my dear, your stratagem worked," he lied, and set her down with an extra squeeze.

"But how did you bloody your face?" he asked.

"Why, I *bit* 'im, that's what! 'E din't understand 'ow young 'uns can wiggle about an' around, an' get loose o' most everythin', so w'en I begun to get peckishlike, I wiggled loose and filled up on their vittles. 'Orful, they was, too!"

Saved by my womenfolk again, Hoare told himself ruefully. First, there had been Eleanor and her upsetting of Moreau's stolen skiff; now it was Jennie and her sharp little teeth. He took the child in another hug, took her by the hand, and led her out of bondage through the low farther door. He knew his way now, and he always would. Bubble and Squeak had embedded it in his innermost soul.

––––––––

Hoare was secretly overjoyed when he and his Jenny appeared in Dirty Mill's lowest wine cellar just as Whitelaw was turning the last few bottles of Hoare's second-best port. After accepting Hoare's hand and holding the child to his chest for a revealing second, the silent servant led him up from the cellars of Dirty Mill, and thence into the astonished arms of Eleanor Hoare.

Chapter XIV

T O MY knowledge, our previous candidate for the post held
until recently by the late lamented Admiral Abercrombie,
who was so summarily dismissed from consideration, has Sir
Thomas Frobisher's interest at heart, ha ha ha, and—as is well
known to all at this table, Frobisher has . . . oh."

At his own gaffe, the First Lord fell silent. For that very night,
Sir Thomas Frobisher's knighthood was about to be stripped
from him. The man himself, his baronetcy still inalienable and in
effect, would be on his way by ship, to Hell or Halifax.

Seeing that he had already carried the day, Mr. Prickett
leaped to pursue his beaten foe. "In my professional capacity, I
must add, my lords, a reminder to this Board of the Act of Parliament of 1768, the Commissions Act, in which it is explicitly
stated that the rank of commander is a temporary one, to be
held only. . . . Er.

"You are required, my lords," he went on sternly, "by the
1768 act of Parliament, to make a decision. Figuratively speaking, of course, a case under that Act stands before you this afternoon. Either you retire Commander Hoare on half pay, or you

advance him to post rank. The rank of 'commander' is one that is purely temporary, created for the convenience of . . . but never mind. Make him, sir, or break him. Make up your mind."

The pride of Sir Thomas Frobisher in his knighthood was inordinate. It was exceeded only by his pride in the baronetcy which had been conferred on his ancestor upon the restoration of Charles I. It was not within the power of the Crown to dissolve the baronetcy; that title inured, not to the individual who might bear it at any particular time, but to the Frobishers as a line.

Sir Thomas's knighthood, however, like that of any other knight, was revocable. While such a thing happened less frequently than a coronation, it happened. A caitiff knight could be degraded. It had, in fact, been the necessary precursor of a man's execution for high treason, in the days when that crime called for drawing and quartering. Since a true knight, it was held, could not commit treason, no knightly traitor could have been a true knight in the first place. Logically, then, the ceremony of knighthood must be reversed before the butchery began.

Sir Thomas Frobisher was not to be dismembered. Once condemned, he was merely to hang. Innocent or guilty, nonetheless, he was to be degraded.

The ceremony took place in the chapel of Henry VII in Westminster Abbey. Only members of the order itself should be present. Nonetheless, though he was no knight and never expected to be dubbed one, Hoare managed to steal into a distant, chilly corner. Since it had been he who disclosed Sir Thomas's treason, he thought it only proper that he witness the result. Moreover, he held the man in great distaste. Throughout the hour before midnight, Knights of the Bath felt their way silently into the choir stalls assigned them, below their knightly banners. Many of the knights in attendance, elderly knights for the most part, were less than agile in the dark. Accordingly, the natural rustle of robes and shuffling of shod feet were punctuated occasionally by a knightly oath and, once, by the crash of a superannuated, night-blind knight into the lectern.

At last, however, the silence in the chapel was complete except for a soft susurrus of breathing. Above, the bells of midnight tolled. At the twelfth stroke, footsteps sounded outside the chapel, and a youth entered, bearing a taper that he used to light the candles—first those at the altar, and then those set at the corner of each row of stalls. As Hoare could now see, the choir was less than half full, it being a time of war and many of the knights, as serving officers, were out of the country. The young man spoke not a word, but finished his task, saluted the gathering with a bow, turned on his heel, and returned to the place whence he had come. The participants waited in their stalls, restless in the dim golden candlelight.

After an eternity, steps sounded again, this time those of a number of men, and the celebrants entered—a short column, led by a heavy, obviously corseted man of middle age, in an ornate cloak. The leader, whom Hoare assumed must be the Master of the order or his representative, had a familiar look. He could be one of several brothers, and Hoare was quite sure he knew the man's family. He carried a velvet cushion, on which rested a pair of gilded spurs. He was followed by several other cloaked figures walking silently in twos, and then by a helmeted man carrying a broadsword at the "carry" as if he were a marine with his musket. Hoare had seen another midnight procession not so long ago, one that, like this one if he was not mistaken, had also included a Royal. But the atmosphere here, instead of being unintentionally comedic, was solemn.

A party of three closed out the procession: two men in back-and-breasts that might have been borrowed from the Horse Guards, dragging a hooded man in gyves with a hood over his head. No, Hoare told himself; whoever the hooded man is, he is *not* Sir Thomas. He was much thinner, and his garments were shabby. He might be a homeless vagrant, pressed into duty for this occasion.

Silently, the guards came to a halt, facing inwards, while their leader stepped in equal silence to the altar before making an about turn. The guards and their charge proceeded on until they stood at the altar's foot.

The Master now walked around the three waiting men, knelt with a grunt, and fastened the spurs onto the captive's heels. Rising and returning to the altar, he nodded at the man with the sword.

Was this to be another sacrifice, Hoare wondered, like the one he had thwarted at the Nine Stones Circle? No. The swordsman bent over and, with sharp chops of his blade, hacked off first one, then the other of the spurs the Master had only just attached to the hooded man's heels. He hurled the cut-off spurs, one after the other, down the length of the chapel, where they clattered against the door.

At another silent signal, the swordsman now made his way up one of the cross aisles of the choir and thrust his way brusquely past three seated knights before halting at a vacant stall. Here, he reached up with the sword and, with an overhead swing, chopped away the staff from which a banner overhung the stall. This, too, he hurled down the aisle; staff and banner slid only half as far as the spurs before coming to a halt.

Finally, at a nod from the Master, the two guards picked up their prisoner, gripping him at the armpits, and thrust him down the aisle. The man uttered a muffled yelp, and yelped again when, one after the other, the guards pushed and shoved him with their booted feet the rest of the way down the aisle and, with the spur and the dishonored banner, out the chapel door.

The Master gave one last nod, and paced down the aisle, followed again by his paired attendants. The entire party vanished. Throughout the ceremony, no single word had been spoken.

Hoare waited in a corner until the last of the somber column had passed out of sight. He made his bow to the altar and followed in their tracks, out a side door of the Abbey. It had grown colder while he was within, and the broad steps were icy. The square was deserted now, except for a dark trio. At first he thought they might comprise the late traveler, taken by a pair of footpads, but then he guessed what was really going on.

The central figure was bent over. "Here, one of you, steady me," he said. "It's slippery underfoot." Each of the footpads gripped a shoulder. Silently, Hoare prepared himself to come to the rescue, and began a cautious tread down the steps. Before he could commit himself to action, he saw that the victim was unbuckling the stumps of the amputated spurs, one by one. He was a lean, red-headed young man with a mischievous face.

"Here you are, gentlemen," he said to his captors. "I see the things have already been cut quite a few times."

"Oh, yes," the taller rapscallion said. "It happens every fifty years or so, so in the interests of economy, we have them brazed back together again and save them against the next unfortunate occurrence. And here *you* are, Mr. Heathcliff. Thank you for an admirable performance."

A small pouch appeared, clinked, and changed hands.

"As agreed, I see. Considering the donor's standing, I hardly need count it. Thank you both. And remember, just mention my name at the door tomorrow evening, and the manager will pass you in at no charge. Standing room only, I fear. Good night, gentlemen."

"I have no choice in this, Hoare," Sir George Hardcastle said. "At least, I am so informed by Mr. Henry Prickett, advocate to the Admiralty. By the terms of an Act of Parliament of 1768 of which he informed me but of which I never, never before heard, I am required either to promote you to post rank, or to let your commander's rank lapse and place you on half pay. The latter fate you hardly deserve, so I must, willy-nilly, inflict the former upon you.

"I must say, Hoare, Mr. Prickett took me most unjustly to task on the matter, I being less than a day on the post when he mounted his assault upon me. Really, I felt myself in all but physical danger. Well, sir, what have you to say?"

The stunned Hoare could do no more than stammer.

"I shall assume that those peculiar noises you are making indicate acceptance. Very good. Go, have your man shift that swab, and invite me to help you wet it."

"I confess, sir," Hoare whispered to Prickett *père*, "that I knew nothing of the Act of Parliament of 1768 that you called to Sir George's attention . . . with such happy results for myself."

"Neither did Sir George, Captain Hoare," Mr. Prickett said calmly. "Nor had I, before I thought of it, as I did on the spot. I wished, if you will allow me a cant term, to 'bounce' him out of a torpid inactivity which was doing justice to neither of you. It served its purpose, did it not?"

"Indeed, it did." Ten years gone, Hoare had given up all hope of being made post. Now, if he survived long enough, he would die an admiral.

"I noted, however," Mr. Prickett said, "that Cratchit twigged. I was not surprised. Cratchit knows by heart every statute bearing upon the Admiralty in the remotest degree, from the days of Mr. Pepys to the present. I would warn you against him, were it not that he appears well disposed toward anyone who will protect him against Lestrade. He thinks the latter lives only to suck his blood and devour his vitals."

"I shall take care to stand guard over Mr. Cratchit, then," Hoare whispered.

"Well, then, let us bury the Act of 1768," Mr. Prickett said, "before it begins to stink. And I must be home betimes, for young Harry leaves for his new ship tomorrow. Good evening, sir."

Chapter XV

A marriage has been announced, and will shortly take place, between the Honorable Anne Gladden, only daughter of Sir Ralph Gladden of Broadmead Manor, Wilts, and Lady Caroline Gladden, and Lieutenant Harvey Clay of the Navy.
—*Naval Chronicle*, 16 January 1806

Made post . . .
. . . with seniority dating from 30 December, 1805: Bartholomew Hoare, Esq., master commanding in *Royal Duke*.
—*Ibid.*, 23 January 1806

*I*N GREENWICH and its environs, for those festivities whose sponsors lacked access to a private ballroom, the Green Man tavern atop Blackheath Hill most often was the recourse. To this place, in April's first soft evening breeze, gathered the friends, naval and otherwise, who wished to celebrate a double occasion: the shifting of Bartholomew Hoare's swab from the left to the right shoulder, and the betrothal of Mr. Harvey Clay and Miss Anne Gladden.

Hoare's silent servant Whitelaw had shifted the epaulet himself several weeks ago, immediately upon Hoare's receiving official word unofficially from Mr. Pricket père that his elevation had taken place. It had been a swab of high quality to begin with; Hoare had determined upon one which would be none of your cheap pinchbeck substitutes for proper bullion but of good English workmanship, a swab suited to the standing of a new commander with reasonably deep pockets of his own and a wife who was also reasonably well off.

And, since the swab was a mere few months old and had all too seldom encountered sea air, it had retained its pristine glow. Indeed, Hoare thought abstractedly as he caught sight of his reflection in one of the windows of the Green Man's ballroom, the swab's glow had brightened upon Whitelaw's shifting it to the uniform's starboard shoulder, as though it shared in its owner's astonished pride. Post captain at last! it crowed to all the world, and all the world paid heed.

Admired by all the world, that is, save the connections of the others being honored this evening, persons of considerable standing for whom Hoare's swab was as the leaves of autumn. They had eyes for the betrothed alone. Tonight, the diminutive Harvey Clay towered above his Anne; the couple was perfectly matched.

"At this range," Eleanor had murmured to her husband that afternoon while they watched the younger pair stroll ahead of them along the path in Greenwich Park, "it merely looks as though the flowers and the trees were half again their usual size."

All evening, Hoare had had but one dance with his own Eleanor. Within minutes of the first less-than-stately air, the younger gentlemen among the guests had commenced flocking to her side, beseeching the next jig or reel or hornpipe . . . the next waltz in particular.

Just now, to be sure, she rested at her husband's side in a dark brown taffeta, heavy black hair in slight disarray, her cheeks flushed, brown eyes aglow, giving off a faint odor of womanly sweat. She looked square, forthright, homely and—to Hoare—utterly adorable.

"It seems you are in good odor among the gentlemen tonight, my love," said Hoare, and immediately was appalled at himself. But the gaffe passed over Eleanor's head.

"I know. Evidently, I spin well. My low balance of power . . . no, that's the wrong term . . ."

"Center of gravity, perhaps?" Hoare whispered.

". . . is perfectly designed, or placed, to make me a solid partner in the brisker dances. That waltz with Mr. Gladden, Bartholomew! Did you see us? And he a clergyman! Really!"

But Prothero of *Impetuous* was at Eleanor Hoare's other side, claiming the favor, and away they went, leaving Hoare without companion. Spying Miss Austen making her way toward his daughter, he took alarm and set course among the wheeling couples to Jenny's rescue.

"And how does Order do?" Miss Austen asked Jenny. From her tone, she was genuinely interested in learning the answer.

"He does very well, ma'am. My new mama says he keeps *me* in order, though I vow I don't understand what she means."

At Jenny's designation of his wife, Hoare found himself inexplicably touched.

"And I'm writing a story about him!" the child continued.

Miss Austen's eyes widened, and she squatted down on the floor, so—Hoare supposed—as to see Jenny eye to eye. "Writing stories is a wonderful experience, isn't it? I write them myself, you know. May I give you a piece of advice about your writing?"

Jenny nodded.

"Put your eyes into it, and your heart, and your soul. Will you do that for me?"

Jenny nodded.

Just then, young Harry Prickett's form hove into sight. He had accompanied his new captain to the ball, on account, it seemed, of his close acquaintance with Hoare himself. Since he looked somewhat at loose ends, and since Hoare knew all too well what a seven-year-old boy at loose ends can accomplish, he went over to him. Miss Austen excused herself to Jenny and followed. A short inconsequential chat ensued.

"But Mr. Prickett," Miss Austen said at last, "I am being neglectful. Have you been introduced to Miss Jenny Hoare?"

That very young gentleman looked ready to burst into bawdy laughter, but before he could do so, thereby running the risk of being called out by his host, remembered where he was and simply said, "No, ma'am!"

"Then permit me to do so, sir. Pray come with me. Excuse me, Captain Hoare." Reaching down, she permitted Mr. Prickett the younger to take her arm. Amused, Hoare watched her steer him easily across the ballroom to where Jenny stood amid a bevy of other unescorted females.

"Miss Jenny?" Miss Austen's clear voice carried easily from the other side of the room, and Hoare listened intently.

"Ma'am?" Jenny gave her bob.

"Permit me to present the son of a very old friend of myself and your parents: Mr. Harry Prickett, of HMS. . . ." She awaited the prompt; it was at hand.

"*Impetuous*, ma'am, thirty-eight," came the treble voice. "Captain Prothero."

"Thank you. Of *Impetuous*."

The lad made his leg, the lass her curtsey, and they rose to eye each other, each waiting to see what would happen next.

"Charmed, Mr. Prickett," the lass said at last. "I believe you were once of considerable assistance to Mr. . . . to my new father."

"I hope so, Miss Hoare." For once, Hoare could hear, the boy was not speaking in exclamations. "Your new father?"

"Oh, yes, Mr. Prickett! My old father was quite different! Shall I tell you about him?"

And the two were off. Later, out of the corner of his eye, Hoare saw that his daughter was brushing some trivial atom of lint from Mr. Prickett's buttoned jacket. With this instinctive grooming gesture, Hoare realized, she was laying claim to him in a manner that was gently but pointedly proprietary. To all the world, Miss Jenny had marked out Harry Prickett as hers.

Hoare still had an apology to make. He wove his way through the dancers to where Miss Austen still stood, unclaimed and solitary among the other returned empties, "dowding it alone," as she had described herself on that memorable evening when he had first met his Eleanor.

"I have done you a disservice in my mind, Miss Austen," he whispered.

She turned to him in surprise. "Why, sir, how is that?"

"I had come to believe you more hard-hearted than one might have wished. Now, having seen the unpretentious courtesy with which you introduced those two children, I happily change my opinion. You are a kind soul, after all."

The lady looked away in embarrassment. On her slightly faded face, her blush made her no more beautiful.

"Between us, sir," she said, "we have much to account for to each other. Will you be so kind as to escort me outside for a moment, where we may speak undisturbed?"

Outside, in the fragrance of the spring evening, Miss Austen stood straight and stared Hoare in the face.

"I, too, have a confession to make, Mr. Hoare, and I wish to make it here and now." Her voice shook slightly. "I was mistaken in my judgment, and you were, at least partially, in the right."

"*I?*"

"I beg pardon, sir. I was using the second-person pronoun in its plural sense. I meant you and my dear Eleanor.

"From our first meeting, in the Graves's drawing room," she went on, "I allowed myself to convince myself that you were no more than the latest in the gaggle of unscrupulous adventurers who had chosen Eleanor—a married woman and a good wife—as their innocent target and were prepared to go to any lengths to achieve their goal. Among them I included the late Edouard Moreau, whom we all knew as 'Edward Morrow,' and Sir Thomas Frobisher. Now, I was certain, I must add you to the number of those against whom I must do my best to protect her.

"It was hardly helpful to my cause, sir, when I began to detect in her a degree of fondness toward yourself that ill became a lady in her position. Not only a wife, but the wife of a gentleman and a cripple.

"In due course, I have learned once again that, no matter how a person may strive to divert one of Eros's arrows from a target he has selected, one never, never succeeds."

"I—" Hoare began, but she raised her hand.

"Let me have my say, sir, I beg. It hardly improved matters," she said sternly, "that gossip reached my ears, first of your involvement with Mrs. Katerina Hay—a new widow as well, like Eleanor!—and then the Prettyman woman. You can imagine my distress."

"I had nothing to do with Selene Prettyman," Hoare whispered in protest, "more than our mutual involvement in scotching Spurrier's plans."

"Such an involvement was close enough to cause talk, I assure you," she replied with a return to the asperity that Hoare had been accustomed to hearing in her tones when addressing him.

"In fact," he went on musingly, as if he had not heard her, "I continue to wonder why she did so. I remain perplexed at the true purpose of her game. Was she working for Goldthwait, do you suppose, or for Sir Hugh Abercrombie?"

"Perhaps she did not know," Miss Austen said. "But, considering what I know of her character, she was most likely to be most interested in maintaining her relationship with the Duke of Cumberland. In feathering her own nest, in short."

Hoare—or at least, so he hoped—suppressed his surprise that Miss Austen was aware that any relationship whatsoever existed between Selene Prettyman and that authentic royal duke, let alone referring to it in conversation with a member of the opposite sex. While Mrs. Prettyman had made no secret to him of her position as Cumberland's mistress, and while Admiral Hardcastle had known of it, it was hardly a subject for open conversation between a single lady of a certain age, such as Miss Austen, and any gentleman.

He smiled. "In any case, she was—and is—far too high a target for me, even had I been so inclined."

But the lady was not prepared to let her prey off the hook as easily as that, and switched to her alternative bait.

"You give me no such assurance, I note, in the case of Mrs. Katerina Hay."

And he could not. Within days of her bereavement, the widow of *Vantage*'s murdered captain had, indeed, seduced him. There was little he could say. He rolled over and exposed his belly.

"Have mercy, Miss Austen," he whispered. "At the time in question, I hardly knew Eleanor."

"That has nothing to do with the case, as you well know, my dear sir," she said with another smile. "It is history now, however . . . or at least I will assume it to be so, unless I should learn anything to the contrary."

Hoare wondered whether Miss Austen's smile was genuine, or concealed a threat that, as far as she was concerned, any betrayal of his wife, her bosom friend, would meet with her severest displeasure. Well, he had lived for some time past, and he supposed he could do so again. Besides, nothing was further from Hoare's mind than betraying the sturdy woman whom he found himself loving more, day by day.

"In any case," the lady said, "I confess myself to have been mistaken from the outset. I could not ask for a more honorable, kindly, loving companion for my dear friend. May we be friends? *Pace?*"

Hoare felt a lump rise in his throat.

"*Pace,*" he echoed. Even had he not been mute, he could not have summoned more than his whisper. Mute, he bowed over Miss Austen's hand. Then, after a pause, "May I invite you to join this quadrille?"

"Of course, sir. With pleasure."

"She has kindled, you know," Miss Austen said as they set to in the first figure.

"What? Who?" Hoare nearly missed his step.

"Your Eleanor, of course. Did you suppose I referred to myself? Or your daughter?"

"But she has told me nothing of this."

"She probably does not know as yet, herself."

"But, then, how do *you* know?"

"It is hard to explain, sir. Something in the expression, I suppose. In the way she looks at your Jenny."

"Dear me," he whispered.

Hoare and Miss Austen came into one figure and passed on to the next.

"You have done it again, I see," he whispered as he sighted two dignified children who, knowing themselves deemed still too small to join their elders, performing their own private pavane, quadrille, or volta off in a quiet corner of the ballroom.

"Sir?"

"Your matchmaking. I do not understand how you do it. First my lieutenant and the Honorable Anne . . . now Mr. Prickett and my daughter."

"It is my métier, Captain Hoare, as it is that of every woman. I cannot help practicing it. I am a woman, and it is the sworn duty of every woman to find a husband for every friend she owns. Besides, I am far from certain I made that match without the help, perhaps unwitting, of another. Or, in fact, that that person was a female. If I recall, you played an equal part with me in the more mature of the two affairs to which I must believe you refer."

"And, ma'am, if as you say, it is a woman's duty to find husbands for all her friends, what then is the duty of a man?"

"Why, sir, to let himself be found. What else?"

Now, at last, Hoare burst into laughter. His laugh could not be heard, for it, too, was mute; a fascinated, poetically inclined maiden, fresh from the schoolroom, had once described it as "like a pair of waltzing snowflakes."

At this point, the little orchestra at the end of the ballroom struck up a cheerful little tune that Hoare remembered from his days on the North America station. It had been quite the rage then, back in '81, until it had been cast into disrepute as the air to which the British garrison of Yorktown marched out to make their surrender to Mr. Washington:

> *"If buttercups buzzed after the bee,*
> *If boats were on land,*
> *Churches on sea,*
> *If ponies rode men,*
> *And if grass ate the corn,*
> *And cats should be chased*
> *Into holes by the mouse,*
> *If the mammas sold their babies*
> *To the gypsies for half a crown,*
> *If summer were spring*
> *And the other way 'round,*
> *Then all the world would be upside down"*

In a glow of mutual forgiveness, Captain Bartholomew Hoare and Miss Jane Austen tripped on down the set behind Mr. Clay and Miss Anne Gladden, to the merry lilt of "The World Turned Upside Down."